WHAT GOES AROUND

A HOTLANTA NOVEL

WHAT GOES AROUND

A HOTLANTA NOVEL

DENENE MILLNER

MITZI MILLER

Point

No part of this publication may be reproduced, stored in a retrieval system, or transmitted in any form or by any means, electronic, mechanical, photocopying, recording, or otherwise, without written permission of the publisher. For information regarding permission, write to Scholastic Inc., Attention: Permissions Department, 557 Broadway, New York, NY 10012.

Copyright © 2009 by Denene Millner and Mitzi Miller

All rights reserved. Published by POINT, an imprint of Scholastic Inc., *Publishers since 1920*. SCHOLASTIC, POINT, and associated logos are trademarks and/or registered trademarks of Scholastic Inc.

Library of Congress Cataloging-in-Publication Data

Millner, Denene.
    What goes around : a Hotlanta novel / Denene Millner, Mitzi Miller. — 1st ed.
        p.   cm.
    Summary: Wealthy and beautiful African American twin sisters Sydney and Lauren must solve a family mystery before their privileged life in Atlanta comes to an end.
    ISBN-13: 978-0-545-00310-0
    ISBN-10: 0-545-00310-5
    [1. Sisters — Fiction.   2. Twins — Fiction.   3. Wealth — Fiction.
4. Fathers and daughters — Fiction.   5. African Americans — Fiction.
6. Atlanta (Ga.) — Fiction.]   I. Miller, Mitzi.   II. Title.

    PZ7.M63957Wh 2009
    [Fic] — dc22

                                                        2008036062

10 9 8 7 6 5 4 3 2   10 11 12 13 14/0

Printed in the U.S.A.
First printing, April 2009
Book design by Steve Scott. Text set in Bulmer, Peignot, and Delta Jaeger.

*For Elsa,
our one-woman street team.
We are so grateful
for your endless optimism
and positive energy.*

1
SYDNEY

"Omigod, this is so not good."

Sydney Duke heard her identical twin sister, Lauren, whisper fearfully as the Lincoln Town Car bringing them home from school slowly stopped in front of their awaiting mother and stepfather, Altimus.

Sydney felt the rush of her heartbeat pounding in her ears and tried to accept that these could very possibly be the last moments of her life. *Well, it's been a good run*, she thought morbidly. There weren't many people who could say that they'd lived as fabulously — or as dangerously — as the Duke twins. For the past ten years, the two had been the reigning "it chicks" of Atlanta's young, beautiful, and progressive African-American social circle: Sydney was the more reserved, politically connected tastemaker and Lauren, the outgoing devil-may-care fashionista. Designer clothes, hot shoes, expensive jewelry, fast cars, exotic vacations — say the word and, thanks to their superwealthy stepfather and social-climbing mother, the Duke twins both owned it and worked it. However, recently, the walls of the glass castle had started to crack.

"Here we are, ladies, home sweet home, and a whole five minutes ahead of schedule," their driver, Caesar, happily chirped in the rearview mirror. The normally outspoken Lauren groaned weakly in response. "Just give me a second to get your gym bags out of the trunk and I'll open your door," he continued before hopping out of the car.

Sydney thought about the events of the past couple of months. First, the girls' biological father, Dice Jackson, was released from federal prison and then rearrested. Then Sydney's so-called perfect boyfriend of four years impregnated Lauren's former best friend, Dara. Add to that Lauren falling in love with Jermaine, a cutie from the wrong side of the tracks, and the combination set off the biggest scandal Brookhaven Prep (and its vicious student-run gossip blog, YoungRichandTriflin.com) had seen in years. Just when it seemed things couldn't get any more complicated, Jermaine's brother was suspiciously murdered . . . and the girls suspected Altimus might be involved.

"Are you ready?" Lauren whispered fearfully as she looked past her sister and out the car's tinted window.

Keisha and Altimus were standing together, filling the arch of the doorway.

"Of course not," Sydney replied with a small shake of her head. Despite the distance, she could see her mother clenching her jaw. Sydney briefly wondered exactly what pictures they would use to eulogize her in the yearbook. She hoped her best friends, Carmen and Rhea, would pick one from her parents' anniversary party — that silver Ungaro dress had done a great job making her butt and thighs look super skinny that night.

"I can't believe they found the number of the phone Jermaine gave me," Lauren whimpered as she looked down at the small cell in her hand. "Did I tell you they called twice from the house? I knew I should've gotten rid of it when Jermaine disappeared from our party, but I was just hoping that he might call. . . . If you want, I'll tell them you didn't know anything about it."

"Shh, Lauren, stop. There's nothing you can do about it now. Just put it away. Everything's going to be okay, I promise. Remember, we're in this together," Sydney said softly as she stroked her sister's trembling hand. She hoped her words sounded more reassuring than she truly felt. In reality, after the melee that broke out at the girls' holiday party over Thanksgiving break, her parents had made it very clear that Lauren was to cut all ties with her boyfriend or there would be hell to pay.

"You go first," Lauren insisted at the sound of the closing trunk.

"What? Why do I have to go first?" Sydney questioned, dropping Lauren's hand like a hot potato.

"'Cause you're the oldest," Lauren responded without missing a beat. She nervously tugged at the diamond heart pendant on her charm bracelet as she looked pleadingly at Sydney.

"Whatever, Lauren, three minutes *so* does not count," Sydney scoffed as the door swung open. Time was up. Sydney took a deep breath, grabbed her gray Marc Jacobs bag, and stepped out of the car.

"It's been a pleasure, ladies. Have a nice day," the completely clueless driver said as he held the door.

"If you say so," Sydney replied with a small smile as she accepted her pink Nike bag. She smoothed her hair, straightened her back, and squared her shoulders. Even if Caesar was the last person to see her alive, at least he could tell the police Sydney Duke looked good. She slowly headed toward the front door.

"Welcome home, ladies," Keisha hissed once both girls were in earshot. Sydney flinched as if she'd been slapped in the face. For a moment, she considered taking Lauren's earlier suggestion and making a bolt for it. But from the fiery look in her stepfather's eyes, Sydney had no doubt that he'd not only catch her before she made it halfway down the driveway, but he just might tackle her to the ground for the hell of it. For sure, if there had been any doubt in Sydney's mind whether Altimus Duke was capable of murder, it was all erased now. She could see why everyone in the hood thought he was as cold-blooded, calculating, and dirty as Marlo, the Baltimore crime lord in the classic HBO series *The Wire*. Sydney shivered.

"Take off your shoes and go straight to the library," Altimus directed with a curt nod of his head.

"Yes, sir," Sydney mumbled as she squeezed by her stepfather's hulking frame into the semi-darkened house. Following his instructions to the letter, she didn't look left or right as she dropped the gym bag, kicked off her Tory Burch ballet flats, and headed silently toward the back of the house. Sydney stopped uncertainly before the closed door. "Um, should we go in?" she questioned, not quite sure she was ready for whatever awaited on the other side.

"No, just stand there like two little dummies," Keisha snapped as she pushed past her daughters to slide open the two doors.

Sydney used the opportunity to turn and slyly shoot Lauren what she hoped was a look of encouragement. "It's okay," she mouthed to her visibly frightened twin. Suddenly, Lauren's eyes bulged and a small gasp escaped. Sydney whipped around to face whatever caused her sister to react. She found her biological father's only sister sitting on the burgundy-colored leather couch, about to pull a Newport out of a half-empty pack. "Aunt Lorraine?" she sputtered.

"As much time as you spent running over to her house behind my back, what's the confusion now, Nancy Drew?" Keisha snapped. "Put the cancer stick out, Lorraine," she ordered, turning her attention to the tired-looking woman wearing an ill-fitting sweat jacket and noticeably worn jeans. "This ain't the eighties. My house will not smell like a damn ashtray because you still don't know any better." Aunt Lorraine audibly sucked her teeth, but she put the cigarette back in its pack.

"Um, I believe your mother said inside," Altimus gruffly reminded the stunned girls as he walked up behind them.

"Yes, sir," Sydney and Lauren responded in unison as they rushed into the center of the gigantic, book-filled room.

Altimus entered and closed the door firmly behind him. "Have a seat," he stated, walking past the twins to stand beside his wife at the front of the room. Lauren quickly grabbed the freestanding seat on the wall opposite the small couch on which Aunt Lorraine was sitting, leaving Sydney no choice but to sit next to the sour-faced woman. Unable to bring herself to make eye contact with Lorraine, Sydney fixed her gaze on the small snag in her tights as she twisted the silver hoop in her right ear.

"Since there's no need for introductions," Altimus began mockingly, "I'll cut to the chase. In light of recent events, it has become, shall we say, necessary for this family to circle the wagons to avoid any more negative exposure. And by family, I mean immediate as well as extended, which is the reason I asked your Aunt Lorraine to be here today."

When Altimus said the word "asked," Aunt Lorraine cleared her throat and shifted uncomfortably in her seat. Sydney tried to sneak a look out of the corner of her eye to gauge if the movement meant anything. However, heat from Keisha's eagle-eyed glare kept her focused on Altimus.

"As you already know, your mother and I have a very long history with your aunt. And while it hasn't always been smooth sailing, there was a time when it was, shall we say, profitable. And so, after much consideration, for her own bene . . . I mean *all* of our benefit, your aunt has agreed to come back to work with us again."

"Excuse me, what do you mean by work with *us*," Sydney blurted out before she could stop herself. Keisha or not, this time Sydney couldn't help but turn and look at her father's sister in total and complete shock. This was the same woman who, not even three months prior, was protecting her own flesh and blood from Altimus and company because she understood the ruthless man was capable of anything. And now that Dice had gone to jail for a murder Altimus probably committed, Lorraine was joining "the team"? A million questions raced through Sydney's mind but the most urgent was — *what the hell?*

"So, yeah, it's just like Altimus said," Aunt Lorraine started before a bout of smoker's cough momentarily rendered her helpless. "My bad," she wheezed. She turned and sipped a glass of what looked — and smelled — like a strong vodka and tonic with lime. "After giving it some, er, um, thought, things just might be better for everybody if we all work together."

"How could you? After all you know?" Sydney demanded angrily. "I — I can't believe you," she stammered in shock.

"Humph, you can believe this — I ain't 'bout to go to war with nobody behind some mess that don't even belong to me," Aunt Lorraine retorted with a smirk. "I'm a businesswoman."

"You see, Sydney dear, that bleeding heart nonsense you and your sister have been pulling around here doesn't necessarily run in the genes," Keisha sneered. "You and Lauren would do well to take a page out of your aunt's book before things get any messier."

"And just what can Aunt Lorraine do for you?" Lauren asked her mother as she looked over at her aunt's sloppy physical appearance.

"You might say, your Aunt Lorraine is going to be helping out in our PR department," Altimus hinted with a sly grin. "There're some people in our old neighborhood that need to see the light when it comes to staying out of the Duke family business. Normally, I would deliver this kind of message in person — there's nothing like a good face-to-face. But as I'm sure you know from your own sneaking around in the West End, we Dukes don't exactly blend in. And with all the heat on, we think your aunt is the right person to get in below the radar and make it known that no one else will get a free pass. And if they rise up against me — in any way — they will be dealt with swiftly. "

Sydney just continued to grind her teeth and glare at her aunt. She couldn't believe that this worthless woman was somehow related to her or her father. "You can give her those looks all day, Sydney, it's not going to change a thing," Keisha snipped. "You and your sister need to cut the crap and get with the program. 'Cause truth be told, you are really becoming serious liabilities up in here. And I'm not having it."

Both Sydney and Lauren were silent as they considered their mother's words. "Does Dad know about Aunt Lorraine helping you spread your message to the hood?" Sydney asked her mother boldly.

"I ain't scared of Dice," Aunt Lorraine replied nonchalantly between sips. Apparently being down with Altimus and Keisha had given her more courage than usual. "This is all part of the game. Shoot, Dice damn sure played long enough to respect it for what it is."

"I take it that's a no," Sydney summarized curtly.

"Listen here, smarty-pants, you can take it however you want," Keisha responded. "But it's time for you to start thinking long term."

"It's really up to the two of you girls how you want this to play itself out," Altimus said as he slowly crossed his arms and leaned against the floor-to-ceiling bookshelf behind him. "You can come to grips with the reality of the life you live, accept that everything your mother and I are doing is always in the best interest of the family, and go back to living the way you've obviously become accustomed to, in which case, there will be no punishments or restrictions; all will proceed normally." Sydney rolled her eyes — as if life could ever be "normal" again. "Or you can choose to fight . . . and lose, in which case, I will confiscate any and every thing I have ever bought for the two of you, from the clothes on your backs to the beds you sleep in. Plus, I will send you both to live in a South American reform school that one of my clients owns and operates, until you are twenty-one. And let's just say that what I've seen and heard of the institution isn't pleasant."

"Ain't no weekly manicure/pedicure appointments or cell phone service to reach your little boyfriend when you're working in the jungle all day, cuteness," Keisha scoffed at Lauren's increasingly reddening face.

"But here's the catch," Altimus continued. "Whichever you decide, it's a two-for-one deal. So if one of you decides to take the hard road, then you're both gonna troop that together."

Sydney was officially floored. Her stepfather was a maniacal dictator and her own mother was willing to send her away to what sounded like a modern-day concentration camp if she refused to sign on to their murderous lifestyle. For a moment, she thought she'd almost rather be homeless in Timbuktu than spend another second with either Altimus or Keisha. Then Sydney glanced over at Lauren, who was fanning herself and gulping for air. There was no way her sister could ever survive a minute in some third-world correctional facility. There was no choice.

"I guess we're on board," Sydney said in a voice filled with defeat. "Just tell us what we have to do."

"Go figure," snorted Aunt Lorraine with a nasty smirk on her face. Shame and anger rushed through Sydney's body. She couldn't believe she, too, had sold out her father so easily.

"Well, let's start with the easiest thing — shut your mouth," Altimus answered without missing a beat. "Stop asking questions about Rodney's murder, insinuating guilt on this family, and all the rest of that rabble-rousing you've been doing. The two of you need to learn to be seen and not heard — ever. If it isn't about school, your friends, or an after-school activity, I better not hear your opinion on the matter."

"Yes, sir," Sydney and Lauren intoned meekly in unison.

"At the end of six months, your mother and I will re-evaluate your behavior. If everything goes well, then perhaps something might be done to help Dice figure out his situation."

"What do you mean by 'help' Dice?" Sydney questioned suspiciously. She knew that the last thing in the world her father wanted was anything to do with Altimus.

"Let's just say that Dice wouldn't be sitting in a cell to begin with if he understood how to play politics," Altimus replied cryptically. "I'm hoping that since you have such a good relationship with him, you'll set the example and show him the way. You'd be surprised how quickly things can turn around when you're on a winning team."

2
LAUREN

Lauren shoved aside the stuffed animals, purses, shoes, and a huge pile of outfits she'd tried on and rejected before school, and plopped down onto her bed. Mouth agape, eyes wide, she was still dumbfounded by Altimus and Keisha's big kumbaya moment with Aunt Lorraine. She looked over at her sister to seek some kind of reassurance that they were, indeed, still breathing, with all limbs intact after what they were sure was going to be some kind of murderous, bloody showdown with the 'rents. But Sydney was in another world, twirling her earring and staring at the tip of her Tory Burch flats. "Um, seriously?" Lauren finally whispered. "Our parents are psychopaths."

"Tell me about it," Sydney said in an equally hushed tone, her eyes still focused on her shoes. "I don't know if I should stay here and be good, or pack a bag and assume an alias."

"Yeah, well, if you choose the latter, just let a sistah know — you're not going to leave me here alone with Bonnie and Clyde."

Sydney chuckled a little and clasped her sister's hands. "Don't think I have much of a choice in that one, huh," she said, finally looking up and into Lauren's eyes. "We're most definitely in this one together."

The two sisters stared at each other for a moment, contemplating what, exactly, that meant. All that other mess — their disagreements about Dice; the hookup between Lauren's best friend, Dara, and Sydney's ex, Marcus, and its unintended pregnancy; Sydney's outing of Donald's homosexuality in front of the family and his subsequent stint at a military school — none of it mattered right now. The twins were in survival mode, and they instinctively knew that they were much better playing nice together than each fighting this battle on her own.

"Well, at least one good thing came out of this," Sydney said, forcing a smile.

"Oh, yeah? And what, exactly, is that? Unrestricted access to Aunt Lorraine? Okay, if you consider that a good thing, but, er, um, I was cool with her being a really distant relative."

"What, you got something against sloppy, chain-smoking, ghetto-queen aunties?" Sydney giggled. "No, seriously, I was talking about what Altimus said about Dice. Maybe he's serious about helping out — you think?"

Lauren rolled her eyes. Sydney knew exactly where her sister was about to head with her standard "I couldn't care less about Dice" comments, but this time Sydney shut them down with a quickness. "And if he's willing to help Dice out, maybe he's willing to help Jermaine out, too."

Now you've got my attention, Lauren thought to herself. "Go on," she said, sitting up.

"Well, since Altimus is in such a benevolent mood, maybe he'd be willing to give peace a chance with Jermaine. I mean, if he's willing to work with Dice, then there's no reason he wouldn't consider you exploring a relationship with your crush, right?"

"You think so?" Lauren said, her eyes widening with each of her sister's words.

"I don't think — I know," Sydney said. "I mean, not once did they say anything to you about the phone. Maybe they're letting that go."

"Yeah, but how do I even begin to ask for that — particularly after what just went down?" Lauren quizzed. "And not for nothing, what do you care about Jermaine anyway?"

15

"I don't know Jermaine enough to care anything about him," Sydney said simply. "But I do know that I've never seen you happier than when you were kicking it with him or more upset about something unrelated to yourself than when you thought your boy was in trouble. Plus, how likely is it that Altimus will do something directly to your man? Seems to me like the best way to protect Jermaine is to keep him close. Plus, he might know something more about Altimus and his involvement with the murder. Next to Dice and us, he's the only other person who knows what's up and can identify with the craziness."

"True," Lauren said, contemplating her sister's words. "But how do I even begin to get Jermaine into the family circle of trust?"

"Come on, you know how to work Altimus and Keisha," Sydney insisted. "Pour on some of that Georgia-peach charm of yours. It's undeniable."

"With Altimus, maybe, but Keisha? I don't know . . ." Lauren began.

"Then just set it up so both you and Jermaine can win Altimus over. Take Jermaine to the dealership. It's a neutral location and public, so there's no way Altimus can do anything to him, and Keisha won't be there to make things hot," she reasoned. "If you bring him here, they might try to bury him under the crape myrtles out back," she smirked.

* * *

Lauren gave herself an hour and a half to work up enough nerve to go to Altimus's office.

"Daddy?" she said sweetly, sitting on the wingback chair positioned in front of Altimus's desk. "Can I ask you something about Jermaine?"

Altimus gently placed his pen on his oversized mahogany desk and folded his hands. "I have to say I honestly don't get your preoccupation with thugs, Lauren, particularly since Brookhaven is full of fine young men with great potential," Altimus said, pausing to rub his teeth together. Lauren could hear them clanking; she tried, albeit unsuccessfully, not to furrow her brow when she peeped her stepfather's temple about to burst through the side of his forehead. She knew that when Altimus ground his teeth hard enough to make his temples jump, he was either pissed or lying or both, and it was clear from the way he was working his jaw that he really wasn't feeling the idea of his daughter dating a boy from the West End. "The Donald fiasco aside, you're usually pretty good about picking 'em. What's this Jermaine got over all the other boys who are about something and doing big things?"

"Jermaine *is* doing things," Lauren said simply, trying her best not to incite any arguments with her stepfather. She didn't want him to say "no" outright without giving her a chance to state her case.

"Really? What exactly *is* he doing?" Keisha asked, chiming in as she walked into Altimus's office with a Diet Coke in one hand, a bag of popcorn in the other — just in time for the show, no doubt.

"I — I don't know just yet," Lauren stammered, mentally kicking herself for sounding weak. She couldn't help it, though; she was still shaken from the afternoon family powwow. This much she did know, though: Altimus and Keisha thrived on intimidation, and now they could smell the faint scent of fear; if she didn't get it together, any second now they were going to deny all her requests to get with Jermaine. *Stop being a punk*, she warned herself. *You got this.* Lauren put a little more bass in her voice: "But no one knows if someone is right for them until they get to know them, right? That's all I want to do. Get to know Jermaine."

"And I guess it hasn't occurred to you that we might have a bit more info about this little boy than you do, huh?" Keisha said, popping a piece of popcorn into her mouth.

"Look, I'm not trying to marry Jermaine and have his babies," Lauren snapped, squaring her shoulders. "He's just a friend I'm interested in getting to know better. That's all."

Altimus glanced at his watch and worked his jaw. He slowly rose from his seat, signaling he'd grown tired of the topic. "Look, I got to get to the office. But I want to meet this Jermaine. Soon," he said.

"Not a problem," Lauren said. "How about tomorrow? I can bring him over for dinner. Maybe we could watch a movie together — you know, kick it for a minute?"

Keisha almost choked on her soda mid-swallow; Altimus reeled back like Lauren had just slapped his face.

"Just kidding," Lauren said, raising her hands in surrender. "Laugh? Ha, ha?"

"Okay, Chris-Rock-Not, don't get your little feelings hurt," Keisha said. "Ain't nothing for him to change his mind up in here."

"Just jokes, Mom — just jokes. I'll talk to Jermaine and we'll figure out when is a good time to meet, okay?" Lauren insisted as she rose from her chair. "Love you, Daddy," she practically sang, laying a smooch on Altimus's cheek. "You're the one."

"Fine," Altimus said and headed out the door. Keisha watched Lauren run up the stairs and straight to Sydney's room, confident her daughters were going to sit and pow-wow over everything that had unfolded.

"Explain to me why you would want that boy around when he's been running all over the West End telling people you killed his brother," Keisha demanded, following Altimus. She popped another piece of popcorn into her mouth and washed it down with a swig of soda.

"You know the old saying, 'keep your friends close and your enemies closer'?" Altimus asked. "Well, let's just say that it'll be better for all of us if the brother of the man I'm accused of killing is an official friend of the Duke family. I'm thinking maybe it'll help the hood quiet down about the bastard that went and got his block knocked off."

Bringing Jermaine to the car dealearship had seemed like a good idea. But when Jermaine walked through the doors of Altimus's Buckhead BMW dealership, pants sagging a little too low, polo a little too long, cap a little too twisted, swagger a little too hard, Lauren did a small sign of the cross and silently asked Jesus to make a way.

"Hey, L," Jermaine said over the ringing doorbells that clanged loudly as he stepped into the showroom.

Lauren put her magazine in the chair next to her and popped up from her perch. "Hey," she said, reaching out to embrace Jermaine. His hug was inviting; he smelled totally delicious. But she pushed him away almost as quickly as she fell into his arms, with one eye on Drew Grier, Altimus's top salesman, and Lisa Cypress, the snobby receptionist who, when potential customers entered the swank dealership, weeded out the wannabes from the ballers before they could get onto the showroom floor.

"Man, it's good to see you," Jermaine said, taking her hands into his. "It's been a while, huh?"

"Too long," Lauren said, a little less nervous as she looked into Jermaine's eyes. "I'm really glad you came."

"I'm glad I could come," Jermaine said. "I thought I'd never see you again, what with everything that's been going on."

"You don't know the half. But let's not talk about that now," Lauren countered as she nervously eyed Drew again. "You know, in front of mixed company and all."

"Oh, yeah, okay," Jermaine said. "Does that mean I can't kiss you, though?"

Lauren giggled. "Boy, if you want to leave here with both your lips attached to that face, you might want to hold off on that."

"Damn," he said, snapping his fingers. "Well, since a brother can't give you a proper greeting, how about you show me around." Her hand still in his, Jermaine made his way over to the black Z4 M coupe standing sentry on the stage of the main showroom. He whistled as he ran his fingers down the sides of the car, circling it like a lion about to partake in a fresh kill. "Dang, a brother would look hot to death in one of these," he smiled, peering into the driver's side window. "What does something like this set you back?"

"I don't know, like fifty Gs, I think?" she said.

"So can I get a hookup since I'm officially dating the owner's daughter?" he asked, smiling and turning his attention back to Lauren. He leaned against the car and grabbed Lauren's hands to pull her closer to him. Lauren, keenly aware that both her father's employees were focusing on her and Jermaine, made a point of keeping a reasonable distance between the two of them.

"Yeah, about the random acts of hookupdom? They don't really do that here in BMW Buckhead," she smirked. "And, um, unless you're planning on taking that baby home with you, you probably shouldn't lean on it — I'm just saying."

"Oh, my bad," Jermaine said, hopping off the car. "This is a hot ride, though," he said, folding his arms and eyeing the rims. "I might have to cop me one of these."

Lauren reeled back and giggled. "Oh, really now? And you just got fifty Gs sitting around for a BMW, huh? That would be quite the upgrade from what you're rolling around in now."

This time, Jermaine furrowed his brow and smirked. "Hey, my ride gets me from Point A to Point B, so there's no need for the upgrade right now," he said. "But that doesn't mean I can't have one eventually. In case you didn't know this about your man, I got big things planned."

"Really? Big things, huh?" Lauren smiled, trying hard now to conceal her nervousness.

"Well, yeah," he said simply. "I'm not going to be in

the SWATS forever. I'm trying to go places, do something with my life."

"And how, exactly, are you planning to do that," Altimus boomed, startling the couple. He walked up from behind; neither of them saw him coming.

"Um, uh, Daddy? This is, um, the guy I was telling you about — Jermaine," Lauren said, laughing nervously. "Jermaine? Say hi to my stepdad, Altimus Duke."

Jermaine snatched his hat off his head and quickly said, "Hello, Mr. Duke." He held out his hand; Altimus let it hang there for a moment, long enough for Jermaine and Lauren to wonder if he was going to reciprocate Jermaine's greeting. After what seemed like forever, Altimus took Jermaine's hand in his, squeezing it so tight Jermaine grimaced. After a few seconds, Altimus loosened his grip and sucked his teeth. Lauren felt faint. It was this mess right here that was going to make the sky part so the Lord could call her home.

"So don't stop talking on my account, Jermaine. Tell me what you're going to do to get in here and make a deal for this beautiful machine of mine. You know, this is a mighty fine vehicle — got a great handle to it. It's a high-performance race car — the ultimate driving machine. Only the most skilled, fearless drivers feel truly comfortable pushing it to its limits."

Lauren wiped her brow but knew not to say a word. Jermaine cleared his throat but was surprisingly unbowed. "Oh, I got skills," he boasted.

"Really, now?" Altimus said, crossing his arms. "Tell me about these, um" — Altimus paused and let his eyes slowly roll from Jermaine's face to his feet and back up to his eyes again — "skills."

"Well, as I'm sure you know, my brother passed away last month and I've been involved in trying to find out who killed him, so my class work and my extracurricular activities suffered some, but it won't be a thing to get my weight back up," Jermaine said confidently. His words made Lauren shiver — partly because she was impressed that her boyfriend was standing up to Altimus, but mostly because she was sure Altimus would just as soon see Jermaine join his brother in the afterlife than continue to let Jermaine disrespect him this way. She shifted from one foot to the other, searching desperately for something to say to cool down the conversational tension that went from simmer to boil in just a few sentences.

"Get your weight up, huh?" Altimus said, his eyes locking with Jermaine's. "What weight, exactly, are you talking about, Jermaine? Surely you're not referring to drugs in the presence of my daughter, are you?"

"No, sir," Jermaine said quickly. "I don't fool with that stuff. You're from the West End, so you know how it can get in the hood, but you also know that it's possible to leave the hood and do something with yourself that doesn't involve illegal substances. I mean, you proved that with your business selling all these ultimate driving machines, right?"

Altimus didn't bother to respond.

"I got nothing but good intentions, Mr. Duke," Jermaine continued. "Right up until my brother died, I was always a straight-A student. I got big plans to turn that into something positive for myself — the kinds of things only a skilled, fearless driver like yourself can accomplish. You can believe that."

Just as Altimus was about to respond, Lisa summoned his help. "Mr. Duke, sorry to disturb your conversation, but you're needed in the office. We have a gentleman who is looking to purchase a 7 Series, but Drew would like to give him some incentives to close the deal."

"I'll be right there, Lisa," Altimus said, his eyes still locked on Jermaine's.

"Yes, sir, I'll let him know," Lisa said.

"But I must say, your daughter," Jermaine continued, smiling at Lauren, who was now as close to physically ill as she could possibly get, "she's been really supportive — helping me get through the death of my brother and all," Jermaine said, folding his arms.

Without bothering to reply, Altimus turned his attention to Lauren. "Lauren, I'll see you back at the house. I'll be working late tonight, but you make sure you get home in time for dinner. Your mother is expecting you." And with that, he turned on his heel and walked away, without so much as a word to Jermaine.

"Okay, Daddy," Lauren called out after him.

"Nice meeting you, Mr. Duke," Jermaine yelled.

Lauren waited until Altimus was out of their view before she turned to Jermaine and let him have it. "What the hell were you doing? Didn't I tell you my stepdad is crazy? Are you trying to get on his last nerve?"

"Come on, Lauren, don't sweat it, okay?" Jermaine said. "And get it right: I'm the one who told you your step-dad is crazy."

"Oh, I see — you've got a death wish, huh?" Lauren stage-whispered as Jermaine took her hand and headed toward the door.

"No death wish. I just wanted your dad to know a little bit about your man, that's all. Where's your coat? Let's get out of here."

Lauren grabbed her coat off the showroom chair and pulled it on as Jermaine opened the door. The Atlanta winter chilled her to the bone, but she suspected her shivers had less to do with the air than what she thought Altimus might do to Jermaine for cutting up. "You know, you really ought to watch what you say to him," Lauren said. "Altimus usually has no problem giving me exactly what I want, but giving him lip isn't going to convince him to leave you and your family alone."

"I'm from the West End, baby — the SWATS," Jermaine countered. "I can handle myself."

"Whatev, straight-A boy," Lauren joked as Jermaine opened his car door for her. "And what was all that 'I get good grades and help in the community' bull about, anyway?"

"What, a brotha from the hood can't be smart and helpful?" Jermaine said as he climbed into the driver's seat and started his engine.

"Ain't nobody say all of that. Dang, why you gotta assume that's the way I think?" Lauren questioned defensively.

"Aw, baby, if I were making assumptions about you, you wouldn't be riding shotgun," he said as he pulled out into traffic.

"Then why are you with me? I mean, with everything you know about my family and what happened to your brother and all the questions about how he died and who killed him, why are you with me?"

Jermaine was silent.

"Dang, you don't even have an answer? Pull this car over, boy," Lauren demanded, punctuating her every word with a punch to his arm.

"Chill, chill," he laughed. "You're going to get us into an accident. But then you know all about crashing into other people's cars, don't you."

"See how you do me?" Lauren said, cracking up. "Why you gotta bring up the car wreck?"

"Well, if it weren't for that car wreck, I would never have found you, so I'm glad you took a brother's bumper out," he said quietly as he put on his signal and slowly pulled into the right lane. He turned into the parking lot of a Kroger shopping center and slowly came to a stop next to a large red minivan.

"What, we going shopping now?" Lauren said, eyeballing the shopping center; she and Jermaine watched as a mom struggled to get her two children and all of her groceries into a car just across the way from Jermaine's.

"Though I'm quite aware of how much you like the pastime, we're not going shopping," Jermaine said, shifting his body to face Lauren. "I have something much more fun for us to do." And with that, he leaned in and kissed Lauren on her lips so gently, she felt herself get a little dizzy. "I've been waiting for way too long to do that," he finally said after a long kissing session.

"I dreamed about this so many times," Lauren said, smiling. "I'm so glad we're back together again."

"Look," Jermaine said, his face turning serious. "You should know this much about me: I'm still real upset about what happened to my brother — I don't think he deserved to die that way. But I don't want to be like him, either. See, his problem was that he didn't want to leave the hood. That's the mentality of a lot of the people I live with. But there are some of us who want to leave and do something with ourselves, and then bring back what we earn and learn to help make the neighborhood better. People outside the hood don't ever see people like me getting good grades, staying out of trouble, trying to do right. And I don't care if they see it in me. What counts is I see it for myself."

Jermaine leaned in and kissed Lauren again. He ran his fingers over her eyebrow and took one more look into her eyes before turning back to the steering wheel. He put the car in drive and pulled out of the parking lot and back onto the street.

Lauren rubbed his arm and snuggled into the passenger seat. Every time she got with Jermaine, she learned something new about him — and herself. She turned each of his words around in her mind as she watched the ATL skyline rise before her and then rush by.

3
SYDNEY

"Okay, seriously, Sydney, you and your sister need to write a freakin' book," Rhea commented randomly.

The three girls leaned against the student lockers outside the entrance of their Fine Arts classroom, watching students pass by as they waited for the second-period bell to ring.

"What are you talking about, Rhea," Sydney muttered in reply as she examined the damaged cuticles on her left hand. Those last couple of weeks of hardcore punishment had wreaked havoc on her normally flawless fingers. And from the looks of her chipped polish, it was going to take several honey and warm paraffin treatments to undo the damage.

"I'm just saying, if a melee ever broke out at one of my parties, please believe it would take more than two weeks for me to convince my parents to let me off punishment," Rhea began as a crowd of boys heading toward the girls came into view.

"Shoot, it would probably take me another lifetime," Carmen co-signed. "The way my parents are about all their precious homes, I'd probably be sleeping in the garage until the day I died."

"Don't get it twisted," Sydney said, measuring her words carefully. She didn't want to give away more than she was willing to explain about the repercussions of the property damage and public humiliation of the entire Duke family that had happened that night. "Altimus and Keisha were not pleased. It took some pretty fast talking and a whole lot of begging. But at the end of the day, it's not like what happened was either of our faults." Sydney's voice faded out as she remembered the betrayed look on Jason's face when Marcus put her on blast for going out on a coffee date with him. Even though at the moment Jason had pretended that Marcus's accusation of Sydney not being over their old relationship didn't faze him, there was no hiding that he was no longer speaking to her. Or even worse, that thanks to the blow-by-blow YRT recap of the night's events, the entire school thought she was a cheater. She immediately began to tug on the diamond stud in her right earlobe. "I mean, who knew . . ."

"Duh, it definitely wasn't your fault," Carmen quickly reassured her best friend. "That's not what we're saying at all."

"Omigod, not at all, Syd," Rhea said as she shook her head. "Don't think that. It's so obvious Marcus is totally jealous of Jason. He was just looking for an excuse."

Sydney smiled warmly at her friends' valiant attempt at damage control. They always managed to make everything seem okay — even when it was so not.

"What's good, ladies," a voice called out from the group of guys that had finally made its way down the hall. The three looked over at Rhea's newly minted boyfriend, Tim, as he sidled up to Rhea for a quick kiss and squeeze of her booty.

"Ugh, Tim." Rhea feigned disgust as she swatted his hand away.

"What? Can't a brother get a little somethin'-somethin' to get him through the day?" he questioned playfully as he wrapped his arms around Rhea's tiny waist. He nuzzled his nose into her neck. "You smell good, babe."

Sydney felt a slight twinge of sadness as she remembered how Jason used to compliment her all the time on the scent of her favorite L'Occitane Green Tea with Mint perfume.

"Lloyd, will you please come get your boy?" Rhea pouted playfully toward Tim's best friend.

"Hey, don't blame me, Beyoncé. You're the one that's got him actin' all crazy in love," Lloyd joked as he yanked Tim back by the collar of his varsity baseball jacket.

Carmen giggled as the boys finally headed off down the hall with Tim in tow. "Not crazy in love! Lloyd Chesquire is a stone-cold fool."

"Girl, yes, he is. Every time we go out on a double date with him and whatever girl of the week he's dating, he has me in stitches," Rhea confirmed.

"I can only imagine," Carmen said with a shake of her head.

"But anyhoo, Sydney, will you tell me how you ever managed to do this whole relationship thing for four years?" Rhea questioned as she smoothed out her fitted pink-and-gray Nanette Lepore sweaterdress. "'Cause I swear, Tim's crazy behind is straight killing me and it's barely been a month."

Sydney nonchalantly shrugged her shoulders in response. The way her relationships were turning out — Marcus knocking up Dara, and Jason acting like he was never going to speak to her again — she felt totally unqualified to offer anyone relationship advice.

"Whatever, Rhea, you love it," Carmen said with a smirk.

"Well, sorta," Rhea giggled as she dug in her silver Cole Haan bag for lip gloss and a hand mirror. "I mean when you get past the whole butt grabbing, he is really cute. . . ."

"So have you asked him to the Sadie Hawkins Benefit or are you still playing hard to get?" Carmen asked Rhea curiously.

"I'm totally making him wait," Rhea giggled in response as she slathered on a sparkly layer over her heart-shaped lips. "You should hear him, hinting hard about it every chance he gets! It's so cute!"

"Is that a new gloss?" Sydney questioned in a subtle attempt to change the increasingly uncomfortable conversation. Considering she didn't have any prospects for a date to the upcoming dance, she really didn't want to hear much more about it.

"Um, actually I bought it a while ago," Rhea responded as she looked at the tube's label. "I think I picked it up that day we went underwear shopping after the pep rally."

"Oh," was Sydney's only response.

Carmen reached over and took the tube out of Rhea's hands. "NARS," she said, reading the label aloud, "very cute. You know that bright red lipstick that Michael absolutely loves on me is also NARS."

"Really? I had no idea," Rhea commented. "And I meant to ask you where you got it the other day. It's really hot."

"Well, I heard NARS is, like, number one on PETA's animal-cruelty list and no one who's remotely conscious is wearing it anymore," Sydney snapped, reaching her breaking point with all of the 'whose-boy-likes-what' talk. Carmen and Rhea stopped short and exchanged guilty looks. "I'm just saying," she continued, knowing full well that her little lie would curtail the boy-relationship-related convo pronto.

"Here you go," Carmen mumbled as she handed the gloss back to Rhea like it was infected.

"Damn, my bad," Rhea replied, shoving it back in her bag.

"Anyway, what time is it?" Sydney questioned, attempting to move on. She glanced at her Cartier tank watch, then down the hall. "I wonder if Mr. Wilkens is out today." She pushed off the locker, stood up straight, and turned to face her friends. "He's never late for class."

"Um, actually I think that's him coming now," Carmen countered just as the burly older gentleman, who looked more likely to coach a football team than instruct students on the intricacies of the fine arts, turned the corner.

"I always love his outfits," Rhea mused, of the tailor-made chocolate-brown suit, bright yellow tie, and spit-shined wingtips Mr. Wilkens wore that morning. "I wonder where he gets them. I just might buy my dad a few of those ties to help soften him up enough to upgrade the sound system in my Lexus. . . . What do you think?"

"Sounds like a plan to me," Carmen said. "I know anytime my mom wants something new, she just buys my father a new set of golf clubs. It's like an unspoken agreement — new clubs equals a new dining room set."

"I swear your mom is addicted to new dining room sets," Sydney joked. "She goes through at least three a year."

"Who are you telling?" Carmen agreed. "Parents are so crazy."

"Seriously," Rhea said with a good-natured smile. "But you know, the apple never falls far from the tree," she added forebodingly.

"I guess," Sydney said.

Just then, Mr. Wilkens arrived at the entrance to the classroom. "Good morning, ladies. I believe that classes are held inside the rooms, not in the hallway. No?"

"Yes, sir," the three intoned as they turned to walk inside the noisy classroom.

"All right, students, settle down. That was the final bell just a moment ago. I'd like everyone in their seats," Mr. Wilkens announced authoritatively as he reached his desk at the front of the room and placed his briefcase on the chair. "Today we're going to review pages . . ." He paused mid-sentence to read something on his desk. "Actually,

Ms. Duke, would you please head down to the athletic director's office?"

Confused, Sydney stopped unpacking her bag to face her teacher. "Is there something wrong?" she asked, wracking her brain to remember the last time she'd ever been called out of class.

"I'm not sure," Mr. Wilkens responded, raising the note that he had been reading toward her. "But it says 'immediately.' So you should probably get a move on."

"I wonder what it's about," Rhea whispered as Sydney grabbed her purple suede Moschino jacket.

"No clue, but wish me luck," Sydney muttered in response as she headed to the front of the room and out the door.

The sound of her hunter green Hogan knee-high boots sounded like rifle fire as Sydney hurried toward the athletic director's office. Even with a pass, she hated being in the hallways between classes. It reminded her of all those scary movies where the unsuspecting beautiful starlet is always getting her throat slashed by a serial killer lurking in an old janitor's closet. She sighed in relief as she finally neared the entrance to the office.

"May I help you?" the middle-aged receptionist sitting behind a huge computer screen inquired sweetly as soon as Sydney stepped into the front office.

Sydney raised her hand to show the note. "Yes, um, my name is Sydney Duke and I was asked to come down to the office immediately. I assume Coach Wiggins . . ."

"Oh, yes, Ms. Duke," the kindly woman said with a nod. "Have a seat, sweetie; I'll inform Coach Wiggins that you're here." She picked up the phone to announce Sydney's arrival.

"Thank you, ma'am," Sydney replied as she took a seat on the cracked black leather couch against the wall. She looked around the room at all the different championship trophies and plaques. Her eyes inadvertently fell on one with her own name from last year's Young Equestrians Championship. With all the drama going on, Sydney couldn't remember the last time she'd been down to the stables to spend time with Thunder, the championship filly her parents had bought her for her fifteenth birthday, let alone lap the ring.

"Ms. Duke," the receptionist called out, breaking Sydney's depressing train of thought. "Coach Wiggins is ready to see you now."

"Thanks," Sydney said politely as she headed to the large office in the back.

"Have a seat, Ms. Duke," Coach Wiggins instructed gruffly from his seat behind the large metal desk.

"Hey, Coach Wiggins," Sydney greeted the bald-headed, heavyset, former All American football player hesitantly. Although she saw him regularly when she was working out in the gym and weight room for her gym credit, she had never actually been called to his office before.

"Ms. Duke, I received a very interesting phone call this afternoon." Coach Wiggins started slowly as he tapped his two pointer fingers together.

"Is that so?" Sydney replied as she wondered what that had to do with her being urgently called out of class.

"Mmm-hmm, it was from your mother," he continued with a straight face.

"For what?" Sydney asked, completely shocked. In the three years she'd been at Brookhaven, Keisha Duke had never called the school about anything besides updating Lauren's portrait in the cheerleaders' clubhouse. "I mean, what did my mother need to speak to you about?"

"Well, it seems that the instructor down at the stable hasn't seen you for your equestrian practice in the past couple of months. And he was concerned that you were no longer interested in riding. So he contacted your mother directly."

Sydney gulped audibly. Had it been months? "I — I mean of course I'm still interested. It's just that a lot of other things have come up." She struggled to find an appropriate excuse for her absence from the early morning private sessions at the stable. The only things she kept coming up with were late nights spent talking on the phone and early morning breakfast dates with Jason when she should've been down at the stable.

"I'm sure I don't have to tell you, but your parents have donated a lot of money to the Brookhaven athletic programs over the last three years," Coach Wiggins continued. "And let's just say your mother made it very clear that if the school wants to continue seeing those generous donations, she expects her daughter to not only be on the equestrian team but to be named captain this spring."

Sydney's mouth dropped open at her mother's not so thinly veiled threat. It was one thing for Keisha to throw her weight around when it came to airbrushing Lauren's picture in a clubhouse, but this was unbelievable. "Oh, my God, Coach, I would never expect . . ."

"Now, don't get me wrong. Based on your show performances last spring, there's no doubt that you were a shoo-in for the spot even before this morning's call. But, as I'm sure you can understand, it's going to be very difficult for the instructors to keep you on the team, let alone make you captain, if you don't start attending your winter lessons immediately."

"I understand," Sydney said as she hung her head in shame.

"While it's the first time I've had the, um, pleasure of speaking with your mother on the phone, let's just say she didn't come across as the type of person afraid to back up her words with action. Am I right?" he asked. Sydney nodded in agreement. "Well, that's just fine, 'cause neither am I. So let me put it to you straight: I assured her that there was no reason to believe that you wouldn't be named captain. And you will — but not because she called over here. Because, as of tomorrow morning, you're going to have your butt down at the stables at seven A.M. sharp, and you're not going to miss a lesson from now until competition season ends. Am I clear, Ms. Duke?" Coach Wiggins stopped tapping his fingers and gave Sydney a very hard look.

"Yes, sir," Sydney squeaked.

Coach Wiggins leaned back in the swivel chair, crossed his arms, and looked at the large, round wall clock to his left. "Well, I'm glad we were able to come to an understanding so quickly. Have a nice day, Ms. Duke."

Sydney stammered as she stood. "Yes, sir. Me, too, sir." And without a second look, she rushed out the door.

"Slow down, sexy, you might hurt yourself in those heels," a familiar voice called out as Sydney rushed down the hallway.

She stopped dead in her tracks. The distinctly New York accent caused the hairs on her arms to stand at immediate attention. She listened as the squeak of what she was sure was a fresh pair of all-white Air Force Ones on the linoleum floor grew increasingly louder. Even when she could feel the heat of his presence burning her back, Sydney still couldn't bring herself to move an inch.

"And Lord knows, we wouldn't want that," Jason said as he gently touched her shoulder. "Right?" he asked teasingly. Sydney finally turned around.

"Hey, J," Sydney answered softly. The two stared into each other's eyes for at least thirty seconds before Sydney cast her eyes downward. "What's going on?" she asked, trying to force a smile to hide how nervous she felt.

"Nothing really," Jason ventured hesitantly. "I was actually chilling in the weight room when I saw your purple jacket pass by. So I stuck my head out to see if it was you. And I don't know, I guess I kinda just wanted to, you know, talk. . . . But if you're in a rush, I won't keep you."

"Naw, it's cool. I'm not in a rush." She struggled to keep her voice light and even.

"True," he responded, looking visibly relieved. "So what are you doing down here? Don't you have Fine Arts class with Mr. Wilkens this period?"

The fact that he still remembered her schedule made Sydney's heart skip a beat. "Um, I do, but Coach Wiggins needed to speak to me about tryouts for the equestrian team," Sydney hedged as she tugged at the scalloped cuff on her jacket.

"Oh, that's right. I forgot that you were on the team last

year," Jason responded. "Guess it's time for you to start practicing again, huh?"

"Something like that," Sydney said as she stole a quick glance at the adorable lips she'd once so easily had access to. "Isn't your season over? Why were you in the weight room?"

"I actually lift year-round," Jason explained. "But today I was down here with the defensive coach putting together my regimen for the Christmas break. He wants to make sure I stay on schedule even when the school is closed."

"Oh, okay, makes sense," Sydney said as she twisted the green leather Chanel cuff on her wrist.

"So, yeah, I had been meaning to call you," Jason started hesitantly as he dug his hands deep down in his pockets. "I wanted to apologize. . . ."

"You don't owe me an apology," Sydney immediately countered.

"Yeah, I do. I was fighting up in your parents' house. I ruined your holiday party. Marcus is a jerk but my parents raised me better than that. I'm really sorry, and, you know . . ."

Sydney put her hand on his arm to stop him. "Jason, listen. I'm really sorry about what happened with Marcus. I should've told you —" She stopped short, took a deep breath, and looked Jason directly in his eyes. "No, actually,

I shouldn't have even gone out with Marcus. I really messed up. I put you in an awful position, and I'm the one who's really sorry. I just hope that somehow you can find it in your heart to forgive me." Her heart pounded in her ears as she rushed to finish her words before she completely lost her courage.

Jason looked at Sydney for a long minute and then he reached out to smooth down a flyaway curl. "I really like you a lot, Sydney Duke."

"I really like you, too, Jason," Sydney said softly, again casting her gaze downward. "I know I didn't act like it but . . . I do. I just made a mistake. I don't know what else to say."

" 'Cause the thing is, Syd, if you still have feelings for Marcus, I can respect that. You guys were together for a long time. What? Like four years, right? Maybe it wasn't the right time."

"Trust, I have no more feelings for Marcus," Sydney retorted with a snort. "I don't think it was the wrong time, I just made the wrong decision. As far as I'm concerned the only reason Marcus and I will ever have to talk again is to plan this Sadie Hawkins Benefit Principal Trumbull is forcing us to do together."

Jason gently raised Sydney's head so that they were looking at each other eye-to-eye. "Good," he said. " 'Cause I think there's something really special between the two of us. Over the past couple of weeks, I've thought really hard about everything and, if you're game, I'm down to try again."

"Omigod, yes," Sydney squealed as she threw her arms around him. "Yes, yes, yes." Sydney turned her face upward and met his soft lips in a passionate kiss.

After a minute, Jason pulled away and looked at her gravely. "But I need to know that you're not going to play me out again. 'Cause I won't be made a fool of again. You feel me?"

"I promise, Jason. I won't," Sydney answered breathlessly. She was so happy, her entire body tingled from head to toe. Suddenly her whole outlook on the upcoming benefit seemed a lot brighter.

"Ever?" he questioned as his eyes momentarily narrowed.

"Ever."

Jason sighed with relief as he put his arm around Sydney's shoulders. "Now, if I can just get your stepdad to forgive me," he mused playfully. "Maybe I'll get an invite to this dance. . . ."

"Please, Altimus is the least of your worries," she answered sourly as she thought about the dictatorship her mother had established overnight in the Duke household.

Jason looked at her curiously. "Oh, so it's your mom that I need to be sucking up to, huh?"

Sydney shrugged and looked away as she tried to get her bitter emotions in check. Jason persisted playfully. "Okay, note to self, send Mrs. Duke a dozen yellow roses ASAP."

"Hey, hey," Sydney playfully punched him in the arm. "The only Duke that should be receiving roses is me! Do you hear me, Jason Danden?"

Jason laughed and pulled her into his arms. "I hear you, Syd. I hear you loud and clear," he whispered as he leaned in for another long kiss.

"Welcome home, Ms. Sydney, your snack will be ready shortly," Edwina said, greeting Sydney as she walked through the garage entryway.

"Thanks, Edwina," Sydney responded with a smile as she pulled off her boots at the door. She skipped happily over to the table and sat down to wait for the elderly maid to prepare her daily plate of fresh fruit and glass of pomegranate juice. Still feeling extra bubbly inside, Sydney pulled out her cell phone and scrolled down to the text message that Jason had sent her moments ago: I feel like the luckiest guy at Brookhaven. XOXO J.

Sydney smiled and sighed, "My boyfriend is so cute."

"I'm sorry, I didn't understand what you said, Ms. Sydney," Edwina apologized as she placed the snack down in front of Sydney.

"Oh, nothing, nothing," Sydney replied as she placed the iPhone down beside the plate and picked up her fork. "Everything looks great, thanks so much."

Edwina smiled slightly. "Enjoy," she said before heading back over to the refrigerator, where she began pulling out food to prepare for the evening's dinner.

Feeling hungry for the first time in weeks, Sydney dove right into her food. "Yummy," she mumbled mid-bite when her cell phone vibrated against the table. Looking down, she saw Aunt Lorraine's house number pop up, and her mood immediately dissipated. Her stomach knotted up as she fought to swallow before answering the phone. "Hello?" she answered hesitantly.

"Hope I'm not catching you at a bad time, princess," Aunt Lorraine sneered on the other end of the line.

"What's up, Aunt Lorraine?" Sydney asked, struggling to ignore the obvious bait.

"Um, I spoke with your father last night. He said that he sent you a letter, but for some reason it got returned. I guess the postman couldn't read his handwriting and took it to another house on the block. I don't know."

"I see," Sydney said simply. Now that her aunt was working for her parents, she refused to show any emotion.

"So he asked me to tell you that he re-sent it and it should be here within the week," Aunt Lorraine continued as if she didn't notice Sydney's curt tone. "I guess I'll send you a text when it gets here so that you can come over and get it."

"That's fine," Sydney responded as she listened to her aunt take a long drag on a cigarette. Like nails on a chalkboard, the sound made her skin crawl.

"Okay, then, I'll let you go —"

"Quick question," Sydney interjected before Lorraine could disconnect the call.

"Yeah, what's up?" Lorraine asked suspiciously. Sydney could clearly imagine the look of distrust on her aunt's face at that moment.

"I was just wondering . . . Did you ever manage to tell Dice that you're back in business with Altimus?" Sydney asked sweetly.

"You're the genius, Sydney — you tell me," Aunt Lorraine snapped sourly before slamming the phone down right in Sydney's ear.

4
LAUREN

"Look, as much as I wish I had the time to stand here and consort with the fans, I really have to run along," Lauren said, pulling her arm away from Cole Waters, who'd practically snatched her off her feet as she sprinted toward the lot where her car was parked.

She peeked at her iPhone: ten minutes before the first basketball dance squad practice, and she still had to pull her hair into a ponytail, slip into her cheer gear, and set up the music for the new number she'd created for the team; but none of this could happen until she actually got into her car and drove to the field house. Walking was not an option — and neither was being late.

On any other day, Lauren would have tossed Cole a little action; she'd had designs on him since before

Homecoming and had thrown enough hints his way to make it more than obvious that she was interested, but he was so tragically distracted. Boys.

Lauren couldn't imagine why she was rating so much attention on this particular day: a couple of the girls from the dance squad were (finally!) showing her the respect due their captain by doing the obligatory lunchroom swarm around the Queen B; the e-mail notifications on her Yahoo account signaled that the comments on her MySpace page were racking up; and now Cole was trying to holler. For sure, Lauren had to admit it felt good to be noticed again. After the whole Thanksgiving holiday debacle and subsequent posts on YRT — many of which made a point of reminding everybody that Altimus was crazy and deranged and that Lauren was all booed up with a ne'er-do-well from the West End — you would have thought Lauren was the president and CEO of the Society of Losers.

If nothing else, Cole was doing a helluva job reminding Lauren of her hot girl social status, which had, in Lauren's mind, taken a tragic dive.

Pleased by the attention, Lauren put on her most seductive smile. "If you didn't catch on by my running, I'm kinda in a rush," she said, looking down at Cole's hand clinging to her wrist.

"My bad," Cole said as he let his fingers linger. "Anything I can do to help ease the day? You lookin' stressed and all, but I can think of a few ways to make it better."

"Is that right?" Lauren smiled, soaking in Cole's words and the muscular legs peeking out from under his basketball shorts — he was on his way to practice. *Have mercy*, she said to herself. As tempted as she was to play, Lauren willed herself to focus. "Well, in case you've been living in a fox-hole for the past month, let me clue you in: I got a man. I mean, this is cute and all, you trying to make me late for practice. But I tossed you the ball a while ago, and you fumbled."

"In case you didn't know," Cole replied without hesitation, "I'm really good at rebounds. Maybe you can work that into one of the cheers you'll be doing for my team."

"Oh, is that what you think we're doing out there, cheering for you?"

"I don't think, I know," Cole said.

Lauren looked at her iPhone again. "Look, I gotta go," she said, unable to contain her smile. "You're making me late — and if you don't stop kicking game, you're going to be late for your practice, too."

"All right, then, I'll holla. Here's my number," he said, grabbing Lauren's phone.

"Boy, give me my phone back," Lauren said, futilely reaching for her cell, which Cole, at six feet three inches, easily held out of her reach as he started tapping at it. "What," demanded Lauren, "are you doing?"

"Chill — I'm just making sure you know how to get at a brother when you get bored slumming on the West End," Cole said, finally holding the phone at a height Lauren could reach.

"Slumming? What's that supposed to mean?" Lauren demanded, snatching her iPhone out of his fingers.

"Give me a call, and I'll explain it. Gotta go — Coach trips if we're late. Use those digits," he said, jogging away before Lauren could respond.

Lauren looked at the phone: It was 3:25 P.M. "Damn, I'm going to be late," she yelled. She watched Cole turn the corner of the hallway toward the gym, shook her head, and took off in the opposite direction, running out the door and into the winter chill.

"Before we get started, we have some administrative items to take care of," Coach Piper said as she fumbled through a stack of papers on the table before her. She looked up just as Lauren, working overtime to position a brown elastic band over her thick hair, clumsily scooted past a few of her dance squad members in search of one of the last of the empty metal folding chairs. "Well, so nice of you to join us, Ms. Duke," Coach Piper said, glancing down at her watch. "Practice started seven minutes ago."

"Sorry," Lauren said, trying not to wince as her bare legs hit the chair's cold metal. "I got tied up."

Coach Piper didn't bother to respond — just tossed Lauren a side-eye and got on with it. "As I was saying, a few administrative things before we get started. As you all know, the vote for captain is coming up next week, and I need you all to start thinking about who should lead the squad. To that end, I thought we should review the standards for being the squad leader, so that you can have it in mind as you all make your decision about the person who will be the face of Brookhaven Prep's basketball cheer team." She got up from her table, a stack of papers in hand. "Pass these down," Coach Piper said, handing the stack to Assistant Coach Pearl Maddie.

A hum moved through the room as the squad members, about a quarter of them newbies who, for the first time, were old enough or good enough to join the team, read through the "Standards of Conduct." Lauren sat back confidently in her chair; she placed the paper on her lap and took the time she was supposed to be reading to text Donald: You still there?

Donald's text came back almost instantaneously: Ugh, these sorry heifas in the yearbook club are going to be the death of me. I'm trying to make my light shine bright today, but they're slowly . . . making . . . it . . . dim.

Lauren giggled as she typed. Stop it! Focus. And then tell me all about it after school. You need a ride home?

Does Tyra rule the world? He responded in eight seconds flat.

"Okay, everyone, settle down. I'm going to run through this quickly so that you can really think about this before the vote," Coach Piper said. Her eyes settled on Lauren, whose fingers were flying so fast over the phone, she didn't notice the coach staring at her. "Um, Ms. Duke — care to stop texting and join us, or should we just wait until you're finished?"

Lauren tapped SEND on her phone and then balanced it on her lap. "Sorry, Coach. I'm all ears."

Coach prolonged her stare-down for a couple of extra seconds for emphasis, and then turned her attention back to the "Standards of Conduct" memo. "'Number one: The team captain must possess leadership qualities and devotion to the squad,'" she read. "'Number two: She must be highly motivated to the improvement of the squad. Number three: She will oversee the team at all times and be capable of organizing fund-raising, charity events, Homecoming, clinics, and banquets . . .'"

That's new, Lauren thought. Prior to now, those duties were carried out by the team manager. *Oh, well, I'll just delegate.*

"'The squad captain must also show maturity, emotional stability, and responsible leadership,'" Coach Piper continued. "'And she must be an adequate role model for her teammates, lead the way in being cooperative with guest teams, and maintain an unimpeachable reputation that represents herself, the squad, and Brookhaven Prep to its fullest potential.' Any questions?"

Meghan Robichaux's hand shot up like a pop rocket on the Fourth of July. "What's the nomination process for squad captain?" she asked.

Lauren's head popped up. The room fell silent.

"Good question," Coach Piper said. "We have a long tradition of great squad leaders, all of whom are vetted by the coaches with the recommendation of the outgoing squad's captain. The coaches and captain then nominate three people, and then the team gets together and decides who should be captain and co-captain. Now, in the past, the outgoing squad captains have always been seniors, so the process was fairly cut-and-dried. But because this past season's captain is now a junior, she has to negotiate the tricky terrain of nominating herself as well as two others who will compete against her for the position. Anyone who is interested in becoming squad captain or co-captain can come into my office and submit your name before we head out to the practice gym. Any more questions?"

Meghan looked at Caroline and Elizabeth, and they

started chattering like three old ladies at a Bingo game. Lauren tried to lean in but between Kayo cackling in her ear and Coach Piper rambling on and on about the fees for the banquet, she couldn't make out what they were saying. But she had the sneaking suspicion that it was a lot of things — none of them good.

"All right, everyone, let's settle down. We have about forty-five minutes to practice the new routine Ms. Duke so graciously coordinated for our first game, which is in two weeks. That is if Ms. Duke had the energy, between texting and all the other wonderful social skills that consume her time, to put it together?" Coach Piper asked, directing her attention to Lauren, who was still a tad dumbstruck by the prospect of having someone compete for her Number One spot.

"Uh, yeah, it's all set," Lauren said. "Ready when you are."

"Okay, then, if there's nothing else, I'll accept nominations in my office; everyone else can go with Lauren out to the gym."

Lauren did everything she could to linger so she could see which traitor was heading to Coach Piper's office; she was trying not to be obvious about it, but that was challenging, considering it was down the hall, in the opposite direction of the doors leading to the gym. Standing in front of the gym doors facing the coach's office, Lauren pulled out her ponytail holder and fiddled with her hair, like she was getting it ready for practice. Then she retied one shoe . . . slowly, then the other. And then, there was the imaginary lint on her Nike gym pants that just needed to be removed, right then, at that moment.

Just when she was about to get a sip of water from the fountain, her iPhone rang — a text from Sydney. The girl had a way with timing. Lauren pulled up the text and read slowly. Her eyes grew larger with every word of the story Sydney had forwarded from an online *Atlanta Journal-Constitution* bulletin:

Breaking news (Atlanta): Prominent Buckhead business-man Altimus Duke, owner of several of Georgia's most successful high-end car dealerships, is under federal investigation for tax fraud and tax evasion. Sources say Duke is accused of bilking the federal government of hundreds of thousands of dollars over the past four years. A spokesman for Duke Enterprises, the parent company of Duke's eleven dealerships, said the businessman would have no comment, except to say that he intended to fight the charges vigorously.

Mortified, Lauren started to text Sydney back but instead made a detour to YRT. The site was prime time for gossip updates — they always made their way to the site just a few hours after school, when all the juicy mess that happened during the day hit the fan. Sure enough, there it was in all its glory; whoever posted the Duke business debacle didn't even bother to put any spin on it — just posted the AJC story with one simple line following: *Inhale, exhale, inhale, exhale, inhale, exhale, namaste.*

Lauren's eyes shot up when she saw Meghan, Elizabeth, and Caroline walking her way, huddled over Caroline's phone. The three of them were whispering and cackling and acting like fools as they tumbled down the hallway, heading for Coach Piper's office. Lauren steeled herself for the madness.

"I mean, really, the 'must maintain an unimpeachable reputation' part alone disqualifies her for the job," Caroline insisted. She didn't make any kind of effort to lower her voice. "A father who rips off Uncle Sam? Cavorting with hood rats and pushing them off on friends and family? Really?"

"Well, maybe she was taking the 'being cooperative with guest teams' part literally," Elizabeth chimed in, peering into a compact mirror to slather gloss on her lips.

"Yeah, whatev," Meghan snapped as the three walked slowly down the hallway. "I don't care if this is the house the Dukes built. I don't see it written anywhere on these walls that Lauren has to be the team captain. That whole Thanksgiving party? Total fiasco. And the gangster tax thing with the dad? Hot mess. And as much as she thinks she's Beyoncé's long-lost sister, she could use a little extra direction on how to cheer off some of those hips and thighs."

"You ain't never lied," Elizabeth laughed as the three walked into the coach's office, one after the other.

Not even the slamming door could snap Lauren out of her shock.

Lauren paced back and forth across the lobby, trying really hard to look like she wasn't fazed by what was going on. But it was clear to anyone watching that she was a wreck — and best believe, everyone was watching.

"All right, then, Lauren, um, see you around," said Eunice Blake as she and her BFF, Chere Baker, tumbled past her and out the door, both of them giggling. Lauren had seen them whispering all the way down the hallway — who were they kidding, like they weren't talking about her? Lauren wanted desperately to reach out and slap them or else melt into the wall. And just where the hell was Donald anyway? He knew she needed to get out of Brookhaven, stat.

"Okay, first of all, breathe," Donald insisted, rushing up to Lauren and putting his arm around her shoulder. "Here, let me take your bag. You lookin' a hot mess."

"Well, wouldn't you have a fever if you found out your father was about to go to the clink?" Lauren snapped.

"Dammit, I got one in jail; do I really need another one there?"

"Alrighty, friend, calm it down, you're talking awfully loud for someone who just had her business put on front street," Donald said, looking around wildly to see who all was listening. "Let's keep the details between us."

"Do the details even matter?" Lauren snapped. "I heard Caroline and them already plotting and planning how they were going to use this to take away my captain status. I mean, can you really imagine me on the squad and *not* in charge? Sweet Lord."

"Are you really going to worry about Caroline, Meghan, and Elizabeth taking your spot?" Donald insisted as he took her hand. "Honey, please. They only put the cute ones up front. You could totally put Caroline's picture up on the refrigerator to discourage late-night snacking — she's so not cute."

"But being the prettiest girl on the team wasn't part of Coach's standards of conduct," Lauren pointed out as she rummaged through her purse for her keys.

"It should be," Donald said quickly. "When is an ugly captain ever acceptable?"

"Donald, I'm being serious!"

"So am I," Donald insisted. "Shoot."

"I can't believe they were just walking down the

hallway, shamelessly talking about me like I was invisible — or worse, like they didn't care if anyone heard them."

Donald stopped short, right in the middle of the parking lot.

"What?" Lauren yelled, her eyes darting all around the cars to see what had startled Donald. "What's wrong?

"I can't believe you just fixed your mouth to say that!" he insisted.

"Donald, what in the world are you talking about?"

"You just said they were talking about you like they didn't care if you heard them," he said.

"Yeah — and?"

"So who do you think they learned that from, Miss Put 'Em in Their Place?"

"True," Lauren said after a brief hesitation. "But still, that doesn't give them the right."

"Nobody ever gets permission to talk smack about somebody," Donald said. "You sure didn't. Those little girls learned how to diss and stomp all over people from the best: Lauren Duke."

"So what you trying to say, Donald — don't hold back," Lauren said, taking off for her car, annoyed.

"I'm not *trying* to say it — I am *saying* it: You're the queen of social climbing, and these little bitches are going to try you every moment they get. You're going to have to fight to keep your captain's sweater and bullhorn. Don't pay them any mind — go get what's yours. And not for nothing? But I think Altimus can more than handle his own, so I wouldn't be too worried about him, either."

Lauren took in a deep breath, squared her shoulders, and pushed the UNLOCK button on her key ring. "I hope you don't have any homework," she said.

"Actually, I have enough calculus and AP physics homework to last me through my third year in grad school," Donald droned.

"Well, bring it with you — you can work on it while we're at Justin's," Lauren said.

"And what in the world are we going to be doing at Justin's?"

"We're going to strategize," Lauren said, ducking into her car. "It's. About. To. Go. Down."

And with that, Lauren started her engine.

By the time she dropped off Donald, drove to her house, and pulled Baby into her parking spot in the circular driveway, the Duke household was in full crisis mode. She could hear Altimus and Keisha in his office, talking in hushed tones. Even though she couldn't quite make out what they were saying, she was sure the discussion involved how all of them were going to end up in the clink. Sell drugs, beat people upside the head with a baseball bat, threaten family members with bodily harm and cell phone monitoring and nobody cares. But mess with Uncle Sam's cut? Even Lauren knew the government wasn't to be played with.

"Oh, hello, Ms. Lauren, can I get you a snack?" Edwina asked, grabbing Lauren's book bag and purse as Lauren flipped off her heels.

"Häagen-Dazs," Lauren said, not bothering with greetings and niceties. "Lots of it."

"Yes, Ms. Lauren, right away," Edwina said.

Lauren walked over to the closed office door and lingered a little, while she waited to hear a lull in the obviously heated conversation. When she heard someone walking toward the door, she quickly knocked, lest whoever was approaching thought she was spying.

Keisha snatched open the door.

"Hey," Lauren said simply when her eyes met Keisha's. They were bloodshot — so red they almost matched the Chanel lipstick that had begun to wear off of her lips. Over her mother's shoulder, Lauren could see Altimus, sitting at his heavy wooden desk, rubbing his temples, his elbows resting on stacks of paper-filled folders.

"Hey," Keisha answered back. "What's up?"

"Um, question of the day, for sure," Lauren said quietly. "I saw the article about Dad."

"I'm sure," Keisha said. She looked at Altimus, then stepped outside his office and shut the door. "Look, we're

63

not going to panic, okay? To hear your father tell it, this investigation is preliminary, and it doesn't prove he did anything wrong. That's the family line if anyone asks, got it?"

"But . . ."

"Look, Lauren, now's not the time to ask questions or give your two cents about anything, okay? Your father and I? We got this. This family has been through far worse things, trust," Keisha insisted. "Now, like I said, keep your mouth shut about this, and let me and your father handle it. No worries. Yet. And if anyone's got anything to say about it, tell them to come see me."

And with that, Keisha stepped back into Altimus's office, and quietly shut the door. Lauren stared at the massive mahogany door, then dropped her head and headed for the kitchen. Her ice cream was waiting.

5
SYDNEY

"Not for nothing, I don't know what's more unbelievable: that you and Jason are back together, or that your parents are even letting you out of the house with everything that's going on with your dad's business," Carmen mused from her end of the three-way call.

Sydney had initiated the call twenty minutes earlier to discuss strategy for her first official-official date with Jason.

"I hate to say it, but Rhea might really have a point about that, Syd. . . ."

"I told you." Rhea happily tooted her own horn. "If it were my mom, she'd have me and my sisters sitting in a twenty-four-hour prayer vigil for her country club membership."

Humph, you'd be surprised at half the things my parents

are capable of, Sydney thought cryptically before responding with the more appropriate, "I guess I'm just really lucky to have the parents I do."

"Totally," Carmen responded, "and —"

"Anyhoo, it's almost seven. So let me . . ." Sydney cut Carmen short.

"Oh, no, my dear. I'm so not hanging up this phone until you absolutely promise to call us the moment you walk back in the door and tell us Jason's reaction to the dress," Rhea threatened.

"Yeah, Syd, after all this prepping, we deserve the blow-by-blow before it ends up on YRT," teased Carmen.

"Okay, okay! Barring all unexpected paparazzi and hidden cameras, I solemnly swear to give my best friends a full account of my date as soon as I get home," Sydney assured her girls. She finished applying her favorite lemon-scented Bliss body butter and pulled out the new gray Calvin Klein sweaterdress Rhea had chosen for her from the silver Saks shopping bag. "Now, let me go before Jason shows up and I'm still standing around talking to the two of you in my underwear," she insisted as she held the dress up against her scantily clad body and tried to envision which of her countless accessories best complemented the form-fitting minidress.

"The way he looked at school today in that adorable baby blue Lacoste shirt and those Sean John jeans, we're probably doing you a favor by keeping you on the phone," Rhea mused playfully.

"Um, Rhea, can you please get your mind out of her man's pants?" Carmen retorted with a snort at Rhea's ongoing joke about Jason's form-fitting football uniform.

"Good-bye, ladies . . ."

"Just tell me you're at least wearing the purple polkadot undies we spent an entire afternoon searching for," Rhea insisted as Sydney disconnected the call with a smile. She could always depend on her feisty best friend to try to get in the last word.

Placing the phone on its base and the dress on her bed, Sydney headed into her closet to dig through her enormous jewelry box. She finally settled on twisted, chunky Cartier bangles and the silver hoop set Keisha had bought on a whim and then handed down to Sydney when she decided they didn't exactly have the same effect as a platinum pair she'd seen Vanessa Williams rocking in *Us Weekly* a couple of days later. Just as Sydney finished securing her second earring, there was a knock at the bedroom door.

"It can't be seven-thirty yet," she mumbled, grabbing a pair of black tights and hurrying out of the closet to find Lauren standing by her bed gently fingering her dress.

"Cute," Lauren commented. "I hope you're wearing the right underwear or that panty line is going to be a situation."

"Thanks for the news flash, Britney," Sydney retorted sarcastically as she shooed her sister away from the bedside so she could sit down. "Um, correct me if I'm wrong, but I don't remember the part where I granted the fashion police permission to come in."

"My bad," Lauren sighed dramatically as she flung herself into Sydney's desk chair.

Recognizing the beginnings of a signature Lauren Duke meltdown, Sydney nervously eyed the iHome clock on her nightstand. With only twenty-five minutes until Jason's scheduled arrival, she still had to get dressed, put on her makeup, and do something with her hair. "Okay, what's wrong?" she questioned as she carefully pulled up her tights to avoid causing a run. "And honestly, with everything going on, do I even want to hear this right now?"

"I mean, I guess it's not *that* big of a deal," Lauren mumbled as she carelessly flipped through the copy of *Vanity Fair* Sydney had sitting on top of her closed laptop.

"Lauren," Sydney paused in the middle of pulling her dress over her head. "I've only got twenty-five minutes. Spare me the dramatics and start talking."

"Fine," Lauren pouted as she closed the magazine and turned to face Sydney. "Well, it's just . . . I was so excited to see Jermaine. You know? Especially after all the craziness,

I just wanted him to hold me and for us to just, like together like a normal couple. . . ."

"Okay, so what's the problem?" Sydney asked over her shoulder as she headed into the bathroom. "Not enough time together?"

"No, no, it's not that," Lauren continued as she followed behind her sister. "It's that Jermaine just won't let the whole 'who killed Rodney' thing go." Lauren sat on the closed toilet lid next to the vanity and examined her fingernails.

"Uh, are you really surprised?" Sydney questioned as she leaned into the mirror and carefully applied her trusty Diorshow mascara. "Jermaine was literally on the run for a crime that he didn't commit. Did you think he was going to get over it that quickly?"

"But *I* wasn't the one accusing him," Lauren insisted, standing up beside Sydney to grab the bottle of Aveeno hand lotion off the counter. "So why do *I* have to deal with the tirades?" she whined. "Why can't we leave it up to the police and move on? I mean, with all that's happening with Altimus and the tax situation, don't I deserve to be comforted instead of always being put on the defensive?"

Sydney stopped applying the second coat of her shimmering lip gloss to look at her sister's reflection in total disbelief. "Lauren, Jermaine's only brother was murdered. Your own father is looking at life in prison until the real killer is brought to justice. And you want to move on?" Momentarily ashamed, Lauren cast her gaze downward. "Seriously? Are you that self-centered?" Sydney continued sharply.

"Whatever, Syd, it has nothing to do with being self-centered," Lauren snapped as she slammed the bottle of lotion down on the counter. "I just need a freaking break. I am sixteen years old. I am not supposed to be worrying about going broke or going to jail. I just want to enjoy my life! And if that makes me a bad person, then" — tears of frustration welled up in her eyes as Lauren took a deep breath — "then I don't know what to tell you. I guess you're just a better person that I am."

"It's not about being a better person, Lauren," Sydney said, quickly softening her tone as she turned to comfort her distraught twin. "It's just that this isn't something we can just ignore and it will disappear. And that sucks. But the good news is, the sooner we figure out who's at the bottom of all this, the sooner it will be over for everyone. Okay?" Lauren sniffled and nodded her head in response. "So instead of getting upset, why don't you go see Uncle Larry? See if he's heard anything new."

"That's probably a good idea," Lauren said softly.

"It's definitely a better idea than you standing here crying on my new dress," Sydney teased gently as she hugged her sister.

"Ha-ha," Lauren said with a smile as she turned to grab a tissue out of the box on the counter. Cocking her head slightly, she looked at Sydney in the mirror. "You look good, Syd."

"Really? I haven't worked out in a minute so I wasn't so sure about the mini . . ."

"No, I mean the dress is great and all; but you look happy," Lauren clarified. "I'm glad you and Jason figured things out."

"Yeah, me, too," Sydney said softly as she felt the butterflies in her stomach. "Now, if I could just figure out this hair," she complained as she started to pull her curls back away from her face.

"No, wear it out," Lauren advised knowingly. "I heard guys from up north totally dig that whole big hair, curly look. Besides, it works for you." Sydney smiled at her sister. "Okay, okay, let me get out of here before your head gets too big for the both of us."

"Forget you," Sydney laughed as Lauren headed out the door. Deciding to take her sister's advice, she fluffed up her curls, slid on a skinny headband, and sprayed some Luster oil sheen for the finishing touch. "Perfecto," she said, stepping back to admire her handiwork. Sydney sprayed her neck and wrists with the L'Occitane perfume, grabbed her lip gloss, and headed back into her bedroom to pack her purse.

"Oh, so I guess you think you cute," sneered Keisha Duke from the open doorway as Sydney stood by her desk disconnecting her iPhone from the charger.

Refusing to make eye contact with her mother, Sydney simply focused on the phone and shrugged her shoulders. "I don't know what you're talking about."

"You don't know what I'm talking about?" questioned Keisha as she stepped into Sydney's bedroom and closed the door firmly behind her. "Well, please, let me break it down for you. I'm talking about that little boy sitting in my living room waiting on you. For some reason, he thinks that the two of you are going on a date."

"His name is Jason," Sydney retorted as she turned away from her mother to throw her wallet and cell into the silver Balenciaga bag on her bed. "And for your information, we *are* going out on a date."

"Is that so? 'Cause it seems to me, I already done told you how I felt about that situation, months ago. But maybe I wasn't clear enough," Keisha sneered. "Here's the deal, princess — your father and I donated a lot of damn money to Councilwoman Green's campaign. Not just this past election or even the last; I'm talking on a continuing basis. Donations, dinners, gifts, you name it, we gave it. And it all equals way too much for you to be 'going out' with someone other than her beloved only son."

"Excuse me?"

"Oh, no, you heard me correctly," Keisha continued as she walked up directly behind her daughter. "Every hand greases the wheel. The security and longevity of our family business depends on making the right connections. And be clear, your little star quarterback sitting in my living room looking crazy ain't part of the program. So you can play dumb as long as you like, but at the end of the day a winning pass ain't gonna save none of our asses from jail!"

Sydney turned around slowly and looked at her mother from head to toe with newfound contempt. "You know what? I really don't care how much money you and my *step*father donated to Marcus's mom's campaign. Everything done in the dark eventually comes to light. And there's no amount of money or greasing palms that's going to save either of you. And remember, I said you, not me!"

"Oh, please, who the hell are you kidding?" Keisha laughed. "You *are* me, little girl!"

"No, I'm not," Sydney retorted angrily.

"Wow, I always thought you were the smart one," Keisha mused nastily.

"Whatever, Mother. You may be able to dictate what goes on in this house, but you can't tell me who to be in a relationship with. And I'm certainly not about to stay with Marcus to help save you, when you wouldn't even stay in your marriage to help save my father!" Sydney snapped.

She grabbed her bag, stepped around Keisha, and headed for the door.

Jason sat nervously on the edge of the living room couch where Sydney's mother had left him. Looking at his watch, he increasingly regretted his decision to arrive five minutes early. Suddenly the door connected to the kitchen swung open and Altimus's figure filled the entire frame.

"Good evening, Mr. Duke," Jason said as he jumped to his feet to offer his hand.

"I don't believe we've met," Altimus replied gruffly, choosing to dismiss both Jason's greeting and out-stretched hand.

"Um, no, we haven't. I mean, not formally," Jason replied nervously. "My name is Jason. Jason Danden. I'm a friend of Sydney's from Brookhaven. I was at the holiday party at Lake Lanier. . . ."

"I see," Altimus countered coolly. "Well, there was a lot going on that evening. You'll forgive me for not remembering you. Normally, in my line of work, I rarely forget a face."

"Oh, it's okay," Jason interjected, secretly relieved that Mr. Duke didn't recognize him from the tangle of bodies involved in the melee at Sydney's holiday party brawl.

"Yet I've never seen you around here before."

"Well, yeah. Sydney and I just started hanging out recently. I'm not from here . . ."

"And just where would you be from, Jason?"

"Well, my folks moved down here about two years ago from New York City. So I just recently started going to school with Syd . . . I mean Sydney," Jason continued nervously.

"I see. And what brought your parents down to Atlanta?" Altimus continued his poker-faced interrogation without so much as a blink of the eye.

"Well, actually *I* did," Jason explained as he ran his sweaty palms down the front of his dark-indigo Evisu jeans. "I wanted to play football in an area where I could easily get noticed by the college scouts, and my coach recommended the Atlanta area —"

"But Brookhaven doesn't win games," Altimus cut him off sharply with a raised eyebrow.

"This is true," Jason concurred. "But there was no way my parents were going to let me go to a school that didn't have a strong academic program, and let's just say Brookhaven has the best reputation by far. So my hope is that over the next year, I can help turn the team around."

"Hmm, I'd have to agree with your parents. Reputation is very important," Altimus said simply. "Sydney has worked very hard to build and maintain her outstanding reputation both academically *and* socially."

Jason cleared his throat and shifted from one foot to the other. "Sydney's definitely a great person. I, uh, I'm looking forward to getting to know her," he started awkwardly.

"So it goes without saying that both Mrs. Duke and I have great expectations for our daughter. None of which will be achieved if she becomes sidetracked."

"Yes, sir."

"And while neither her mother nor I would ever propose to choose who our daughter spends her time with," Altimus continued, "I'm sure you can understand *my* concern after years of walking into this room and greeting the Honorable Councilwoman Green's son, Marcus — you do know Marcus Green, don't you?"

"Yeah, I know him." Jason bristled at the mention of Sydney's ex-boyfriend.

"Well, then, I'm sure you can understand how I might feel about finding you here now," Altimus continued unapologetically.

"Understood," Jason responded from between clenched teeth.

"As long as we're clear," Altimus concluded just as Sydney bounded down the staircase into the living room. She paused at the end of the staircase for effect. Altimus reflexively clenched his teeth.

"Hey, J!" Sydney rewarded Jason with a huge smile as she unknowingly interrupted the tense moment.

"Hey, Sydney, you look nice," Jason responded, grateful for the opportunity to escape from Altimus's well-executed scare tactics.

"Thanks — so do you." Sydney paused for a moment to take in Jason's jeans, buttoned-up shirt, and fresh pair of Nike Air Force Ones. Even though the jeans were much baggier than his infamous uniform pants, Jason still looked really good.

"Altimus, did you meet my friend Jason?" Sydney inquired, oblivious to the tension in the room.

"Yes, I did," Altimus responded. "As a matter of fact, Jason and I were talking about future prospects when you came down."

"Of what? The Brookhaven team?" Sydney looked quizzically at Jason for a clue to what her stepfather was talking about.

"Something like that," Jason answered vaguely with a slight smile Sydney couldn't figure out. "You ready to go?" he asked.

"Yeah, my shoes are at the door," Sydney answered as she headed to the front door in search of her black-and-silver Gucci ballet flats.

"Cool," Jason said. "It was nice to meet you, Mr. Duke." He turned and offered his hand again.

"I'm sure," Altimus responded drily and walked away.

6
LAUREN

Lauren felt around the bottom of her purse, reaching past her makeup bag, iPod, two notebooks, a few tubes of M.A.C Lipglass, a compact, a couple of purple pens, and a gaggle of school papers, until her fingers hit the pile of coins collected in a jingling lump beneath a piece of stale, half-opened Orbit Bubblemint. She peeled off the quarter that was stuck to the gum and rolled the coin between her fingers. Honestly, she didn't even know how much it cost to make a local call from a public phone these days; heck, she didn't even know public pay phones still existed, really. But there was one, right there at the corner of the McDonald's parking lot, as ancient a relic as Uncle Larry's house, which she was about to call to warn its owner that she was on her way over. He wouldn't be happy about it. Never was. But visit she must.

Lauren needed some intel, and right about now, Uncle Larry was the only one in the family she could turn to without repercussions or a cuss out.

Lauren pulled up Uncle Larry's contact info on her iPhone and punched his number into the sticky keys on the pay phone. As she raised the receiver to her ear, she secretly wished she was afflicted with Sydney's perpetual (and annoying) habit of carrying antibacterial hand sanitizer and wipes everywhere — Lauren was sure the phone harbored some kind of nasty toxic cootie that would make the side of her face break out into some kind of funky, incurable rash. She held the phone as far away from her ear as she could without ruining her ability to hear. Uncle Larry answered after the second ring.

"Hey, Uncle Larry, it's Lauren," she said.

"Oh, hey, doll, how you been?"

"Good, good," Lauren said. Cutting to the chase, she quickly added: "You up for some company?"

"Um . . ."

The hesitation in Uncle Larry's voice made Lauren immediately regret asking permission to visit; he was two seconds away from shutting down her drop-by. She was going to have to do some fast talking. "Look, Uncle Larry, I really need to see you. I have some interesting updates for you — things you need to know."

"Lauren, now isn't a good time, sweetie —" he began.

"I promise, I'll only be a few minutes," Lauren said, cutting him off. "I'm right around the corner at the McDonald's. No one knows I'm here, and I called you from a pay phone so that the call can't be traced. . . ." Lauren insisted.

"Lauren, this isn't a good time," Uncle Larry repeated simply.

"Look, Unc, I'm going to just come over to your house for a few minutes. . . ."

"No!" Uncle Larry shouted. "Don't come here, okay? I need you to stay where you are."

"But I need to see you, Uncle Larry — I really need your help."

"Then I'll meet you where you are," he said. "Just don't come here. You said you're at the McDonald's?"

"Yes," she said simply.

"What you driving?"

"A black Saab."

"I'm on my way. Don't get out of the car, hear me? Not even to get fries. Just pull around toward the back and sit tight. I'll be there straightaway."

In no time at all, Uncle Larry was easing his black Cadillac into the space next to Lauren's, which was hemmed in by an oversized Dumpster that absolutely reeked of rotting food and sour milk. The stench and the gust of cold air that rushed into the car when Uncle Larry climbed in delivered a one-two punch from which Lauren struggled to recover. She pressed the digital temperature button until it read 80, and snuggled into her coat. Uncle Larry peered through the side-view mirror and peeked out the rear window, clearly nervous; he was giving Lauren the shakes.

"Uncle Larry, you're kinda bugging out — don't worry, nobody knows I'm here," Lauren said.

"Lauren, the whole block knows you're here," he said, slamming the door behind him. "I need you to understand that you can't just drop by when you feel like it. The block is hot, sweetheart, and your Uncle Larry is trying to keep cool. I don't want no part of this now, I told you that before."

"But a lot has happened since the last time we talked, and I really needed to tell you about it," Lauren said, quickly surmising that she should wait a few minutes before asking his advice about Jermaine's brother. "Altimus —"

"See?" Uncle Larry said, peering out the mirrors and windows again, "that's what I don't need to know about. Altimus."

"Uncle Larry, take it easy — it's good news, kinda," Lauren said.

"Good news, huh?" Uncle Larry said. "Did Rodney

come back to life or something? Because that would be the best news right about now. Otherwise, he's still dead, we still don't know who killed him, and the entire West End thinks one of your fathers had something to do with it."

"But —"

"But, hell," Uncle Larry said, cutting his niece off. "You're in the middle of some serious mess, Lauren, and you're dragging me into it."

"I didn't drag you into anything," Lauren said, a little louder than she'd intended. "You came for me that day at Pride and offered your help — I didn't ask for it. So no matter how much you say you don't want anything to do with this, you made yourself a part of it."

Uncle Larry was taken aback by Lauren's gruffness; honestly, he didn't know the girl had it in her, but he should have figured. *This*, he said to himself, *is Keisha's child.*

"Now, I came over here to give you some news and to see if you could help me sort through what it means," Lauren said. "It's about my Aunt Lorraine."

Uncle Larry just stared blankly at Lauren.

"You know who she is, right?"

Uncle Larry folded his arms.

"She's my real father's sister," Lauren said. "She lives here in the West End, and my father, Dice, has been —"

"He lives with her, I know that," Uncle Larry said as he settled into the leather seat. "Lorraine is a real piece of work."

"Yeah, well that piece of work is working with Altimus and my mom," Lauren said. "I don't know exactly what she's going to be doing for them, but it's got something to do with helping Altimus get himself off the hook for the murder."

"Wait, Lorraine is in on this now?"

"Exactly — weird, huh?" Lauren said. "All these years she's been standing by Dice and keeping her distance from Altimus and my mom — I assume because she knew what they did to Dice and what they could do to her if she got mixed up in the madness. Now she's all down. She even came to our house a few days ago, like she was there to kiss Altimus's ring or something. I swear it was like a scene straight out of *New Jack City*. The only thing missing was the Rottweiler and the chain."

"She wasn't there to kiss your father's ring — Lorraine was there because of Keisha," Uncle Larry muttered cryptically, almost as if his words were intended only for him.

"Keisha?" Lauren said. "But Altimus . . ."

"Look," Uncle Larry said, waving his hand. "My sister is many things, chief among them a winner. She will not lose. She's like Malcolm X in that regard — by any means necessary."

"I don't follow you," Lauren said, confused.

"What I'm trying to tell you, doll, is that you need to fall back on this — give everybody some room to breathe and figure out what's what," Uncle Larry said.

"But I can't do that, don't you see?" Lauren demanded. "I feel like I'm the one who can't breathe. I'm sneaking around the West End, watching over my shoulder trying to see who all is looking at me and watching what I'm doing. I'm afraid to talk on the phone, my sister is a mess, my parents have lost their minds and are dragging our family members into their madness, and Jermaine? He's treating me like I'm one of the detectives from *Law & Order*, like I have all the clues and the answers. It's driving me crazy!"

By the time she finished her rant, Lauren's heart was beating so fast and hard, she was sure anyone looking could have seen it pounding through her sweater. She was absolutely done with everyone telling her to be quiet — to sit back and wait for the adults to handle it. Their words made sweat pop from her brow, it got her so angry, because all of the adults were doing a piss-poor job of giving up the info and getting her life back to normal. She could feel the lump in her throat as she struggled to find the words to say this to Uncle Larry. But the only thing her body would conjure were tears — tears she did not want to cry.

Uncle Larry shifted his body so he could look Lauren in

the face; he watched the first tear, then the second, fall from her eyes. "Look, I didn't mean to upset you. That's not what Uncle Larry does."

"Then what does Uncle Larry do?" Lauren demanded. "Because right about now, you're the only one who can actually *do* something. My parents have no idea I even know you exist, so you can make moves without anyone knowing you're involved."

"It's nice that you're so confident in my skills, darlin', but I'm not so sure it's that easy," he said.

"I'm seeing that much, Uncle Larry. I know it's not easy. But Jermaine and his mother deserve to know who killed their fam, and my father — my real father — deserves not to have to rot in prison for something he didn't do."

Suddenly, Lauren got quiet. Had she really suggested out loud that Dice was innocent?

"I hear you loud and clear," Uncle Larry said quietly, putting his hand on Lauren's. "I got my eyes wide open and my ear to the street on this, Lauren. I got your back."

Lauren took in a deep, long breath and swiped at the tears on her cheeks. "Thank you, Uncle Larry. Thank you so much," she said, taking his hand in hers. "I swear to you from the bottom of my heart, I'm so grateful. Anything you can do, it's appreciated."

"Yup," Uncle Larry said. "But one more thing: You can't keep dropping by, okay? I need more notice than this, hear? Seriously, little girl, you don't know what you're up against coming here. This is the lion's den, sweetheart. You're easy prey, no matter who your daddy is."

Lauren just nodded.

"Now, you need to get on — go on back to Buckhead and let me figure some things out. I'll be in touch." And with that, he stepped out of Lauren's car, slammed the door, and watched as she put her car in reverse, pulled out, and got on down the road.

When he could no longer see her car, his eyes settled on the value menu; high cholesterol and blood pressure be darned, the Big Mac combo was practically whispering in his ear. Moments later, he was telling the surly girl behind the register just that. "Hold the onions, though, doll — can't stand them things," he told her as she punched his order into the register's buttons.

"Make that two Number Ones, but I want the onions on mine," a familiar voice called from behind Uncle Larry. The register girl tossed him the side-eye; Uncle Larry whipped his head around to see for sure if the voice belonged to who he thought it belonged to.

"Oh, hey there, Smoke," Uncle Larry said nervously. "Fancy seeing you here."

"Yeah, man, you know, can't beat Mickey D's when you got the taste for those good fries, huh?"

"Yeah, you know that's right," Uncle Larry said,

rubbing his stomach. "Say, man, I'm getting my food to go, but you're welcome to order — my treat."

"Oh, say word?" Smoke said, smiling. "Your treat, huh?"

"Yeah, man, go 'head and get you something to eat — tell the lady what you want."

Smoke turned to the surly girl and winked. "What up, Trina?"

"Hey, Smoke, what can I get for you?"

"The Number One with the onions," he said. "You know how I like it, don't you, Trina?"

Trina rolled her eyes, punched in the order, and stalked her way over to the fries.

"So I thought you were supposed to be taking it easy with the fast food, what with your health and all," Smoke said, folding his arms.

"Yeah, you know . . ." Uncle Larry said, trailing off.

"I know my mother would be worrying you to death if she saw you up in here supersizing Big Macs and fries and such," he smirked.

"Yeah, your mom always was a worrier," Uncle Larry said quietly. "This little hamburger and fries ain't gonna kill me."

"Yeah, man, ain't nothing wrong with a fry every now and again," Smoke said. "But maybe you oughta meet your friends at the health food store — that way you can get you some vitamins and vegetables or something after you finish up your little talks."

Uncle Larry didn't say anything — just blinked.

"Who was your little friend?"

"Who do you think it was, Richard?" Uncle Larry asked, putting a little more bass in his voice.

Smoke frowned. "Well, judging from the 'Duke Two' license plate in the back and the 'Duke Dealers' plate in the front, I'm going to assume it was one of the Duke girls," he said. "What she doing in these parts?"

Under any other circumstance, with any other person, Uncle Larry would have come up with a good lie or simply told the inquirer to mind his own business. But this wasn't just your average inquirer; this was Smoke. Lies didn't work well with him. They'd known each other much too long for that.

"That's my niece," Uncle Larry said simply. "She comes around every once in a while to check up on me."

"Really, now?" Smoke said, cocking his head to the side. "Your niece? How about that — I learn something new every day. And here we are, practically family. How come I've never seen her at your house before?"

"Her mama and I had a falling out, so we're just kinda getting to know each other is all," Uncle Larry said, keeping his explanation as simple as possible.

"Humph," Smoke said, his arms still folded. "Well, it's good to keep in touch with family, huh?"

"Well, that depends on who your family is," Uncle Larry said. "Like I said, her mama and I don't have much dealing with each other. The young'un just wanted to reach out to her ol' Uncle Larry. Simple as that."

"Yeah, simple," Smoke said.

Surly Girl stalked her way back to the register, two bags in hand. She dropped them unceremoniously on the counter. "Ketchup?" she practically growled.

"No, none for me," Uncle Larry said.

"I'll take a few packets," Smoke said, peering into his bag to grab a fry.

Surly Girl pushed a few packets across the counter. "Next," she said, peering around the two men to get to the next customer.

"Good seeing you, Trina — give a brother a call sometime," Smoke said. She ignored him. Then Smoke turned to Uncle Larry.

"I just stopped by because I saw your car parked out back, and I figured I'd come on in and holler at you. My mother's been on me to stop by the house."

"Yeah, yeah, it's good to see you, Smoke. How's your mama doing?"

"She's getting along all right," Smoke said.

"Well, tell her I said 'hey,' " Uncle Larry said, picking up his bag.

"Will do," Smoke said. "By the way, that Duke car was hot. Maybe I ought to go down to the dealership and see if they have any more like it. Maybe I could cop one."

Uncle Larry held his breath and then sighed. "You could do that, but you know the Dukes can be hard on the pockets."

"Yeah, but they serve a brother well," Smoke said. "They serve a brother real well."

Uncle Larry stared blankly at Smoke, clutching his meal. He didn't say another word.

"You enjoy your lunch now," Smoke said. "Trina made the fries nice and salty, just like you like 'em."

And with that, Smoke disappeared into the winter chill.

7
SYDNEY

"I don't know, it just doesn't add up," Sydney sighed in frustration as she cross-checked the most recent Sadie Hawkins savings-account statement with the growing list of expenses for what felt like the hundredth time.

"What are you talking about, Sydney?" Marcus questioned tiredly. "You've gone over the same twenty line items for the past three hours. Let it go, it's already been an hour since we adjourned the committee. I'm not sure you're aware, but it is a Friday night."

Sydney cut her eyes so hard, Marcus cringed. "Um, yes, I am very aware that it's a Friday night. And please believe I have somewhere to be, too, Marcus," she spat back. "But I'm not about to half-step on my responsibilities because you want to hurry up and catch Albertson's midnight sale on baby formula!"

"That was uncalled for," Marcus retorted. "And for the record, I wasn't implying that I had somewhere to be. I was just pointing out that you're nitpicking. If we're a couple thousand dollars off, it's fine. All these figures are estimates. Something will come in lower than expected."

Sydney could feel her blood pressure rising with each breath. "Marcus. It's not just the missing money; it's the principle. I need to understand where the discrepancy is happening. Did we not collect all the letters of intention? Did I miscalculate them?" she questioned, waving her hands dramatically in frustration. "I've never had this happen before on any of the committees that I've led. The Benefit is only two weeks away and . . ."

Marcus gently grabbed ahold of Sydney's hands. "Syd, re-lax. Seriously," he said slowly as he looked her in the eye. "We can go over the numbers as many times as you need to feel comfortable, but I'm telling you, there's nothing to give yourself a heart attack over just yet. I'm here and I got this."

Sydney stared at Marcus's hands covering her own. Everything rational in her brain told her that she should be pulling her hands away in disgust, but for some reason, the warm pressure of his touch seemed like just what she needed to calm her nerves. *Omigod, I forgive him. I'm finally over it*, Sydney thought, noticing the lack of anger and, even more important, romantic tension. She inhaled deeply, exhaled slowly, and smiled.

"Okay, just one more time and then we call it a night. Deal?" she asked, eager to finish and go spend time with the guy who actually made her hormones react.

"Deal," Marcus agreed as he slowly removed his hands from Sydney's and picked up his BlackBerry to check the time. "Okay, it's nine o'clock; we're outta here no later than nine-thirty, agreed?"

"Fair enough," Sydney replied amicably as she picked up the stack of donor promissory notes and vendor invoices and handed them over to Marcus. "You read them off and I'll double-check the account."

"Okay, drill sergeant," Marcus teased with a mock salute.

"Whatever," Sydney laughed. "For someone trying to get out of here, you sure got a lot of jokes."

"Hey, I laugh to keep from crying," Marcus said as he pulled his long locs up into a ponytail in one sweeping motion.

"Mmm-hmm, I sure hope you laugh and count at the same time," Sydney mused as she turned back to the statement. "Hey, do you see a withdrawal receipt for the second? I don't think I went to the bank that day, but it says here that five hundred dollars was withdrawn."

"Maybe Principal Trumbull moved some money around," Marcus offered as she started searching through the pile.

"Maybe . . ." Sydney said as she highlighted all the withdrawals she didn't recall at first sight. Deep in thought, she didn't even hear the conference door open.

"What's up, Sydney?"

Startled, both Sydney and Marcus looked up like deer caught in headlights. "Oh, hey, J," Sydney responded in surprise. As Jason stood in the doorway assessing the situation, Sydney grew increasing uncomfortable. Marcus defiantly stared back at the other boy. She pushed her chair back and stood up.

"I thought you said you'd be finished by nine?" Jason questioned uncertainly. "Am I interrupting something?"

"No, no, you're right," Sydney said as she walked over to Jason to give him a quick hug and kiss. "There's a small discrepancy with the numbers, so Marcus and I had to stay a little later and go over everything."

"Oh, true. So about how much longer you think it's going to be?" Jason asked.

Sydney looked at her watch. "Um, gimme about fifteen, twenty minutes?" she asked sweetly.

"All right, babe, I'll be in the truck," Jason replied evenly. He leaned down to kiss Sydney on the cheek and whispered in her ear, "I'm not waiting more than twenty minutes." He backed out of the doorway before she could even react. Slightly bewildered by his tone of voice, Sydney watched Jason walk away without so much as a backward glance.

"I guess you weren't kidding about those plans, huh," Marcus muttered sourly.

Still reeling from Jason's abrupt departure, Sydney turned around with a confused look on her face. "Huh? What did you say?"

"Nothing. Do you still want to do this? Or do you need to go?" he asked pointedly.

"No, it's fine. Let's just hurry up and finish." Sydney headed back to her seat and tried to find her place. "Now, where was I?" Sydney struggled to concentrate on the figures, but Jason's threat kept running through her head. She looked at her watch and wondered how many minutes she had left. And more important, whether he would make good on his word and leave her stranded.

"Well, we were going to go over everything one more time," Marcus started slowly. "But to be honest, maybe you should just prepare the deposits for tomorrow and start again on Monday when everything clears."

"Yeah, maybe you're right," Sydney said as she opened the money pouch with all the checks and deposit slips. "Hey, do you see the calculator anywhere? I need it to add up everything right quick."

Marcus scanned the cluttered table and easily spotted the half-hidden instrument directly in front of Sydney. He reached over and grabbed it. "Okay, Sherlock Holmes, this was right in your face. You've clearly checked out," he said. "Why don't you go ahead and let me do tomorrow's deposit, and you can handle the one on Tuesday, okay? Just sign the slip so I don't have any issues at the bank."

Partially embarrassed and very much relieved, Sydney nodded. "Okay, that'll work." She scribbled her signature on the slip, stood up, put on her Burberry minitrench, and grabbed her extra-large burgundy Botkier saddlebag. "Thanks, Marcus," she said as she put her folder with the committee notes in the bag and tossed it over her shoulder. "I owe you."

"Yeah, you do," Marcus replied simply as Sydney headed out the door.

Sydney lightly tapped on the truck's window to get Jason's attention. Noticing her standing outside the passenger door, Jason quickly unlocked the doors, jumped out the driver's side, and ran around to open her door. "Thank you kindly," she said as she sat down inside. He closed her door without a word and headed back over to his side. Jason jumped in the car, buckled his seat belt, and turned on the engine. "Sorry about that, there's a little bit of discrepancy with the funds and —"

"You said that already," Jason said curtly as he turned on the radio.

"Okay," Sydney said hesitantly. "Um, is something wrong, J?"

"You tell me, Syd," he responded while staring straight ahead.

"I have no idea what you're upset about, Jason," Sydney said honestly. "I know you had to wait a little while for me to come out of the committee meeting —"

"Actually, Syd, the 'committee meeting' has been over for the past hour," he retorted, using his fingers to accentuate his point. "The reason I know is because I ran into Cornell and his girl, Delria, at the BP gas station. And he had just come from picking her up. So really, I've been sitting out here waiting for you to finish hanging out with Marcus for the past twenty minutes."

Sydney was at a complete loss for words. "That's not what . . . I wasn't just hanging out with Marcus. I was working — *we* were working on finalizing the expenses," she corrected.

"Really? 'Cause you guys looked extra cozy up in there to be discussing some numbers. Not to mention the way you jumped when I walked in the room. Seemed to me like somebody was feeling pretty guilty."

"Guilty? I didn't do anything to act guilty about," Sydney responded defensively. She turned her entire body to face him. "You just surprised us, that's all. I told you that I would call when I finished. So you walking in like that was unexpected."

"Honestly, I'm really not feeling the whole working-late-with-Marcus thing," Jason stated as he pulled the brim of his Yankees cap down on his stormy face.

"Jason, I already told you. No, I *promised* you that there was nothing between Marcus and me except for planning the Benefit," Sydney said slowly, hoping that her words would penetrate the cloud of anger that felt like it was suffocating her.

"And not for nothing, what's up with the outfit? Do you always dress like you're going to the club for your committee meetings?" Jason continued his angry rant.

Sydney looked down at the purple-and-white BCBG minidress. The truth was, she'd changed into it just for Jason, but now she felt like a fool. "I didn't think it was that short . . ."

"If you say so, but I don't need my girl sitting up in a room wearing some skintight minidress with her ex."

Sydney tugged uncomfortably at the hem of the designer frock as she made mental note to donate it to Goodwill immediately. "I wasn't sitting up in the room with my ex, we were working."

"And I don't like the way he was looking at you. I'm not

stupid; that shit is disrespectful," Jason continued as if Sydney had never said anything.

"Babe, I swear, there's nothing going on," Sydney pleaded. "You have to believe me. I'm not doing anything to jeopardize our relationship ever again."

Jason looked at Sydney. "You already lied to me once, Sydney. I just don't know if I can deal with this. . . . I'm just not —"

"I know, I know, and I'm sorry, but please, Jason. Nothing was going on." Sydney's voice started to rise. She grabbed his right hand as she felt the tears well up in her eyes. "You're the only one I want to be with, I swear."

Jason inhaled deeply and exhaled slowly as he stared into Sydney's frantic face for what seemed like an eternity. Finally, he said, "Fine, I'll let it go. But you gotta figure that working arrangement out 'cause that can't happen again."

"Okay, babe, I will," Sydney responded.

"You know I'm only mad because I care," Jason said, trying to justify his outburst. He reached out and softly wiped Sydney's tears from the corners of her eyes. "I don't want you to cry, but you can't get me mad like this." Sydney nodded silently. "Anyway, let's just go get something to eat. Okay?"

"Okay," Sydney said softly as he leaned in to kiss her forehead.

"That's my girl," Jason said with a slightly triumphant tone as he started to back the truck out of the parking spot. Sydney turned and looked out the passenger-side window.

"So then we went to dinner and it was like nothing ever happened," Sydney said with a confused shrug as she finished recounting Jason's bizarre outburst to Rhea and Carmen over sips of her Starbucks caramel latte the next day.

"Wow, that's a lot," Carmen said as she stirred her vanilla frappuccino.

"Yeah, I know," Sydney agreed. "And that whole twenty minutes comment. . . . Do you guys think he would have left me if I'd been late? Like, seriously?"

Carmen shrugged her shoulders and took a long sip. "I mean, I hope not," she offered after she swallowed.

"I mean, you've seen my BCBG minidress. Do you think it's skintight?" Sydney asked.

"No, not at all," Rhea responded from behind her favorite Gucci shades. She pulled her hair up into a bun. "But honestly, from the sound of it, you could've been wearing a potato sack and he would've had something smart to say."

"Huh? What do you mean?" Sydney questioned her friend.

"I mean," Rhea started slowly. "Jason was being a boy. He's insecure about your ex-boyfriend so he was throwing a temper tantrum."

"Good point," Carmen co-signed.

"I guess . . ." Sydney started. "But he seemed like he was really about to break up with me."

"Oh, I don't think that," Carmen countered with a shake of her head. "Why would he get back with you just to dump you? Now, that's crazy."

"Yeah, I think you're taking it way too personally," Rhea said as she sipped her green tea and stifled a yawn. "I'm sorry; I was out late with the boy."

"You guys are probably right," Sydney said, although she was clearly unconvinced. "I guess I'm just not used to this whole dating thing. I mean, being with Marcus for four years really kept me out of the loop."

"Yeah, I totally wouldn't stress it too much," Carmen replied as she turned to look out the window. "I remember when I first started dating Michael. He used to trip every time my phone rang. Now it's like he wouldn't even care if I was on the phone with freaking Chris Brown. Or what's the name of that cute boy from Day 26?"

"Ugh, as if any of the boys in Day 26 were ever cute!" Rhea countered with a laugh. Sydney smiled at Rhea's reaction.

"Whatever, silly, my point is," Carmen said, pointedly ignoring Rhea's sarcastic comment, "everyone goes through it. And then, just like that, they stop. And you almost wish they cared enough to get worked up."

"I hear you, but I don't remember Marcus being like this," Sydney said doubtfully. "Jason seemed really angry with me."

"But remember, Syd," Rhea offered. "Marcus never had any competition. When the two of you got together, it was like Beyoncé and Jay-Z. Who else could you have been with that was equally fly? Had Jason been around, it might have been a different story."

"Good point," Carmen nodded. "It's a totally different ball game now."

"And not for nothing," Rhea continued. "It's kinda cute that he got that worked up. I think he really, really likes you."

"Well, when you put it like that . . ." Sydney said, finally starting to come around.

"For sure," Carmen said as she finished up the last of her drink. She stood up and stretched.

"You're finished already?" Sydney questioned as she slowly sipped her latte.

"You know how greedy I am," Carmen laughed over her shoulder as she headed over to the trash with the empty container and used napkins.

"So how was volunteering today?" Rhea inquired.

"It was really good, thanks," Sydney said. "I was a little tired 'cause we didn't get home from dinner until, like, almost eleven o'clock, but overall it was fine."

"True. I didn't get home until almost one o'clock myself," Rhea said. "David Harris had a bunch of guys from the team over, so we were hanging out there."

"Sounds like fun," Sydney said.

"It was, actually," Rhea admitted. "At first, I was nervous because I don't really know any of the other girlfriends, but Tim stayed glued to my side the whole night, so it was cool."

Carmen returned to the table and sat down. "What was cool?"

"The get-together at D-Harris's house," Rhea explained. "That's where Tim and I ended up last night after I left the committee meeting."

"Ah, I see," Carmen said as she opened her purse and started digging around for her lip gloss. "Michael and I went back to his parents' house and watched *Iron Man* for, like, the hundreth time," she said with an eye-roll. "I swear, that boy is such a comic book freak."

"Back to his house, huh?" Sydney teased as she finally finished up her latte. "Is there something we should know, Carmen? Don't make me call Harold and Cheryl!"

"Girl, please. I already told you he and I are taking things very slowly. I am not trying to become the next Dara up in Brookhaven Prep," she said sarcastically.

"I know *that's* right," Rhea agreed as she stood up and

gestured to Sydney to pass her empty cup. "I'll be right back; I need to use the restroom."

"Well, Carm, just keep me posted," Sydney said as she passed the cup and used napkins to her friend. "Inquiring minds always want to know."

"Speaking of inquiring minds," Carmen said as Rhea walked away. "Is everything okay with your family? My mom was reading the article about what's been going on with the IRS and she said it sounds like they're really trying to set an example with Altimus. I know I was teasing you the other day, but she made it sound kinda serious."

"Honestly, I haven't even read the stories," Sydney lied as she pulled her Tom Ford sunglasses over her eyes to avoid Carmen's gaze. "Altimus and my mom are really confident that everything is going to be fine. So you know, I just have to trust them."

"I understand," Carmen said with a nod. "I don't want to stress you. I was just a little worried. You know you can tell me anything."

Sydney paused as she thought about the IRS auditor who had set up shop in her stepfather's home office the past week, and the strict $150 monthly spending limit that Keisha had imposed on her AMEX that very morning. She took a deep breath and forced a smile. "Of course," Sydney said as she reached out to pat Carmen's hand reassuringly. "Of course I would tell you."

8
LAUREN

"My God, not again," Donald said, flopping down on the floor while his friend queued up the music for the thousandth time. He and Lauren were in the middle of a pow-wow on how to make Caroline play the rear on the dance squad — a four-hour session that involved three strawberry-banana smoothies, several packages of Ritz crackers with American cheese slices, two humongous bags of gummy bears, a pack of grape Now and Laters, and at least thirty rewinds of a TiVoed episode of *106 & Park* featuring throwback videos by Beyoncé, OutKast, and Thug Heaven, meant to provide a little inspiration and more than a couple of moves for Lauren's choreography. "It's hot already, goodness. If you do the damn thing one more time, you're not going to be able to shake it fast at practice tomorrow."

"Okay, seriously? I'm gonna need you to stop acting like you're the one doing all the work," Lauren snapped, pushing the PAUSE button on her Bose stereo.

Lauren was on a mission — a righteous one, indeed. Word on the curb was that Caroline, the sophomore basketball dance squad member with the hots for Sydney's ex, was coming for Lauren's Number One spot, and she would be damned if she was going to just let somebody come in and steal her head cheerleader-in-charge title. About this much, Lauren was clear: She wasn't about to go down without a fight.

"You're going to need me to walk into practice and show those girls a thing or two if you want to continue riding on the team bus to the games," Lauren snapped at Donald, who, though he'd graciously agreed to watch and give feedback, was now too overloaded with sugar to put in critical work. "Stay. Focused."

"True," Donald said, popping a red gummy bear into his mouth. "You know how I feel about the backseat of the squad bus. It makes me feel all warm and fuzzy inside when I'm bouncing around back there."

"Easy," Lauren laughed. "That was a mental image I just don't need."

"Okay, okay," Donald giggled. "Let me fix the mental, then. Caroline? With the squad captain's bullhorn? Not good."

"I know, right?" Lauren said, huffing and rubbing her sore knee. "I'm going to need to do a little bit more than go in there with jacked Beyoncé moves to get the team to vote for me — that much I know."

"Come on," Donald insisted. "They'd be fools not to vote you captain."

"That's the problem," Lauren said. "They *are* fools. Haven't you read YRT lately? My entire existence is under question now that stories about Altimus's business are being downloaded directly onto the site. I swear, don't people have anything better to do than get in my family's business?"

"Um, not really," Donald deadpanned.

"Exactly," Lauren said. "Just today, Elizabeth Chiclana raised her hand in Econ and asked Mr. Siegret to explain the difference between the penalties people and businesses get when they fail to pay their taxes. I swear, if I wasn't walking with King Jesus? The devil would have won today."

"Mmm, well, I didn't want to tell you this, but since you're already having the pity party . . . there was an entire conversation over chicken wraps in the lunchroom today about how much intel you had on the Dara and Marcus situation."

"See what I'm saying?" Lauren said, snatching another Now and Later out of the package. "How am I supposed to get past all of that? I mean, we're still on Dara? Damn."

"You know how you get past all of it?" Donald asked without hesitating. "You go in there and you show them why you're still the one who should be in charge. Look, your skills on the dance floor are undeniable, and no one can choreograph like you. Shoot, if you ask me, you should get back with your agent and see if you can try out for a few more video features — give those scalawags something to really talk about."

"Uh, yeah, about the video ho tryouts? I'm so not there," Lauren said. "The last thing I need is another YRT post about my after-school exploits."

"Okay, then give them something to talk about. Go into that practice tomorrow and do what you do best: Show your ass."

"I do know how to do that, don't I?" Lauren giggled. "Okay, but you gotta pay close attention, young 'un. Should I toss in a front twist after the jump or leave this part as is?"

"Come on, girl, you know I don't know nothing 'bout birthin' no dance moves!" Donald said, chewing lazily on another gummy bear.

"Whatev, just pay attention," she said, punching PLAY on her stereo.

Lauren tiptoed to the tiny refrigerator tucked in the corner of the hot-pink Duke cheerleading clubhouse lounge and opened it as gingerly as possible. But still, the sound of her Nikes squeaking across the pristine white tile and the shifting of the water bottles in the refrigerator door made her headache pound even harder. She'd been fighting the migraine all day, but four bathroom passes, two Aleve, a cup of herbal tea, and a visit to the nurse's office later, and Lauren was still rubbing her temples and sending up silent prayers to God begging him to "take the pain away, so I can show these wannabes how a true dance captain gets down." Under normal circumstances, she would have sent a text to her mom, imploring her to put in a call to the school nurse; an early release, an afternoon nap, and an episode or two of *Law & Order: SVU* would have been fitting recompense for the trauma her body was going through, and Keisha, God bless her soul, would have been too preoccupied with her Wednesday afternoon nail salon visit to care if Lauren dipped out of a couple of classes. But there was no time for the zone-out.

Lauren reached into the refrigerator and grabbed the Tupperware container full of cucumber slices she kept stashed for occasions such as these. A twenty-minute power nap in the plush recliner with the cucumber slices on her eyes would work wonders on her headache and surely take away the puffiness that had settled just under her lower eyelids; she'd wake up refreshed and ready to show those heifas just why she was, and needed to remain, the dance squad captain.

Lauren settled into the recliner and set her iPhone alarm for 3:20 P.M.; that would give her about ten minutes after she woke up to change into her gear and go over the new steps in her head before the rest of the team hit the locker room to get ready for practice. But no sooner had she placed the soothing cucumbers on her eyes and rested her head on her special pillow than she heard a stall door in the bathroom slam shut.

"Who's that?" Lauren said, bolting upright. The cucumbers tumbled between the chair's arm and seat cushion.

There was no answer.

"Who's there?" Lauren demanded, her heart racing. She stood up slowly; her eyes darted around the room in search of something — anything — that could serve as a fitting weapon against whoever was creeping around in the bathroom. She settled on a baton that lay on a counter not too far from where the noise had come. She grabbed it and headed for the bathroom, half scared, half amped to beat down any intruder.

Holding the baton like a bat behind her left shoulder, Lauren pushed open the bathroom door with her foot; it slammed against the wall. "Whoever you are, you better come out now!" she yelled.

"Just give . . . me . . . a sec." A girl's voice came between breaths from behind the adjacent stall. And then she hurled. Hard. And coughed. "If you didn't notice, I'm . . . a little . . . preoccu —" She couldn't finish. More hurling.

Damn. Gross. Dara.

Lauren rolled her eyes at the mere thought of her former best friend. What was she doing here anyway? She'd quit the squad and then embarrassed both Sydney and herself by showing up with a megaphone to the twins' holiday party to announce her baby bump. Specifically, Marcus's baby bump. And she still had the nerve to show her face in the House that the Dukes built?

Dara flushed the toilet and slowly walked out of the stall, making a beeline for the sink. Without so much as a side glance in Lauren's direction, she splashed cool water into her mouth and then dried her hands with one of the crisp flowered hand towels in the basket gracing the counter. And then she picked up her purse and started heading for the door. "Excuse me."

"Yes, excuse you," Lauren snapped. She didn't budge from her position in front of the door, leaving Dara little room to squeeze by. "Maybe next time you can keep your nasty baby business in the main building and out of *my* locker room."

"Look, I came here because I didn't think anyone would

be here," Dara said, her eyes stuck on the baton Lauren rested on her left shoulder.

"What'd you do — throw up all over the bathroom stall so we have to tiptoe around your mess?" Lauren demanded. "You're not slick."

Dara shook her head and looked down at her Cole Haan ballet flats. "It wasn't supposed to be like this," she said quietly.

Lauren gripped the baton a little tighter; her former best friend was really trying to test her today, and she was so not in the mood.

"You do understand that, right?" Dara questioned.

"Understand what, Dara? That you deliberately slept with my sister's boyfriend, bragged about it to the entire school, and crashed my holiday party with the news that you and Marcus are about to become proud, teenage, unwed parents? What else is there to understand, sweetie? Oh, hold up — I know: You're a tramp-ass hooker who has no idea what it means to be a true friend. But I didn't need you to come here to tell me that."

Dara rubbed her hand over her brow; Lauren noticed that it was shaking. Dara's tears were inescapable.

"Look, I know I deserve everything you're throwing at me and then some," she said, swiping away the tears.

"Uh, you think?" Lauren snapped.

Dara started to answer back but instead let out a sob.

"Are you kidding me, Dara?" Lauren seethed. She could feel her head getting hot. "You know what? You're pathetic."

"You're right," Dara said. "I'm not going to argue with you about that."

Lauren cocked her head to the side and looked quizzically at Dara. What in the world was she up to?

"I betrayed your trust, your family, and, above all else, our friendship," Dara continued, swiping at more tears. "I lay awake at night thinking about what I've lost — how important you are . . . were to me. How much I miss us. I'm carrying around this baby, and everytime my stomach flutters or I get nauseous or I see you in the lunchroom, I'm reminded about how my hooking up with Marcus so wasn't worth it. You, Sydney, even I deserved better than this. I just wish . . ." Dara continued and then stopped herself.

Lauren stared at Dara, gape-jawed. She wasn't quite sure how to respond — what to say. Her anger was still palpable, but another emotion subtly and unexpectedly started creeping in: empathy. Lauren didn't know what was coming over her.

"You know, all the character flaws you said made him a crappy boyfriend — his sneakiness, his lying, his better-than-thou/playa attitude — are all of the things that he used to convince me that *I* was the one he wanted," Dara reasoned. "I fell for the hype. I really believed him, Lauren. I

113

guess a big part of me still wants to believe it," she added, rubbing her burgeoning belly.

"But that was my sister's man," Lauren said quietly. *"My sister."*

Dara nodded and, after a beat, said just as quietly, "But you always made it seem like he didn't matter — like what they had didn't matter. And honestly, I didn't think it was going to go this far." Lauren shook her head and looked away. "I'm about to become someone's mother," Dara said, her voice trembling. "And, quite honestly, I don't know what to do, who to turn to, how to get through this. And I'm too tired to fight anymore. I miss you," she added quietly. "I miss us."

Lauren loosened her grip on the baton and slowly placed it on the counter. She looked hard into Dara's eyes, unsure of what to do — what to say. She had to admit that she missed her best friend, too. Nobody, after all, knew as many of her secrets — well, except Donald and her sister.

Just as she got a mental image of Sydney in her brain, Lauren's iPhone pierced the silence, startling both her and Dara; Lauren looked in the direction of the ringtone. Keisha Cole's "Let It Go," bounced off the concrete walls. It was Sydney.

Lauren gave Dara a slow, toe-to-head once-over with her eyes and sucked her teeth.

"You know what? That's my sister calling," Lauren

snapped. "I'm going to take that. But I want to thank you for sharing your come-to-Jesus tale. It was, um, inspiring. Do me a favor, though, will you? Save the talk about how Marcus talked his way into your boomchickiwawa for some-one who gives a damn."

9
SYDNEY

"Thank you so much for coming in this evening," Dr. Mitchell greeted Sydney at the door of Better Day Women's Shelter with a tight hug. "I was worried you weren't going to make it."

"No problem, Dr. Mitchell," Sydney said as she stepped into the common area of the shelter and took off her light-weight D&G studded leather jacket. "I apologize for being late. There was an accident on Piedmont, and traffic was at a standstill for at least twenty-five minutes."

"Oh, I hope no one was hurt," Dr. Mitchell mused as she closed the door.

"Well, from what I could see, no one was being taken away in the ambulance that arrived at the scene," Sydney said as she hung up her jacket in the closet. She turned and

looked at the slender middle-aged psychologist who
as both on-site therapist and den mother to the shelter residents. "So, where did they decide to hold the meeting — in
the rec room or the conference center?"

"I do believe everyone is gathered in the rec room,"
Dr. Mitchell answered. "After discussing it with Shirley,
we both felt that it was important that the setting be infor-
mal enough for all the women to feel comfortable sharing."

"Good point," Sydney concurred with a nod as she
smoothed her hot-pink DKNY V-neck T-shirt. "I'm really
excited about these new weekly roundtables. I think discussing their individual experiences and problem solving
with other survivors will really help a lot of the women.
After all, no one knows what it really takes to make it out
more than a fellow survivor."

"Exactly. And, you know, the long-term goal is to eventually get women who have come through the shelter and
are now successfully independent of their abusive partners
to come back and speak as well," Dr. Mitchell added.

"Oh, that'll be amazing," Sydney said as she stole a
quick glance at her vintage black-faced Movado watch.
Jason expected her to be home for their customary good-
night call by 8:30 P.M. If Sydney intended to make that
deadline, the meeting needed to get started ASAP. "Did the
food arrive okay?"

"The delivery guy just left about ten minutes ago,"

Dr. Mitchell said with a smile as she adjusted her black-and-white textured suit jacket. "He even set up the table, which I thought was so nice. I tell you, everything looks great."

"Perfect," Sydney said happily. "I was a little worried because I wasn't here to direct the setup but I'm glad that it all came together." Dr. Mitchell nodded in response. "So I'll just head down and see if they've started," Sydney said as she began easing away from Dr. Mitchell.

"Okay, dear. I'll be down just as soon as I finish locking up the admin office. If they haven't already, please tell Shirley I said it's okay to start without me," she responded with the signature smile that had put many a frazzled and frightened woman at ease when she first arrived at the shelter.

Sydney nodded as she turned and walked down the hall. As she neared the rec room, she could hear the voice of the senior resident assistant asking the ladies to have a seat and prepare to begin. "Ladies, ladies, we have a lot that we want to cover, so let's get started," Shirley said in her booming voice. Almost immediately, there was the sound of chairs scraping the floor as everyone grabbed a seat. Even though she was barely five feet tall, when Shirley spoke, people listened. Sydney entered the room from the back. She waved to Shirley as she headed up the side aisle toward the front of the room. "First of all, I would like to thank you for coming out to our first weekly 'Sister Share' meeting," Shirley greeted the diverse-looking group of women. "As you know or may have figured out by now, Better Day is a temporary living facility for survivors of domestic violence."

"No, really? 'Cause I just thought we all liked living in a dormitory for grown folks," responded Rita, a longtime on-and-off-again resident who seemed to have a knack for always finding boyfriends who liked to use her as a punching bag. She and her cohorts exchanged a round of high fives and laughs.

"Okay, enough from the peanut gallery," Shirley continued with a patient smile. "As I was about to say, the goal of Better Day is to serve as transitional housing where survivors receive the services and support they need to start their lives over. And perhaps the biggest part of that process is the emotional healing. So in addition to one-on-one counseling, we are now offering group sessions where survivors can share their experiences with other women in a safe space. Our hope is that, together, we can help ease the pain and problem-solve new and different ways to avoid going through the drama again." There was a short round of genuine applause from the ladies. Shirley looked at Sydney. "Now, before we begin tonight's session, I would like to take a moment to thank one of Better Day's favorite volunteers, Sydney Duke. Thanks to Sydney's constant campaigning, Better Day just secured *another* corporate donor. Hence, from now on, Sister Share session dinners will be exclusively provided by our favorite local Kroger." This time Shirley led the loud round of applause.

Surprised and slightly embarrassed by the mention, Sydney waved away the praise. "Honestly, it's the least I could do," Sydney stated modestly when the ladies quieted down. "You guys are an amazing group of women, and I just want each and every one of you to see that in yourselves."

"Hopefully, these gatherings will help with that," Dr. Mitchell stated from the back of the room when she had finally entered.

"I agree," Shirley co-signed. "And with that said, do we have any volunteers to, as Rita is so fond of saying, jump things off?" An immediate hush fell over the room as the women started looking every which way, reluctant to be the first one to talk about what landed her in the shelter to begin with. Finally, a hand timidly raised in the back of the room.

"I'll go," asserted a small voice. All heads turned in time to see Mary, a particularly introverted and almost reclusive petite woman in her late twenties, stand up.

"Why, thank you, Mary," Dr. Mitchell said approvingly.

Noticeably uncomfortable, Mary cleared her throat for

an extended moment. "Um . . . I was, um . . . my boyfriend hit . . . I was abused by my boyfriend." Mary struggled momentarily to form the words. "My boyfriend, Shane, physically abused me for five years." The woman sitting next to Mary reached out to touch her arm sympathetically. "Whenever he got angry, Shane would smack me, twist my arms, shake me, punch, and one time he even kicked me," she continued as the tears welled up in her eyes. "Shane got angry at least three times a week."

Sydney struggled to keep her face neutral. Whenever she heard these stories, she was always so shocked. She couldn't imagine anybody, least of all a boyfriend, ever laying his hands on her. She looked down at her watch again.

"But it wasn't always like that. In the beginning, he was the most loving and protective boyfriend a girl like me could ever imagine," Mary asserted. There were several agreeing grunts and head nods from the girls in the group.

"I know that's right. It always starts out really good," an older woman from Mississippi named Lucy chimed in.

"Or maybe I just missed the signs," Mary continued, her voice growing stronger. "The first time, he questioned me about an outfit I was wearing. It was just a regular sundress. But he made it seem so scandalous, the very next day I gave it away to my best friend. . . . I really liked that dress. But I didn't want to upset him." The women in the room all nodded in agreement. "Then the paranoia. He was constantly accusing me of trying to play him out. From the very beginning, he was so suspicious. He warned me that if I ever played him out, he would lose his mind." Mary paused and looked at the women with a wry smile on her face. "I guess I should've believed him, huh?" The room erupted in a chorus of "You ain't neva lied" and "Preach, my sista" catcalls. Looking up from her watch, Sydney softly gasped. Every word Mary said felt like a direct jab to her gut.

"Are you okay?" Shirley leaned over and whispered in her ear with concern. "You look like something just struck a chord."

Sydney struggled to plaster a smile on her face. "Oh, no, it's, um, I just remembered that I have a geometry exam in the morning. And I totally forgot to study," she replied, hoping her lie sounded halfway believable to the extra-perceptive mother of three.

"Mmm-hmm, okay, if you say so," Shirley said with one eyebrow cocked. "Well, then, you probably should get going, huh?"

"Yeah, I should probably go," Sydney whispered without looking Shirley in the eye. Luckily, the entire room was now so focused on Mary's story that they hardly noticed Sydney creeping along the side of the room toward the back entrance. Just as she closed the door gently behind her and turned to walk away, the door reopened and Dr. Mitchell stepped out as well.

"Leaving so soon?" she asked. "I was hoping that you might be able to stay and have dinner with the ladies. They always enjoy your company so much."

"Oh, yeah, I, um, just remembered that I have this test tomorrow," Sydney repeated her lie. "So I really . . . I just can't stay. . . ." Sydney twisted her oversized silver hoop earring around and around.

"I see." Dr. Mitchell nodded her head gently. "Well, let me say thank you again for all your help, it really makes a difference. In a way, you've become a role model to some of these women."

"I'm hardly a role model," Sydney muttered as Mary's words rang in her ears.

"Oh, but you are," Dr. Simmons countered. "Even as old as some of these women are, they look at you, the life you're leading, the healthy relationship choices you make, and they aspire to find that strength within themselves." Sydney felt sicker by the minute. She prayed her face was doing a better job of behaving normally than her flip-flopping stomach. "But I don't want to keep you," Dr. Mitchell concluded as she put her hand on Sydney's shoulder. "Thank you again for getting Kroger to donate the dinners; it really makes all the difference. I will see you next Saturday, bright and early?"

"Yes, ma'am," Sydney squeaked out.

"Get home safely," Dr. Mitchell offered as she turned back to the door and left Sydney standing frozen in place.

From the other side of Lauren's semiclosed door, Sydney could hear the sound of Mariska Hargitay yelling at someone to freeze before she blew his head away. Sydney raised her hand to knock and then hesitated. *What am I doing*, she thought, miserably. If she went inside and told her sister what was said at the session, not only was she violating the trust of the women, but she was also voluntarily putting her relationship issues with Jason on front street. And Lord knew, Lauren was hardly the person she wanted passing judgment on her when it came to relationships.

Sydney turned to walk away. Halfway down the hall, she heard Lauren's door open. Sydney turned around to see Lauren shuffling out into the hallway. "What's up, Syd," Lauren greeted as she stopped to scratch her right arm. "When did you get back?"

"Oh, hey, L," Sydney returned the greeting. "About five minutes ago."

"Hmm, true," Lauren said lazily as she turned to look back into her room at what Sydney presumed was a crucial scene in the episode. "I was just chilling out, watching *L&O* as usual. But I think I'm getting my period 'cause I'm really craving something sweet." Lauren looked back at her sister. "Wanna join me?"

Accepting the invitation as a sign from above, Sydney didn't hesitate. "Yeah, actually, I would," she agreed with a nod.

"Really?" Lauren said, somewhat surprised that her calorie-conscious twin wanted to scarf down dessert. She stopped to wait for her sister to walk back to her so that they could head downstairs together. "So, can I tell you, I saw Dara the other day . . ." she started hesitantly.

"Ugh, who hasn't? I feel like every time I turn a corner I see her gloating face," Sydney grumbled.

"Yeah, but let's just say she wasn't exactly looking so great when I saw her," Lauren mused quietly as she remembered the pathetic look on her former best friend's face.

"Really?" Sydney said excitedly. It was good to know she wasn't the only one going through it.

"Yeah, she was actually pretty sad looking. I guess she's having morning sickness or something. . . . I haven't the slightest. But it didn't look fun," Lauren answered as the two descended to the lower level.

"Why do you sound like you feel bad for her or something?" Sydney questioned defensively.

"Oh, no, not at all," Lauren quickly clarified. "It's

totally what she deserves. I'm just commenting. You know I have absolutely no love for her."

"Oh, okay," Sydney said, giving her sister the serious side-eye as they entered the kitchen.

"Good evening, Ms. Sydney and Ms. Lauren. Do you need help with something?" Edwina asked as she jumped up from the kitchen table, where she was flipping through a copy of *People en Español*. Prepared to put together whatever the young ladies' hearts desired, the petite woman hurried behind the floating island.

"Hey, Edwina," the two girls greeted their longtime live-in housekeeper.

"Lauren's greedy butt has the munchies," Sydney teased as the two headed over to the table and sat down.

"Call it what you want, but there's a bowl of Chunky Monkey with some warm caramel sauce that has my name on it. Right, Edwina?" Lauren said as she lazily stretched her arms above her head and then adjusted the mint-green boxers she was wearing.

"Coming right up," Edwina replied as she turned to the double-door Sub-Zero refrigerator.

"So are you still down to share?" Lauren questioned Sydney with a mischievous gleam in her eye.

Sydney could feel her booty getting bigger just talking about the calorie-filled dessert. "Um, maybe I'll just take a couple of bites of yours," she said with a cautious smile.

"We can't all be future *KING* magazine cover candidates up in here."

"Whatever makes you happy," Lauren laughed; she knew her older sister could never hang when it came to chowing down. "Speaking of what makes you happy," she teased in a conspiratorial tone. "How is Jason? Are you guys, like, totally in love? 'Cause I've seen the pictures on YRT, and the way he looks at you is *so* serious."

"Funny you should ask," Sydney hedged as she looked down at her fuzzy purple slippers.

"Uh-oh, I don't like the tone of that," Lauren said as the smile quickly vanished from her face.

"No, nothing like that," Sydney backtracked. "It's just that this relationship is so different from what I had with Marcus."

"Well, duh, Syd! Jason is a fine-ass, popular, normal guy, and Marcus is a pompous, patchouli-oil-smelling, wack loser," Lauren quickly rationalized as Edwina placed the large bowl of ice cream and two spoons in front of the two girls.

"There you go, enjoy," she said politely.

"Thanks so much, Edwina," Sydney responded as she looked at the monstrosity her sister was already busily scarfing down.

"If you need anything else, I'll be in my room," Edwina said, quietly stepping back.

"Okay, thanks, Big E," Lauren said between mouthfuls.

"Good night, Edwina," Sydney replied as she scooped up a small spoonful. "Anyway," she continued. "So basically, Jason is really great. It's just that he really won't let the whole Marcus thing go."

"Ugh, you don't have to tell me about men not wanting to let stuff go," Lauren said with a frustrated roll of her eyes.

"But there's a difference between him being frustrated and talking about it and him getting mad at me because of the situation," Sydney tried to explain.

"What do you mean, 'getting mad'?" Lauren asked curiously. "What is there to be mad about? Marcus was a bad decision, let's all move on."

"Right, that's what I thought, too, but . . . let's just say Jason has a temper that seems to flare up any time I'm within fifty feet of Marcus. And it makes him act all weird. Like he accused me of wearing a tight dress to the last Sadie Hawkins planning meeting to turn Marcus on or something. . . ."

Lauren almost choked. "You in a 'tight' dress? Seriously? Do you even own anything 'tight'?"

"I know, right?" Sydney mused as she twirled the same spoonful around in the bowl before finally putting it in her mouth. "But here's the thing. I had this Sister Share session at Better Day earlier this evening."

"What's a 'Sister Share' session?" Lauren asked curiously.

"It's when the women at the shelter sit down and tell their stories to one another so that they can get support and problem-solve how to move forward. . . ."

"Ah, okay," Lauren said as she neared the bottom of the bowl. "Sounds good."

"Yeah, it was. But listen, so I'm there and this girl Mary gets up to talk. Now mind you, Mary's not that old. I think she's, like, twenty-eight."

"Twenty-eight is way older than us," Lauren mused as she eyed Sydney's melting spoonful.

"Lauren, will you just listen?" Sydney said sharply before continuing. "So anyway, Mary was saying how when she first started dating her boyfriend — mind you, this is the same boyfriend that flipped out one day and broke several of her ribs and her nose — he used to be really jealous of her ex-boyfriend. And he used to make comments about her clothes and stuff. That's kinda bizarre that it sounds so much like what Jason is doing, right?"

Lauren looked at her sister thoughtfully. "Yeah, that is crazy," she finally said after a moment. "I mean, he's so cool, I can't see . . ."

"But that's the thing. None of these women ever thought the guy they were with could be capable of hitting them. And then you find them dropped off in a ditch," Sydney blurted out before she even realized what she was saying.

Lauren's eyes widened. "I don't know, Syd. You're, like, the smartest person I know. If your gut is telling you there's a problem, maybe you should listen," she cautioned, changing her tune.

"I'm not saying there's a problem," Sydney started to backtrack, suddenly worried that she'd said too much. The last thing she wanted to do was make her sister think she was about to become an after-school special. "I guess it was just that moment got me a little weirded out. Like you said, Jason's too cool to ever do something crazy."

Lauren raised an eyebrow suspiciously and seemed about to say something when Sydney's back pocket rang. Sydney grabbed her iPhone and looked at the message from Marcus that had just popped up: FYI: I'm on top of the banking situation. Took care of the deposits, don't worry about the Sadie Hawkins account, we're all good. MG. She sighed loudly as she put it down on the table.

"What's that about?" Lauren questioned suspiciously.

Sydney rolled her eyes. "It's just some Sadie Hawkins Benefit drama. I will be so glad when this party is over. It is the bane of my existence."

"Ah, okay," Lauren said as she picked up the empty bowl and headed over to the sink.

"Hey, before I forget," Sydney said, standing up from the table and heading over to her sister's side at the sink. "Have you heard anything from Uncle Larry?" she whispered over the running water.

Lauren shook her head. "Nope, sure haven't. But I'm sure if there was anything, he would let us know. We probably just need to resume life until something actually happens."

"You're so right," Sydney said. "Clearly, I'm becoming, like, totally paranoid," she joked wryly.

Lauren turned off the water, shook the excess moisture off her bowl, and put it in the dishwasher. She grabbed a paper towel to dry her hands and turned to face her stressed-out-looking sister. "Sydney, seriously? You gotta relax. Everything is going to be just fine." She put her arms around Sydney, gave her a tight squeeze, and whispered softly in her ear, "I promise."

10
LAUREN

The staccato of the synthesized horns in Ludacris's "Number One Spot" bounced around the gym walls — the beat so deep that if you bothered to look at the basketball net and the bleachers, you would have seen the two of them rattling about like Melyssa Ford's badunkadunk in an old BET music video. But it wasn't the nets or the bleachers or even trifling video girls that everybody was watching. No, today, Lauren was putting on a show worthy of a Top 10 YouTube video — and all eyes were on her.

Decked out in skintight, hot-pink Nike leggings and a matching tank top knotted at the waist to show off her belly button, Lauren mouthed the words to the song as she gyrated and swirled her hips, sat into a perfect knee bend, then hopped back up and popped her butt with the conviction of a woman who was expecting some tips for her hard work.

For sure, overprotective adults with more conservative leanings may have likened her dancing to a Magic City–worthy spectacle, but Lauren knew her constituency: This was what moved crowds, and who was Lauren to disappoint? This was the kind of routine the squad had been rooting for toward the end of last year's basketball season — the kind of dance that, if the squad put its back into it at halftime, surely would work the good students of Brookhaven Prep into a tizzy. She had choreographed most of the moves under Dara's watchful eyes a year ago. Lauren had created it specifically to make her mark on the squad, which, under the direction of the prior dance squad coach, Ms. Bruchette, looked a little too old-school and proper for most of the students' taste. Coach Bruchette had them out there bumping a technical, mechanical two-step to Earth, Wind & Fire, while all the dancers and their fans were fiending for the squad to get low. Alas, despite the most vociferous outcries from Lauren's teammates, Coach Bruchette wasn't having it.

But today was a new day. Coach Bruchette had left the dance squad position and her gig at Brookhaven Prep to become the assistant vice principal at Brookhaven's rival, The Galloway School. And the new coach was considerably younger, cooler, and clearly open to new ideas, seeing as she was trying to revamp the squad and get the girls to pick a new team captain. Lauren was all for revamping, but she wasn't about to see herself erased as the head dancer. So she put her back into it — to remind her squad mates that nobody could do it better than she could.

Lauren twisted one knee in and then the other and rocked her hips from side to side, circled her body around, and launched into a cartwheel/somersault/backflip combination that made a few of her onlookers, who were standing around pretending to stretch but really watching her every move, gasp with glee. Well, most of them. Caroline Morrison and Trina Beddleman, who had all but attached themselves to Sydney's ex's left and right thigh like the trifling cleanup chicks they were, were both off to the side shaking their heads and clucking in each other's ears, trying their best to goad a few of the other dancers, most notably sisters Meghan and Lexi Robichaux, to join in.

Lauren pretended not to notice; she turned toward the control booth and signaled Lucy Thompson, a junior she'd personally recruited for the dance squad after watching her rock it in their Modern Dance class last semester, to start the song from the top.

"Lauren?" Delia Lawrence said, approaching her fellow squad member with the utmost care, half her attention on the anti-Lauren crowd, the other on the Queen B herself.

"I don't mean to pull you out of your zone, but I need to ask you something."

"Shoot," Lauren said, using the back of her hand to wipe sweat from her forehead and brow.

"Well, I did a couple of practice front flips earlier, and I think I might have pulled a muscle in my thigh," Delia shouted over Ludacris, whose rich, lusty baritone once again was warning all within range of the Bose speakers not to "slip up or get got." "You have any tips for getting rid of a leg cramp?"

"Did you warm up?" Lauren asked in her normal voice, forcing the girl to move in conspiratorially closer. This made the anti clique cluck a little louder. Lauren tried her best to ignore them. "Because that's what any good dancer needs to do first and foremost to prevent injury — warm up first, then stretch. Before I got here, I ran around the track twice to get my blood flowing, and then I stretched before I started working on the new routine." She actually ran only halfway around the track — it was too cold to be out there freezing her behind off — and the stretching wasn't really all that drawn out, but whatev. It sounded good.

"Yeah, I didn't really give it much time," Delia said. "I had a meeting with the Art Society Club and I didn't want to be late to squad practice, so instead of warming up I just got to it, you know?"

"Yeah, well, that's why your leg is hurt," Lauren said simply. "Lie on your back and pull your knee to your chest, then rub it. It'll go away eventually. If it's still sore, go to the clubhouse. I've got a special leg-warming wrap I keep for occasions like these. Wrap it around your leg, but not too tight, or else you'll cut off your circulation, and that'll make it hurt worse."

"Bet," Delia said. "Good lookin' out. Oh, and that dance routine is the fire — it's for us?"

"I hope it is," chimed in Kayo Childers, a dance squad vet who joined the team around the same time as Lauren. Two of her girls, Rachel Brown and Brooke Redd, flanked her.

"Mos def it's for us — and that's what your team captain is for," Lauren said before turning her back and signaling Lucy to start the music again.

"You have got to teach us that one," Kayo said breathlessly.

"It's easy — come on, I'll show you," Lauren said, explaining some of the moves. With Kayo, Rachel, and Brooke lined up behind her, she counted down, "five, six, seven, eight," and then the gyrating began.

"All right, all right, ladies," Assistant Coach Maddie said, storming onto the court just as the group began to drop and pop it. "Let's focus, people. Cut the music," she demanded, signaling Lucy. She waited until Ludacris's voice faded out before continuing. "Okay, so we've got about four more practices before our first game, so we need to get it together. First, some team business: Coach Piper is out with the flu. Get those flu shots, people! We can't have half the team sidelined with an illness that could have been prevented. If you're afraid of needles, get the nose spray. It works — I know.

"In the meantime," Coach Maddie continued, "Lauren Duke will act as captain until we can hold the official vote."

The coach might as well have hammered Lauren in the head. *Did she say "act"? I'm supposed to "be" the captain, not "act,"* Lauren screamed inside of her head.

"Wait, so we are going to take a vote at some point, right?" Caroline pouted.

Lauren rolled her eyes and folded her arms. "That's what the coach said," Lauren snapped, backed up by giggles from Kayo and her girls. The room fell dead silent; the rest of the squad members seemed to lean in a little closer.

"Oh, I'm just trying to make sure we're all clear what's going on here," Caroline said.

"Um, maybe it needs to be said more slowly so that you can get it right: Coach Piper is sick, and we're going to pick the captain when coach is here," Lauren said, dragging out each of her words.

"We're not going to 'pick' anybody — we're all going to vote, unlike in the past . . ." Caroline began, Trina nodding in agreement.

"In the past, it was clear who was the leader of this squad, just like it is now. Formalities, sweetie. This is all about formalities," Lauren retorted.

"Uh-huh — I got your 'formalities,'" Caroline said.

"Ladies, ladies, please — not here, not today," Coach Maddie said. "It's simple: There will be a vote, and anyone who thinks she's able to lead this team will be able to participate in the elections."

"Sounds simple enough," Lauren snapped.

Coach Maddie gave Lauren a hard-eye and then turned her attention back to her clipboard. "We have the Candy Crave coming up next week. Now, normally the captain and her co-captain would be responsible for pulling this together, but since the position has been up in the air, we need to —"

"I've already started working on it, Coach Maddie," said Lauren of the dance squad fund-raiser, one of their biggest. On Candy Crave day, the squad members would fan out through the halls of Brookhaven Prep with special bags full of candy — Snickers, Now and Laters, Hubba Bubba, Red Hots, Skittles, MilkyWays, Hershey's Kisses, and more. They'd sell the candy at a ridiculous markup and add hundreds of dollars worth of cash to the squad's fund-raising account. Lauren had meant to go buy the candy over the weekend — to show initiative. But, well, she had to help Donald with his shopping therapy on Saturday, and then on Sunday, her parents dragged her to church and to brunch, and by the time they got back home she just needed a nap, and then dinner, and then she had to get her nightly beauty ritual on earlier than usual because there was that *Law & Order: SVU* marathon she wanted to watch. She made a mental note to give Edwina a list so that she could hit up Sam's or Wal-Mart or wherever you get candy at a discount these days. "We should have the candy ready to split into the bags by Monday."

"Seems like we should have the candy Friday so we can split it all before the weekend," Trina chimed in. "I mean, the sale is on Tuesday, and I'm not planning to be up all night Monday trying to get this stuff done at the last minute."

"Well, that's what your fearless captain is for," Lauren smirked. "While you're relaxing, I work. It's no joke leading the team, but I do what I can," she added, raising an eyebrow and admiring her nails.

"I hope to see that for myself real soon," Caroline snapped.

"Whatev," Lauren snapped back. The tension in the room was palpable; it was clear the squad was divided up into two sides — the Lauren camp and the Caroline trough — and it was obvious by the way they were standing who was on whose side. You could practically draw a chalk line between them.

"Okay, ladies, enough," Coach Maddie said, raising her hands as if in surrender. "The fund-raiser is Tuesday. Lauren, thank you for taking the lead on this. Please let your squad know when you need their help; don't try to take all of this on yourself, okay?"

"Sure thing, Coach," Lauren said, her eyes still on Caroline.

"Okay, now, let's get to work. We've got to get the new girls up to speed on some of our classic routines and then get to work on a few new ones, so I hope everyone's warmed up," Coach Maddie said.

"Actually, Coach, I was working on a little somethin'-somethin' during warm-ups," Lauren chimed. "I already started teaching a few of the girls the steps. I'd be happy to show it to you, and maybe we could use it as the beginning of the new halftime show."

"All right, loving the initiative, Ms. Lauren — let's see it," Coach Maddie said, smiling.

Lauren gave Lucy the go-ahead to get the music going; within minutes, the entire squad was standing behind her, taking her cues — following her lead.

Just the way it should be.

* * *

"That was a cute little dance you pulled together, girl," Meghan said, walking up behind Lauren, who was toweling off in front of her locker. "Maybe the next time you find yourself on the set of a Thug Heaven video shoot, you could whip that out — you know, get your shot."

Lauren put her towel in her locker and sighed. "You know, it must really suck to be stuck playing the background all the time."

"I wouldn't really know much about that," Meghan said. "Maybe you could give me some lessons."

"Oh, it wouldn't be a problem for me to school you," Lauren said, her raised voice drawing the attention of the rest of the squad. A few of the girls slammed their lockers and leaned in to the catfight, tossing wild glares and shoulder shrugs at one another. They were seconds away from taking bets on which of the girls would win in an all-out brawl. The locker room fell dead silent. "But since I never play the rear, my lessons would be all about how to win."

"It won't be with that hood rat twirl you were forcing on us today," Meghan snapped. "I have to admit, I feel a little dumber after watching it."

Lauren took a step forward and smiled. "Wow, I really didn't think it was possible for you to be dumber. But you know, since I'm trying to let my light shine bright today, I'll refrain from going there. Instead, I'll give you some of my friendly advice: Why don't you focus your energies on getting that job at the drive-thru at Checkers and leave the big-girl work to the pros."

"Funny you should bring up Checkers," Caroline chimed in. "Isn't that how boys in the hood pay the rent? You know, I hear it's the perfect cover for the weed and crack sales."

"I wouldn't know about that, seeing as I don't deal in weed or crack," Lauren snapped. "Is there something you want to talk to us about, Caroline? Because you are aware of the dance squad prohibition against drugs, right?"

"Oh, I'm well aware of the rules," Caroline said, stepping in to stand directly next to Meghan. "We all know about those. It's those unwritten rules that can get a little tricky. You know, 'Thou shalt not be seen in the SWATS if one wants her family's reputation to stay intact,' and 'Thou shalt act like she's got some home training,' and, oh, there's my personal favorite: 'Thou shalt not consort with hood rats and dough boys, lest you want to become one.'"

"You know what?" Lauren said, getting in Caroline's face.

Kayo stepped between the two and gently pushed Lauren back. "She's not worth it, Lauren, for real. Don't bother."

Caroline flung her weave and turned to face Meghan. "You know what? Unlike some people in the room, I'm really not one to debase myself like this, so I'm going to go

142

ahead and hold my head up like a girl with some class. Maybe someone can watch my moves and learn a little."

"I know that's right," Meghan laughed, tossing a high five to Caroline for good measure. "Come on, let's go — I'm tired of wasting my damn breath in this locker room full of thick-headed posers."

Lauren smirked and turned back to her locker; she grabbed her oversized Marc Jacobs hobo and her Brookhaven Prep dance squad gym bag and slammed the locker door shut. "You ready, Kayo?" she said. "I've got things to do, places to go, people to see. Later for this mess."

"Yeah, sure. Just give me a minute," Kayo said, staring at Caroline and Meghan. "Anything else?" she asked the two.

Neither answered — they just stalked out of the locker room, a few of their minions in tow.

"That's what I thought," Kayo said. "Come on, girl, don't pay them any mind."

"Girl, please, ain't nobody studying Caroline or Meghan or any other one of those heifas," Lauren said. "Instead of being all up in my business, she needs to be figuring out how she's going to handle that not-so-cute face, the slight verbal disorder, and anger management."

Kayo and a few of the other girls who'd been hanging on every word laughed. "Give me a minute, I have to go to the ladies' room. Why don't we all meet outside; we can talk details on the Candy Crave on the way to the parking lot, k?"

"Sounds good," Lauren said. "See you outside."

For sure, Lauren had won that round, and she was grateful for Kayo's assistance, but too many of the dance squad members were getting out of pocket, and she didn't quite know how to respond to the madness. Between the insistent YRT postings, the ridiculously personal outbursts from the girls who used to admire her, and the pressure at home, Lauren was feeling like she had lost absolute control over all the things she once ruled with an iron fist. Did Caroline really come out of her face like that? In front of the entire locker room of dance team members? And just who in the hell emboldened her anyway? Lauren had seen her sniffing behind Marcus a couple of times, like she was trying to get with him. Which would most certainly make her a sloppy mess, chasing behind a boy who cheated on his girlfriend and got the sidepiece in the family way. *Yeah, that's it right there*, Lauren thought to herself. *Unbelievable.*

As quickly as she connected the dots, Lauren whipped out her iPhone and punched in Sydney's info; her sister was going to want to hear about this, for sure. Coming to a stop right at the entrance to the clubhouse, Lauren dropped her gym bag and gingerly placed her hobo on top of it, then prepared her fingers for texting. Just as she'd typed in the words You are not going to believe this some movement caught her eye. She looked up momentarily and then back down at her text, and then, suddenly, back up again. So loud was her gasp that Kayo, Rachel, and Brooke, who all were within mere feet of her, wrinkled their brows. Lauren slammed her back against the wall, the cold tile every bit as shocking as that which her eyes had just taken in.

"What?" Brooke asked, walking up behind Lauren. "Dang, you all right?"

Hell no, Lauren wanted to say, but then she would betray what she wished she hadn't seen: Jermaine, in all his hood-tastic glory, sitting on the front bumper of his car. What in the world he was doing there Lauren didn't know. Maybe he had news for her? Perhaps he got lost? Or maybe Altimus threatened him and he was looking for Lauren to protect him? Whatever the reason, he was there, and Lauren did not need this. Not today.

"Um, nothing," Lauren said, "accidentally" kicking her Marc Jacobs onto the floor so that she could pick it up. "I, um, was in the middle of texting Sydney and almost dropped my phone. I just got this back from after an eternity's worth of punishment, and I'm not trying to break my baby now that she's back in my possession."

"Uh, okaaaay," Brooke said, looking at Lauren like she was two steps off the deep end. "You need some help? You

145

look like you're about to fall to pieces or something. Let me get one of your bags."

"No, I said I got it!" Lauren said a little more loudly than she'd intended. She picked up her bag while she tried to think fast about what to do. For sure, walking up to him and giving him a hug and kiss and acting like they were a couple just wasn't in the cards right now — not after the hellish practice with half the squad giving her the side-eye over her questionable hood associations. What would be said behind her back — and to her face — about the boy in the long white polo, baggy, sagging jeans, and a baseball cap twisted to the side, sitting on top of a broke down car in the middle of the parking lot? Unannounced? Wasn't no way.

"Can you get the door?" Lauren asked. "God, can you believe Caroline's wack ass trying to come for me?" she added, trying hard to adjust her tone and preoccupy them with chitchat so they would focus on her and not the boy sitting outside.

"I mean, I don't know if she'd gotten an extra shot of courage juice or what, but she was really bugging out, wasn't she?" said Kayo, bursting through the door. Lauren walked out right behind her, huddling next to her and in front of Brooke and Rachel, praying that her positioning was shielding her from Jermaine's view.

"She got an extra shot of courage juice, all right,"

Brooke insisted. "She got that special Marcus juice — thinks she can just say anything to you because she's picking up your sister's sloppy seconds."

"Yeah, you better get Syd on the case and let her know she needs to tell her ex to take control, because he's making everybody look really messy right now."

Lauren, barely paying attention to the advice, turned her head in the opposite direction from where Jermaine was standing, praying with every step that the angels made her invisible to Jermaine and rendered him mute so he didn't, have mercy, call her name out in front of folks. She dropped her head down so far, her chin almost touched her chest. And then she messed up and snuck a peek.

Their eyes met.

He was smiling.

Lauren kept walking — just looked the other way.

"So you gonna tell your sister what's up, Lauren?" Kayo asked. "Because this madness has got to stop."

Distracted, Lauren didn't answer her at first. "Um, yeah, I guess," Lauren said. "But you know, I don't really try to get all up in Sydney's biz — I got enough headaches."

"I know that's right," Brooke agreed, using her key-ring remote to unlock her candy-apple red BMW 325i. "Let somebody else deal with the sloppiness. You need to focus on keeping your job as captain, because I will not be answering to anybody's Meghan and Caroline. I swear, geriatric patients in the ICU got more moves than those two. I'm trying to get a little Ludacris in my life."

"Yeah, well, I'm doing what I can," Lauren said, finally arriving at the driver's side of her Saab. She unlocked the door and tossed her bags in the front seat, all with her back to the direction in which Jermaine was sitting. She couldn't get the key in the ignition fast enough and almost slammed her own leg in the car door.

"All right, then," Kayo said over the din of Lauren's engine. "You in a rush or something? Why don't you come with us to Maddy's for a strawberry energy shake?"

"Um, I just gotta get home," Lauren rushed. Just then, her iPhone rang. Jermaine. "My, um, mom's got something for me to do, and Mr. Peters gave me enough homework to get me into Harvard. I swear, I don't know how I'm going to get to it all," she said, putting her car in gear. "Okay, smooches, ladies. I'll see you tomorrow."

"But we didn't talk about the fund-raiser," Kayo said as Lauren screeched out of her parking space.

"I'll hit you on the MySpace," she said, pulling away, her left hand on the wheel, her right on her phone.

"Hello?" she said, answering her phone as she pulled to the corner of the street. She caught the light. Damn.

148

"Yo, what's the rush?" Jermaine asked, his deep voice rumbling more quietly than usual.

"What? What are you talking about? Who is this?" Lauren asked, feigning ignorance.

"Who you think it is? It's the guy who spent the last half hour in the parking lot waiting for you."

"Jermaine?" Lauren asked, trying to sound surprised.

"Yes, it's Jermaine."

"What's up, love?" Lauren said cheerily.

"What's up? You tell me," he said. "Why'd you walk away?"

"What are you talking about?" Lauren said, staring at the light as if her sheer willpower would make the darn thing change from red to green.

"I was outside. You saw me. You kept walking, got in your car, and left," he said, the anger in his voice now fully apparent. "Why'd you walk away?"

"Jermaine, I don't know what you're talking about. I just got out of dance practice and I was with my girls, talking. Why would I walk past you? You came all this way to see me?" she asked, trying to sound seductive. "Aw, I miss you!"

"Well, why don't you come back and hang out with me? We can go grab a bite to eat, maybe go —"

"Um, sweetie, I can't," Lauren said, still watching the

light. Finally, it changed. Lauren gunned the gas. "I got my girls in the car. I have to drive them home and then get back to my house to do some homework and stuff. As much as I'd love to . . ."

Jermaine watched Lauren's car pull past the parking lot — past his car. Clearly, she was the only one in it.

"Nah, nah, it's okay. I should have called first," Jermaine said, walking slowly around the car to the driver's side. "You're a busy girl."

"Sometimes, I guess," she said. "I'm sorry, sweetie. Don't be mad, okay?"

"I'll be all right," he said. "Maybe another time. I'll holla."

Jermaine pushed the END button on his Treo and threw his phone on the passenger seat. The phone landed hard on the bouquet of hot-pink roses lying on the dark brown leather, damaging their delicate petals. Jermaine stared out over the steering wheel, his eyes landing on the huge black letters on the side of the building: THE DUKE HOUSE.

This was Altimus's house, and he wasn't welcome.

11
SYDNEY

"Okay, you have officially converted me," Sydney laughed as the closing credits started to roll across the huge flat-screen TV in front of the couple. "*South Park* is *the* funniest cartoon ever!"

"Hey, I told you, Syd," Jason said with a sly smile as he grabbed the television control and lowered the volume slightly. "Gimme a chance and I'll have you rocking bamboo earrings and fluorescent-colored Nike dunks, too!"

Sydney immediately made loud retching sounds and covered her mouth as if she was going to vomit. "Oh, God, I think I'm going to be sick," she protested with a giggle.

"What?" Jason questioned in feigned surprised. "Like you don't have a lifetime supply of Rocawear baby T-shirts to match in your closet? Stop playin'!"

"Humph, not even on a dare," Sydney replied with a sarcastic roll of the eyes. "Why, if I didn't know any better, I'd think you were confusing me with my BET-crazed sister, Mr. Danden!" Sydney playfully pouted and turned away from her boyfriend to look out the huge bay windows into her spacious back patio.

"Aww, come here," Jason coaxed sweetly as he wrapped his arms around her from behind and leaned in to lightly kiss her on the back of her neck. As his warm lips gently pressed into the soft spot behind Sydney's left ear, he slowly ran his fingers up and down her arms.

"No, just forget it." Sydney continued her charade although she could feel her resolve weakening with each kiss. "Obviously, I'm not the one you want," she said as she played with the frayed edging on her rose-colored Tracy Reese cinch-waist jacket.

"Not only are you the right one," Jason whispered in her ear as he gently turned Sydney around to face him. "You're the only one I want." He stared deeply into Sydney's eyes as he stroked her face.

Sydney smiled shyly as she looked at him. Any and all concerns about his bizzaro behavior were wiped from her mind. She relaxed under his touch. "I'm glad," she finally responded.

"You are so beautiful. Do you know that?" Jason questioned huskily. "I love the curls of your hair, the way your eyes light up when you smile, the softness of your touch when we're holding hands. . . . I swear, just looking at you walk into a room turns me on."

Sydney playfully punched Jason's arm. "Uh, hello, T.M.I! You're gonna make me self-conscious! I'll never be able to walk in a room without thinking you're getting a hard-on!" she teased.

Jason laughed at his own blunder. "Oops, def too much information, huh?" he admitted as he sat back bashfully on the plush, moss-colored couch.

"Definitely," Sydney said as she leaned over and kissed Jason gently on the lips. "But it's okay, because I think you're pretty cute yourself, Mr. Danden," she whispered softly, mere inches from his face. She could taste the trace of cinnamon on her lips from Jason's stick of Big Red gum. She leaned in again, and this time they exchanged a more passionate kiss. Sydney could feel Jason slowly massaging circles on her scalp. Tingles ran up and down her body like electricity. Sydney was always amazed at how much better Jason kissed than Marcus. When they finally pulled away, she involuntarily smiled.

"Whatchu smiling about," he asked in an exaggerated 70s accent.

"You make me really happy," Sydney smiled contentedly. She rested her head on his shoulder and nuzzled the crook of his neck. The smell of his Creed Green Irish

Tweed cologne filled her nose. Sydney hugged him tightly from the side.

"Is that so?" Jason asked with one eyebrow cocked.

"Unfortunately, yes," Sydney teased. "I tried my best to fight it, but alas, it seems that I have a new boyfriend who makes me really happy."

"Hmmm, I see. Although to be perfectly honest, that doesn't seem like such a horrible thing, Ms. Duke. In fact, some might actually call it a beautiful struggle."

"Uh, okay, Talib, is that what you'd call it?" Sydney laughed at the look of surprise on Jason's face because she'd caught on to his backpack hip-hop reference to rapper Talib Kweli's album title. "Bet you didn't think I knew that one, huh?"

"You never cease to amaze me," Jason said with a huge smile.

"A well-trained woman always retains some mystery," Sydney chided with a raised eyebrow of her own.

"I see. Well, you're not the only one with something up the sleeve tonight," Jason said forebodingly.

Sydney immediately straightened up. "Oh, yeah, is that so? And just what are you hiding from me, Jason Danden?"

Jason smiled and stood up. He walked over to the black-and-purple Billionaire Boys Club hoodie he'd taken off earlier and started digging in the pockets. He turned and looked at Sydney over his shoulder with a mischievous smile.

"What? What is it?" Sydney asked, becoming increasingly excited. She sat on the edge of the couch in anticipation of Jason's surprise.

When he finally stopped digging around, Jason turned and faced Sydney with his left hand behind his back. "Relax, Syd, you gotta learn how to enjoy the suspense," he teased as he headed back over to the couch.

"If you don't show me . . ." Sydney jumped up from her seat and grabbed at his hand. Jason easily eluded her reach. She stomped her right foot in a mock temper tantrum. "Jason Danden, if you don't stop being mean to me, I'm going to call my daddy," she threatened playfully.

"Well, dang, when you give a brother an ultimatum like that . . ." Jason feigned fright and finally pulled his hand around for her to see. "And this whole time I thought you liked me. . . ."

"Omigod," was the only word Sydney could utter as her mouth dropped open at the sight of a coveted red Cartier box. She froze in place.

"Wow, are you shell-shocked already? 'Cause you haven't even seen what's inside yet," Jason responded. He slowly opened the box to reveal an 18-karat pink-gold LOVE bracelet.

"Jason," Sydney started slowly as she stared at the beautiful and extremely significant piece of jewelry. "I don't know what to say," she continued at an obvious loss for words.

"Just keep saying that I make you happy," Jason answered as he removed the bracelet and held it out to Sydney. "I know I've been a little harsh with you about the whole Marcus thing. And this is not to say sorry, but rather to show you that it really only happens because I care about you. I wouldn't get upset about your clothes or the way he was looking if I didn't care about you."

Sydney twisted the diamond stud in her right ear. For some reason, hearing Jason's explanation only kicked up Sydney's uncomfortable memories of Mary's speech. "But this bracelet," Jason continued, completely unaware of the slight twitch in Sydney's left eye, "is a symbol of our unity. Once it's locked on, the only way you can take it off is with the tiny screwdriver that I'll wear on my chain next to my cross." He pulled out his chain with the tiny golden screwdriver attached from under his long-sleeve white T-shirt to show her. Sydney forced a smile. Jason locked the bracelet on her left wrist with a soft snap. "It's my way of saying that nothing — or no one — is ever going to come between us," he concluded seriously.

"Wow, thank you, Jason," Sydney said softly as she fingered the perfectly fitting bracelet. "I absolutely love it."

Jason leaned in to kiss Sydney. "I'm glad," he said as he held her tightly. Sydney could hear his heart beating in her ear as she leaned against his chiseled chest.

Sydney pulled away slowly to look up at his face. "No, this is a really big deal. I'm totally surprised."

"Yeah, I know at first it seems like a lot," Jason replied. "But I expect a lot from you. And since nothing in life is really free . . ."

Sydney paused as she considered his words. For a second, it almost seemed like he was justifying his behavior with the expensive bracelet. Trying to shake the queasiness in her stomach, Sydney forced herself to focus on the awesome present and the amazing moment they were sharing. She stood up on her tiptoes, wrapped her arms around Jason's neck, and planted a lingering kiss on his lips. "Say no more," she said, looking into his dark brown eyes. Jason just smiled.

"Don't forget to send me a text message when you get home," Sydney reminded Jason as she walked him to the Dukes' front door. As she swung her hand, she could feel the weight of the bracelet.

"I won't," Jason replied as they reached the foyer. He stopped and turned back to give her a tight hug. "I'm really glad you like your gift," he said softly as he raised her hand so that he could look at it once more before leaving.

"I do, I really do," Sydney responded truthfully.

"Good, because I meant every word of what I said earlier — nothing or no one is going to come between us," Jason responded.

Still feeling conflicted by the intensity of his words, Sydney remained silent as she slowly pulled away.

"I'll talk to you later, babe," Jason said, opening the front door. Then he walked out and hurried toward his truck. He gave her one last wave before jumping in, starting the engine, and driving off into the night. Sydney sighed softly as she closed the door. She looked down at the bracelet and shook her head. "What am I going to do with him," she mumbled under her breath. Caught up in a daze, she turned and headed up the stairs to her bedroom.

"May I have a word with you, please," Altimus's deep voice suddenly rumbled from behind. Sydney was so frightened she almost tripped up the stairs.

"Omigod, Altimus, I didn't even know you were still down here," Sydney said when she regained her balance. "You scared the heck out of me!"

"My apologies," Altimus replied simply as he looked at Sydney expectantly. She immediately turned around and headed back downstairs. "I assure you, this won't take long," he said as he turned away. Completely clueless, Sydney followed silently behind her stepfather to his office.

He held the door for her to walk in before him. Sydney could feel his eyes burning holes in her back as she took a seat in the chair facing his desk.

"So, what's going on," Sydney asked hesitantly when Altimus finally took his seat behind the desk facing her.

"Well, like I told you, your mother and I have been monitoring you and Lauren to see if you girls finally grasped what it means to be part of the Duke family," Altimus began slowly. Sydney mentally reviewed the events of the past two weeks and, to the best of her knowledge, she hadn't done anything too, too terrible. "And I'm pleased to say, you girls have not disappointed us," Altimus continued. Even though Sydney felt the tension in her back decrease slightly, she knew better than to completely relax.

"Okay," she replied as she pulled the lapels of her jacket closer across her chest. "So what does that mean?"

"It means that, as promised, I'm going to give you the money to bail your father out of jail," Altimus said with a smug grin. He sat back in his chair, crossed his arms over his chest, and waited for her reaction.

For the second time that night, Sydney's jaw dropped. "You're going to *what*?" she asked, certain that her mind was playing a cruel and unusual trick on her.

"You heard me correctly. I'm going to give you

whatever funds you need to bail your father out of jail," Altimus repeated. He so obviously loved every minute of Sydney's confusion.

"But — but, why? I don't understand. . . . Why would you help my father?"

"Because I'm a man of my word," Altimus replied simply. "I told you and your sister that if you guys held up your end of the bargain, this is what would happen," he said with finality.

Sydney could feel her heart racing. Never in a million years had she expected Altimus to really bail Dice out of prison and definitely not so soon. Almost immediately, she could feel her adrenaline start to rush. "How much is his bail? When will he be free?" Her questions all rushed together.

Altimus shrugged. "I have no idea. I guess that will depend on when you get all the information together," he said.

"Excuse me?" Sydney asked.

"Well, you're the new Nancy Drew, right? And needless to say, neither your mother nor or I are stepping a foot near anybody's jail. So whenever you figure out how much money you need and get back to me, it's yours."

Is this some type of test? she wondered, searching Altimus's eyes for the deception. "But I don't —" she began to counter.

"Sure you do," Altimus cut her off sharply. "The same way you found yourself all up in my business, I know you can figure this out." Altimus stood up and looked at her. "Although I have to say, I'm looking forward to hearing how Dice feels about his lil' Ladybug bailing him out with my money," he snickered.

A chill ran through Sydney's body. She knew the offer was a setup. Not only did she have absolutely no clue how to bail her father out, but if and when she figured it out, she would still have to explain where she got the money. Tormented, Sydney shook her head slowly. "I don't know if I can do this," she mumbled.

"Well, when you figure it out, let me know," Altimus replied. "With that said, you and I are finished for now." Sydney sat dumbfounded as her stepfather passed by and exited the room. As the door closed behind him, Sydney hung her head in frustration.

"Think, Sydney, think," she muttered to herself as she incessantly twisted her diamond stud. "What would Dice want?" she mumbled, trying to envision the decision her father would make. Obviously, he would never want anything from Altimus. But if he was out, not only would they be reunited, but he could help find clues that would ultimately indict the real killer and clear his name for good. God only knew all the terrible things that were happening to him in jail. And he would have to remain there as long as it took for the slow-ass cops to solve the case . . . if they ever did. Sydney's stomach turned at the very thought of losing her father all over again. Would it be so bad to use Altimus's evil money for good? Especially if, together, they were able to turn it around and use it for good? No, it just couldn't be.

Sydney gritted her teeth and stood up. She knew what she had to do — get her father out of jail. Now the only problem was, how? It wasn't like she could just call Carmen and Rhea and ask them for the CliffsNotes on how to post bail. She didn't know anybody who would have intimate knowledge of the Georgia jail system . . . except Lauren. It hit Sydney like a ton of bricks; her sister's boyfriend had been arrested and released for the same crime. Without a second thought, Sydney rushed out of the room and headed upstairs.

"Lauren, are you here?" Sydney called out urgently as she burst into her sister's empty room. "Hurry, it's an emergency!"

"What happened? What's going on?" Lauren asked as she came racing out of the bathroom with her hair pinned up and her favorite avocado-and-honey mask slathered on her face. "Is the house on fire?" She immediately grabbed her new Gucci trench coat and started to break for the door.

Frantic as she felt, Sydney couldn't help but laugh at her sister's bright green face and impulse grab. "No, there's no fire," she said, struggling to contain the giggles. "I just need to talk to you about something."

Realizing that her sister was laughing at her, Lauren held up her middle finger. "Forget you, Sydney." She tossed the coat on top of a pile of clothes on her bed and headed into her bathroom. "What the hell do you want, anyway?"

Trying not to step on any of the clothes or numerous pairs of shoes strewn all over the floor, Sydney cautiously ventured farther into the Lilac Spring–scented bedroom. "I need to know how to bail somebody out of jail," she said simply.

Lauren turned away from the mirror in which she was examining a new pimple on her cheek. "Excuse you?" she asked sharply.

"I said, I need to know how to bail somebody out of jail," Sydney repeated.

This time, Lauren looked around as if there were a hidden camera somewhere in the room. "Okay, what the hell is going on?"

"It's not a prank, Lauren," Sydney said. "Altimus just offered me the money to bail Dad out of jail, and I'm gonna do it," she said, trying to make herself seem a hundred times more secure than she really felt.

Lauren suddenly grabbed Sydney, pulled her into the bathroom, and shut the door. "Have you lost your cotton-picking mind?" she hissed. "You cannot take money from that man to bail out Dice. This is a setup. He's going to have Dice killed, frame you for the murder, and then send me off to a nunnery! Omigosh, I just saw this same thing on an episode of *Law & Order*! Don't do it, Syd!!!"

"Lauren," Sydney said as she looked at her overly dramatic sister. "This is bad, but this is not a made-for-NBC television show. Remember, Altimus said that he would help get Dice out if you and I fell in line. Well, apparently, we've been doing a pretty good job of acting like the world isn't totally crazy. So according to him, he's just keeping his word."

Lauren gave Sydney a hard side-eye. "And you really trust him?"

"To be honest, I'm more worried about what Dice is going to think when he realizes that we accepted Altimus's money to get him out," Sydney said quietly. "But if this is the only way for him to be free, then . . ." Sydney took a deep breath and squared her shoulders. "Then I'll just have to worry about that later."

Lauren didn't look quite as convinced. "Okay, if you say so . . ." she said hesitatingly. "And exactly how are we going to get him out? We're not really going down to the jail, are we?" Lauren questioned with a look of disdain.

"I don't know," Sydney admitted. "I was thinking that you could call Jermaine and ask him how this all works —"

Lauren shook her head. "No way," she cut Sydney off sharply.

Sydney looked confused. "Huh, but why? I'm sure he would be able to tell us," she pressed.

"Um, let's just say I'd rather not get him started on the whole 'who shot Rodney' thing again," Lauren answered as she turned back to the sink and started to wash off her mask. "Have you tried looking online?" she asked from under the water.

Sydney sensed there was more to it than Lauren was willing to share, but she didn't bother to push. "No, Altimus just told me about the money two seconds ago," Sydney explained. "I came running right up here."

"I see," Lauren said as she used a soft white towel to pat dry her face. "Well it is 2009. I'm sure we can find something about it online. You have the name of the jail, right?"

"You know I do," Sydney said wryly.

"Okay, well, let's make it happen," Lauren said as she finished applying her Kiehl's facial moisturizer. After putting the bottle away, she nodded toward the closed bathroom door. Sydney turned and opened it so that they could both walk back out. "Hop on," Lauren said as she headed directly over to her bed and climbed up into the middle of the plush mattress. Sydney crawled up beside her. Lauren grabbed her open laptop off the nightstand. "So I guess we should just Google it, huh?"

"Probably," Sydney replied as she leaned over her sister's shoulder to see. "The name of the jail is the Fulton County Correctional Facility." Lauren quickly typed in the information and pressed ENTER. There were fourteen hits for the search. Sydney pointed to the very first URL. "I think that's it," she said hopefully. Lauren clicked on it and the girls waited for the page to load.

"This is, like, so surreal," Lauren said as the colorful home page of the Fulton County jail opened up. "Even the prisons have dope Web sites nowadays." Sydney simply grunted as she scanned the site for information on posting bail. "Oh, wait. There's something called a prison roll call, let's see what this is," Lauren said as she typed in Dice's full name. Moments after pressing ENTER, his booking picture popped up. Lauren gasped. "Ewwa, he looks a mess! I am so not related to that man!"

"Will you shut up?" Sydney snapped. "How the hell did you think he was going to look after getting dragged out of his house and arrested in the middle of the night?"

"My bad," Lauren replied meekly. "I was just saying . . ."

Sydney sighed in frustration and stood up. "You know what, Lauren, I don't get you. The things that you worry about? It's, like, so ridiculous. Our father is in jail, accused of a crime he didn't commit. We have an opportunity to get him out, and you're stuck on the way he looks. Don't you understand that this is bigger than that?"

Feeling chastised, Lauren just looked at the screen. "I didn't mean anything by it, the words just popped out, Syd. You don't have to, like, kill me."

Sydney shook her head. "Can you just type 'bail' in the search box?" she finally asked her sister quietly.

As soon as Lauren typed the word in, a laundry list of instructions popped up. Sydney quickly scanned the list and stood up. "Okay, thanks," she said simply as she headed to the door.

"I didn't mean anything by what I said," Lauren pouted.

"I heard you the first time," Sydney replied without turning around. And then she walked out the door.

12
LAUREN

"Oh, and don't make any plans for after choir practice tomorrow — you're all mine," Donald gushed as he gingerly put his knapsack into his immaculately maintained locker. He grabbed his blazer and picked and swiped at imaginary lint on the shoulders before tucking himself into it and checking his mustache and hair in the mirror he'd hung on the locker door. Lauren's hot-pink lipstick kiss dotted the mirror's corner. "I've got to hit Phipps Plaza to find the perfect gift for my new boo, and I just can't do it without you."

"Um, okay, time-out," Lauren said, shaking her head and shifting from one foot to the other. Her pink round-toe Louboutins were literally squeezing the blood from the tips of her toes. She'd said a silent *Thank you, Jesus* when the final bell rang, because it meant she could hobble to her locker for the wholly inappropriate, but comfortable, yellow Chanel ballet flats she'd been dying to change into since about third period. Alas, they just didn't go with her House of Dereon jeans and purple Proenza Schouler belted sweater, but they'd make do for walking to her car. If Donald would keep it short and let her get to her locker, that is. "You're taking me too fast," Lauren insisted. "Who is this new 'boo'?" What happened to the Morehouse boy you were cavorting with at the Jack and Jill luncheon last week?

"Oh, honey, come on, that wasn't serious — he was just a beautiful distraction. My new booby boo holds the key to my heart," Donald said, waving his hand dismissively, and then pointing to a picture of his latest conquest. He was Latino, with dark almond-shaped eyes and long, curly red-streaked hair that swept over his eyes. Four round earrings hung from his lower lip — each of them a different color and size. His muscles peeked from beneath the tight gray spandex jeans that hugged his thighs and waist; a black T-shirt that hung just down to the top of his pants read, COME TO THE DARK SIDE. WE HAVE COOKIES.

Lauren raised an eyebrow. "Name?"

"Jose Lexy," Donald said. "I call him Sexy Lexy."

"Alrighty, then," Lauren said slowly, struggling for words. "He's, um, a goth Mexican?"

"Actually, he's from El Salvador — not everyone you

see with olive skin and dark hair is an illegal from across the border."

"Wow — let the record show that I never questioned his legal status," Lauren said, raising a finger and laughing. "So, um, details."

"Oh, he was too cute — mixing smoothies at that sweet ice-cream shop down in Little Five Points. I was just parched from the shopping and needed a quick liquid fix, and there he was behind the counter, fingering the bananas. Too sexy, my Sexy Lexy. He's not all that smart, but he has his moments of brilliance. He'll do. For now."

Lauren rolled her eyes and shook her head. "Okay, then. So Sexy Lexy is working it enough for a Christmas gift, huh?"

"You betcha!" Donald said, shrugging his shoulders as he giggled. "Let's just say his cookies are well worth it."

"Please," Lauren said, lifting her hand. "No more, *no más*. My virgin ears are starting to singe."

"Uh, huh, speaking of virgin, how's Jermaine?"

"Ugh, I'll have to fill you in on that drama another time, but it can't be now because my feet are k-i-l-l-i-n-g me, and I need to change out of these shoes, pronto," Lauren said. "And about tomorrow: No can do. The decorators are coming to put up the Christmas lights and trim the tree, and for some reason, Altimus and Keisha want to have a kumbaya moment with the neighbors once everything is lit. There's gonna be eggnog. You in? Say you are, because I'm not going to be able to take Keisha and Altimus prancing from one neighbor to the other. The mere thought of going it alone makes me want to throw up a little bit in my mouth."

"Ewwa, sucks for you," Donald said, wrinkling his nose. He slammed his locker shut. "Then let's go now," he said, grabbing Lauren's elbow. "It's Friday, your sked is clear, and you're working those H.O.D. jeans. Let's go be cute at Phipps."

"But my feet . . ." Lauren started.

"Oh, we'll buy some cute new comfortable shoes at the mall — you'll live," Donald said, locking his arm into the crook of Lauren's. "Shall we?"

Phipps Plaza. Shopping. New shoes. Who was Lauren to resist? She did need to pick up some makeup and a new pair of Spanx for the upcoming Benefit next week, and she just couldn't think of a time in her schedule when she'd be able to make it back over to the mall, so what better time than now? "Let's go," she bubbled.

Within minutes, Donald and Lauren were headed down Peachtree Road NE, taking in the bright, crisp Christmas lights dotting the specialty shops and sidewalks crowded with holiday shoppers. It was a time of year that always made Lauren's stomach twirl; Buckhead literally buzzed with the electricity that came from the throngs of people who descended on the chichi town and its two main malls in search of the perfect present. She could do without the present hunt — she always got hung up on what exactly to get people who pretty much had everything they could possibly want and then some — but she always managed to reward her hard work with a few presents for herself. Okay, a lot of presents. But who was counting?

Donald pulled Lauren's car up to the valet stand and waited for the skinny white guy dressed in a tragic, standard-issue red Christmas blazer and black earmuffs to open his door. "Oh, aren't you a dear," he said, giving a halfhearted smile. "The keys are in the ignition. Merry Christmas," he added with a quick wave and a body glance that swept from the top of the man's head to the tip of his black sneakers. Donald pressed a five-dollar bill into the man's hand. "Take good care of my friend's baby."

"Yes, sir, thank you, sir," the man said, rushing around the car to open Lauren's door. "Don't you worry about a thing."

"So," Donald said, turning his attention back to Lauren after giving the man's butt a look-see, "tell me about what's going on with Jermaine."

"First things first," Lauren said, standing aside so Donald could open the door leading to the main entrance of Phipps Plaza. "I haven't had the chance to tell you about Dara and her trifling, preggers behind."

"Ewwa, what you know no good about Dara?" Donald asked, taking Lauren's hand and picking up the pace of his stroll. His shopping sense was leading his legs to Hugo Boss; he was thinking a hot pair of sunglasses would be mucho appreciated by Sexy Lexy. "Do tell."

"Well, let's just say that her love child with my sister's ex is a little less than loved," Lauren dished, leaning into Donald and running her hand across his muscular arm.

"Ooh, are we surprised by this?" Donald asked, gazing at the mannequin in the Giorgio Armani display window. "I mean, anybody could have guessed that baby was the product of a hit-it-and-quit-it hookup gone terribly wrong. But I always thought Dara was one fry short of a Happy Meal. She wouldn't know she was being played if you slapped her with a Monopoly board."

"Well, to hear Dara tell it, she thought it was much more than that, the dumb ass," Lauren smirked. "I mean, come on. After all the conversations we had about Marcus and how fake and over-the-top he is with that up-with-the-people posing and stuff, she still fell for his foolishness. Now she's praying to the porcelain god and he's ho-hopping with Caroline and company."

"Ugh," Donald said, doing a massive mock shiver. "At least Syd is recovering nicely. That hottie Jason Danden could get it, fo' sho'."

"Um, yeah, something tells me that Mr. Footballer shot

caller ain't switch-hitting for the other team — sorry, baby," Lauren laughed, leaning into her friend as they strolled past a line full of rowdy little kids waiting to take a picture with Santa Claus.

"Humph, you'd be surprised about them little boys on the football team," Donald giggled. "Let's just say some of them are quite comfortable in those tight little pants for a reason — hut one, hut two! Omigod, we have to sit on Santa's lap — come on, let's get in line," Donald insisted, pulling Lauren toward the end of the massive procession.

Lauren stopped short and would not budge. "I absolutely cannot walk another inch in these shoes," Lauren said. "They are squeezing the life out of me. Seriously, I think they're going to have to amputate my pinky toe. And my feet are much too cute for corns and bunions. We gotta get to Saks, pronto." Lauren took another step, and pain shot like a razor through the tops of her toes. "On second thought, Juicy is closer, isn't it? Let's go there. They have those cute, bedazzled ankle rain boots. They'll look a little crazy but like I mean it. Anything to get my feet out of these shoes and into something comfortable, without looking like a fashion tragedy."

"Not even on your worst day, but you know I'll never turn down a romp at Juicy," Donald said. "Shall I lead the way?"

With Donald doing everything short of carrying Lauren to help her walk, the couple weaved through countless shoppers slogging through the mall with arms full of Tiffany, Nordstrom, and Saks bags, husbands and boyfriends who clearly weren't into it, and crying, snotty babies ready to get out of Dodge. Despite the onslaught of attitude, though, there was an air of glee everywhere — couldn't be helped with the twinkling trees and gaudy gold-and-white decorations hanging from literally every corner of the building. Christmastime indeed.

Lauren was giggling about Donald's predictions of what Dara and Marcus's baby would look like when they walked through the double doors of the Juicy store; the hee-hee haw-haw came to a dead stop when Lauren looked up and saw Brandi walking out of the dressing room toward some roughneck posted up on the couch like he was at home watching a football game with the remote in one hand and a beer in the other. Or a dough boy out on the bench waiting for the next customer.

"What?" Donald asked, tugging on the arm of his friend, who wouldn't — couldn't — budge.

Lauren couldn't find the words.

"Lauren? What the hell?"

"Shh," she said, staring wildly at Donald. "Look, let's just go."

"But what about . . ."

"Well, well, if it isn't Altimus's baby girl," Brandi called out. "Fancy seeing you here."

"Yeah, um, hey, Brandi," Lauren said meekly. "What up?"

"Going somewhere?" Brandi asked, strutting toward the door. She touched her boy's knee on the way over.

"Uh, no, not particularly — just getting a little holiday shopping in," Lauren stuttered.

"Yeah, me, too," Brandi said, looking down at her Juicy sweat suit. "I just love early presents, don't you?"

"Uh, yeah." Lauren shrugged, sneaking a glance at Donald.

"So, who's your special friend?" Brandi said, tossing her chin at Donald. "You two looking awfully cozy together."

"This is my friend Donald," Lauren said simply.

"Your friend Donald, huh?" Brandi said, giving him the once-over. "Isn't that special. He buying you some early Christmas presents, too?"

"Who, Donald?" Lauren laughed nervously. "No, no, he's not here to buy me anything. He's, um, picking out presents for a friend of his."

"A friend of his," Brandi said, her eyes shifting from Lauren to Donald and back to Lauren. "Well, speaking of friends, let me introduce you to mine — I'm so rude sometimes." She turned back toward the dressing room.

"Ki'anna, Dre, Lisa, Fly," she yelled out, making everyone, including the already jittery saleswoman cowering behind the register, jump. "Come here," she continued yelling, waving her friends over. "Come meet Altimus's girl."

With a quickness, the four of them shot over to where Brandi, Donald, and Lauren were standing, each looking more angry than the next. Though her instincts told her to let go of Donald's arm, she held on for dear life, feeling a little woozy by the sheer number of people — people who were friends of her man's ex — who were now crowded around her. Lauren felt very, very small.

Brandi cleared her throat and folded her arms. "Lauren Duke, this is everybody. Everybody, this is Lauren Duke, Jermaine's, um, lady, though it looks as if she may have moved on."

"What? No, no," insisted Lauren. "This is my friend Donald — emphasis on *friend*. You know, boy? Road dog? Ace?"

"Uh-huh," Brandi said. "Sure, and, um, has Jermaine been introduced to this 'friend' of yours?"

Lauren squared her shoulders; she was ready for a hasty exit — ready for this to be over already. "Look, I have some shopping to do, and obviously, so do you and your friends, so why don't we just all go on back to what we were doing. I didn't come in here for any trouble; I came for the boots."

"Oh, trust, sweetie, won't be no trouble from this end, either," Brandi said. "If you stop causing it."

"If *I* stop causing it?" Lauren asked. "You're the one who's got me surrounded in the Juicy store."

"Girl, ain't nobody surrounding you. We're just having a friendly chat. And as a mutual friend of your man — Jermaine, I mean, not Donald — I thought you should know that it's time you opened your eyes and realized what's going on. I mean, we're not surprised that Altimus is all mixed up in Rodney's beat down and all, but we didn't know how deep the dirt goes in your family."

Lauren sucked her teeth and sighed. "Look, I don't know what you're talking about. . . ."

"I'm sure, sweetie," Brandi said. "Go on ahead and keep that pretty little head in the sand. But the hood knows what's up with the Dukes and the extended family. . . ."

"Look," Donald interjected. "Really, we're just going to get the boots. . . ."

"Yo, who asked you, playboy?" Fly boomed, stepping toward Donald. "You not about to stand here and disrespect my girl."

Donald shrieked and put his hands up to his face like he was blocking a punch; Lauren reared back. Brandi and her friends let out a series of huffs and giggles and head shakes.

"Oh," Fly said, a little more tenderly. "I see, I see. Y'all were here to buy the boots. Who are the boots for, homegirl here, or you?"

Donald didn't dare open his mouth; Lauren squeezed his hand in hopes that it would calm him. *Hold on, Donald,* she said to herself. *It'll be over soon, hopefully without us being carried out on a stretcher.*

"Like I was saying," Brandi said, turning serious again. "I'm beginning to think Jermaine could teach your family a thing or two about class and how to be legit."

Lauren's eyes narrowed to slits.

"What, you didn't know?" Brandi asked. She leaned in some more. "Yeah, Rodney may have been the wild child, but Jermaine is The One. While y'all are spending Altimus's dirty money, he's getting the grades, scoring the points on the court, working with the kids, taking care of his mom, and doing the right thing — trying to be somebody special. No, matter of fact, he *is* special — to all of us."

"And what makes you think he's not special to me?" Lauren insisted, albeit with a tone much less threatening.

Brandi's friends groaned; she sucked her teeth. "If he's so special, why you locking fingers with ole Armani boy, here?" Ki'anna asked.

"He must be some kind of prince of Buckhead or something," Lisa chimed in.

"But, you know what?" Brandi said. "Jermaine is *our* prince, and we're tired of girls like you coming around and slumming it with thugs to get mommy and daddy mad, and then going back to your big houses and your cozy little lives up under the people who forgot where they came from and ain't interested in doing anything but staying clear of the hood. Jermaine is ours."

"Look, I don't want any trouble," Lauren said. "Jermaine is my friend, too."

"Did. I. Stutter?" Brandi said, getting in Lauren's face.

"Excuse me, you're going to have to take this somewhere else," said one of the saleswomen, cautiously creeping up on the group. The walkie-talkie in her hand squawked; a deep male voice warned that security was on the way.

Mortified, Lauren raised her hands in mock surrender. "No, no, we were on our way out — it's okay," she told the woman.

"Yeah, so are we," Ki'anna said.

"Not without paying for that," the saleswoman snapped, pointing at the lime-green sweat suit Brandi was rocking.

"Yeah, we're gonna take that — and all that other stuff she tried on, too," Fly said, whipping his finger in the air. He pulled out a wad of cash like he was going to hit the saleswoman off right there at the door.

"You're going to have to come to the cash register with the clothes so that I can ring them up," she said.

"Okay, Lauren, let's head for the car — don't want to miss that appointment, right?" Donald grinned nervously.

"Yeah, see you around — but not in the West End, correct?" Brandi said through clenched teeth.

Lauren simply turned on her heel and grabbed Donald's hand.

"Oh, and tell your Uncle Larry the crew said what up," Fly said.

Uncle Larry? Lauren asked herself. *What the . . .*

Before Lauren could begin to consider how Fly knew her uncle, Donald snatched her arm and practically dragged her out of the store. "Come on, dammit," he said, looking over his shoulder wildly. "Are you waiting for them to tear us from limb to limb?"

"Donald, I'm gonna need you to calm down," Lauren said, doing her best to walk fast, despite her sore toes.

"We could go to the valet and get the car and skedaddle, but I'm afraid they might catch up to us there. I think we should make a break for one of the restaurants."

"They may be heading to dinner after the big Juicy splurge," Lauren said, hobbling alongside Donald as best she could.

"Right. My guess is they'll be grubbing at Johnny Rockets or Chik-fil-A," Donald deadpanned. He reached into his jacket pocket and pulled out his iPhone. "We should head over to TWIST. I'll give my uncle a heads-up to let his staff know not to let anyone who looks like they're from the set of *Menace II Society* through the front door."

"And what if they're still here when we leave?" Lauren asked nervously.

"Good point," Donald acknowledged. He thought for a moment. "Okay, I'll have my uncle send a car that'll meet us out back. We can have some tapas and a cocktail and head out before they figure out we disappeared."

"Wait," Lauren said, stopping short. "Not another step." She braced herself on Donald's arm while she snatched off her Louboutins. Under any other circumstance, Lauren would never have run barefoot anywhere but the beach. However, desperate times called for desperate measures. The stilettos were dangling from her fingers when she and Donald rushed to a waiting booth in a quiet corner toward the back of the dining room. Almost as quickly as they were seated, their waiter brought over steaming plates of the roasted herb gnocchi, the crispy calamari, the beef-and-olive empanadas, and two miniburgers.

"I'll have the peach martini," Donald said nonchalantly, like he'd been ordering liquor for years.

Lauren gave him the side-eye. "I'll have a Sprite, thanks."

"Look, sweetie, I just almost got my behind whipped in the middle of Phipps Plaza, like we were walking through Greenbriar Mall. I have never."

"I know, I'm still shaking," Lauren said. "Every time I run into that girl, she comes this close to stomping me to a pulp," she added, holding her thumb and pointer finger together. "I just can't figure out what about her makes me such a punk. I mean, I stared her down and gave her a piece of my mind once, but . . ."

"But she's, like, a foot taller and from the West End — no need to explain," Donald said.

"Yeah, but I don't usually back down for anyone. And then I run into Brandi, and all of a sudden I'm ready to scream like a little girl. I can't call that."

"The question is, why do you keep running into her?" Donald asked.

"What do you mean? She lives in the West End, near Jermaine. They hang out in the same places. . . ."

"Yeah, but if you didn't go see Jermaine, you wouldn't have to deal with the cast of *New Jack City*. Aren't you tired of her? I mean, really, is Jermaine worth all of this?"

"He's a good guy," Lauren said weakly.

"Yeah, but good enough for you that you can take the beat down from his friends and yours, too?"

Lauren thought about how she ditched him after dance

squad practice rather than introduce him to her girls. Remembering the look on his face made her stomach queasy.

"I like him a lot, Donald — the first guy in a long time that I've even remotely considered calling my boyfriend," she said. "Well, the first one who really is my boyfriend. You don't count."

Donald laughed and took a bite of his empanada.

"I think he's worth fighting for," she added.

"Uh-huh — but is he worth getting your ass kicked for — that's the question," Donald said, barely letting his martini hit the table before he took a sip. He swallowed hard and took another sip. "Altimus and Keisha can't stand him, your father is in jail because of him — well, kinda — and the first and last time any of our friends peeped him, he was running through your lake house like an escaped convict. I'm just trying to figure out what you're hanging on to, because at this point the only connections y'all got are a couple of kisses, a funeral, and bail money."

"Wow, you just took a left and went all the way there, huh?"

"Donald is always going to tell the truth, baby," he smirked, popping a piece of calamari into his mouth.

"Yeah, I guess that's why I keep you around," Lauren laughed. "You'd be the perfect boyfriend for me. I need to figure out how to bump off Sexy Lexy."

"Oh, please, not until after Christmas," Donald cooed. "I'm looking forward to my thank-you after I get him those shades. I guess I'm going to have to make it back over here to get those, huh?"

"You can go back out there if you want to," Lauren started.

"Nah, I'm just fine right here with my girl and my snacks and my drinks, thank you," Donald laughed. "You couldn't pay me to go back out there — not today, not now."

"I feel you on that one, fo' sho'," she said. "Fo' sho'."

13
SYDNEY

"Okay, I am so torn right now," Rhea grumbled from the oversized massage chair on Sydney's right-hand side. She slammed closed the copy of *The Vow* that she was reading.

"What's wrong, Rhea?" Carmen asked as she placed a copy of *Essence* on her lap and leaned forward from her own seat to look at her friend with concern.

"You know my indecisive ass is still debating which dress to wear tonight. And I just realized that I have to make my decision before she puts on my polish," Rhea said with a splash of her foot in the bubbling aqua-colored whirlpool. "If I go with the sparkly dark blue that I saw in *CosmoGIRL!*, I might be doing too much with the magenta Richard Tyler strapless. But if I do the neutral, flesh-tone pink, it'll be a wash against the crimson Armani full length."

"Hmm," Sydney murmured as she envisioned the two dresses Rhea had purchased for the night's highly anticipated event. Although the two dresses were completely different styles, her BFF looked absolutely hot in both choices. So she totally understood the dilemma.

"Personally, I think a Sadie Hawkins deserves a little flash. I mean, how often do the girls get to choose their dates, right?" Carmen questioned, picking up her magazine again. "Go with the hot pink," she voted as her nail technician gently massaged the soles of her feet with the sweet almond-scented lotion.

"Wait a sec, what color suit is Tim wearing? That might help," Sydney said as she lifted her feet out of the water so that her own technician could begin trimming her nails and cuticles.

"Square or round?" the cute Hispanic woman asked before she began clipping away.

"Square with rounded sides, please," Sydney replied absentmindedly.

"He's wearing a dark gray Hugo Boss suit," Rhea said. "We picked it out together about two weeks ago."

"In that case, definitely go with the hot pink," Sydney stated authoritatively.

"Are you guys sure?"

"Absolutely," chirped Carmen. "Hot pink with great makeup and hair and a neutral nail is the only way to go."

Sydney nodded affirmatively. "If you're totally married to a dark nail, I think I saw this amazing dark-silver Chanel polish in the last issue of *Elle UK*." She tried not to wiggle her toes as she thought about her own dress for the night. Originally, she wanted to go with a gray three-quarter-length halter dress she found in Bloomie's, but on second thought, she realized that the gray would clash with her bracelet, so she switched up to a golden Elie Saab number that she found on the pages of last month's *Vanity Fair*. With a sparkling natural-colored sheer overlay on top of the nude-colored silk, the one-shouldered beauty made Sydney look like she was wearing a cluster of stars. She couldn't wait for Jason to see her later that night.

"Done, done, and done," Rhea said, finally closing the case on her clothing dilemma. "Excuse me," she said, leaning forward toward the blond-haired woman working on her feet. "Can you please see if you guys have a dark-silver Chanel polish?"

"I know just the one you're thinking about," the woman confirmed with a crooked smile. "I'll be right back."

"See, everything worked itself out," Carmen mused as she handed Sydney the copy of *Essence* and picked up the issue of *In Touch* she had stashed at her side.

"Thank you very much," Sydney said as she immediately flipped to the cover story on Raven-Symoné.

Rhea's nail technician returned and handed the bottle

to Rhea for her approval. "So did I tell you guys that Tim's older brother booked him a huge suite in the Ritz-Carlton downtown?" Rhea asked casually as she handed the bottle back to the blond woman with an approving nod.

"What?" Carmen almost dropped her magazine in the tub.

Sydney's head snapped toward her best friend. "Are you serious? You're going to spend the night at the Ritz with Tim? Omigod, you guys have only been dating for, like, two seconds," Sydney blurted out.

"Relax, you two." Rhea laughed at her friends' scandalous assumptions. "He's totally throwing an after party there, that's all. There's no way in the world my mom would let me spend the night out with some boy I just met."

Sydney released an audible sigh of relief. "Thank God! For a second, I thought we were going to have to call your parents and stage a bootleg A&E *Intervention*."

"Don't ever play like that again," Carmen warned. "Or I might lock your fast butt up in a closet until you get married!"

"No need to worry about me and Tim just yet," Rhea laughed briefly. "He's still trying to figure out how to get to second base without getting his little feelings hurt." All three of the girls groaned in sympathy. Then she sobered up and looked at her friends. "But what about you? Carm, you've been dating Michael for almost four months. And

Sydney's got the new golden handcuff. I know you guys have at least talked about it with your boyfriends."

What an appropriate description, Sydney thought as she looked down at her bracelet and remembered Jason's cryptic words, "nothing in life is really free." Although they'd engaged in some pretty intense kissing sessions, so far Jason had been a total gentleman. But at the rate the relationship was going, she wondered how long that would last.

"Obviously, we've talked about it," Carmen admitted. "And yes, nosey, we've made it past second base. But he's really good about waiting until I'm comfortable trying anything more. Although, honestly, every time I look at Dara, I move further and further away from ever being ready. Who really wants to be a statistic?"

"You're so right," Rhea nodded. "I mean, my mom totally took me to the GYN right after I turned sixteen just to get my first checkup, but that certainly wasn't the wild-out pass. She was very clear that I had to respect my body because no one else was going to do it for me."

"Things between Jason and me are definitely intense," Sydney said. "But I'm not ready to make that move. Bracelet or no bracelet, I don't want to rush into anything that I can't get out of, you know?"

"I know that's right," Carmen co-signed with a smile. "Although, I must say, it is a beautiful piece of jewelry."

"Amen to that, my sister," Rhea chirped as she settled back into her seat.

"You guys are soooo retarded," Sydney said with a laugh.

"Uh-uh, not half as retarded as Essence Dervay is gonna look if she wears the dress that she was spotted trying on at Dillard's," Rhea objected. "I saw the photos on YRT and trust, it's a situation!"

"Oh, I missed those," Carmen whispered gleefully. "Was it really bad?"

Rhea gave her a look. "Let's just say, if it was me, I would schedule an intervention session my damn self."

Sydney fought to control her giggles. "You guys! Stop! That is so not nice," she chided, looking around nervously. After spending the last couple of months as a regular on YRT, she was extra sympathetic to the latest gossip-blog victims.

"My bad," Rhea said as Carmen let one last giggle slip.

Sydney shook her head and reopened the magazine. "So back to the Ritz," she said, steering the conversation toward the evening's activities. "Are we all invited, or is this, like, some baseball-team-only thing?"

"Of course you guys are totally invited," Rhea insisted. "His brother only booked it last night so he hasn't had a chance to tell that many people, but I think it'll be fun."

"Works for me," Carmen said with a smile. "At least I'll

get some wear and tear out of the six-hundred-dollar dress my parents bought me," she said, referring to her sapphire-blue Nicole Miller strapless full length.

"True," Sydney said as her green Hermès Kelly bag started buzzing. "Oh, God, I hope this isn't my mom," Sydney complained. "When I left the house this morning to get my hair done, I threatened to chop it all off just to scare her. I'll bet she's on the verge of a freaking breakdown," Sydney laughed as she dug through her handbag for the iPhone. When she finally pulled it out, the caller ID read: PRIVATE NUMBER. "Hmm, I wonder who this could be," she mused as she answered the phone.

"Sydney speaking," she greeted the unknown caller formally.

"Ms. Duke?" a familiar voice questioned on the other end of the line.

"Principal Trumbull?" Sydney questioned, clearly taken aback.

"What's wrong?" Rhea whispered with a concerned look on her face.

Sydney looked at her girls and mouthed the words, "I have no idea."

"Yes, how are you," Brookhaven's longtime principal continued in his characteristically formal manner.

"I'm okay," Sydney responded hesitantly. "Is everything all right?" She looked at her favorite red-banded

Michelle watch. With only five hours until the big event, she couldn't imagine what might've prompted this call.

"Actually, Ms. Duke, there seems to be a bit of a problem at the bank," the principal continued. "You see, when I went to verify the amount of money raised, the balance was fifteen thousand dollars below the balance that you submitted two days ago in our final meeting."

"Fifteen thousand dollars!" Sydney struggled to keep from jumping out of the massage chair. Her heartbeat started racing uncontrollably and she struggled to catch her breath.

"Yes," Principal Trumbull continued gravely.

"But how can that be? Who would take it out? I'm the only one with access to the account. I don't understand," Sydney said as she gave her girls a weak smile. She waved her hand dismissively and mouthed, "It's fine, a little mix-up. No big deal." Thankfully, they both nodded and went back to their respective reading material without a second thought. Sydney cleared her throat.

"I'm aware that you are the only one besides me with access, which is why I immediately asked for a copy of the last withdrawal receipt," he continued.

"And," Sydney demanded.

"And the slip had your signature on it, Ms. Duke," Principal Trumbull said quietly.

Sydney covered her mouth to contain the gasp. Luckily

her technician had just finished the final coat of clear on her Ballet Slippers pink toes. Sydney stood up abruptly and faced her friends. "I'll be right back, you guys," she said, and without waiting for a response, headed to the reception area in search of privacy. Finding a secluded corner, she took a deep breath and started again. "Principal Trumbull, I assure you I did not withdraw fifteen thousand dollars from the Sadie Hawkins savings account," she insisted.

"Ms. Duke, this is a very uncomfortable situation for us all. Obviously, I believed you to be a truthful young lady. Otherwise, I wouldn't have appointed you as co-chair. But in light of recent circumstances . . ."

"Did you ask Marcus? He'll tell you," Sydney asserted, as notes of desperation crept into her voice.

"Yes, I did call Mr. Green. And, needless to say, he, too, assured me that he had no knowledge of the situation. And although he was certain there had to be a mistake, he reiterated that, as we all agreed in the initial planning meeting, you were the only one with signing power."

Sydney started to tell Principal Trumbull that Marcus had just made a deposit the other day, but she stopped herself just in time. There was no point in getting both of them in more trouble for disobeying the principal's rules. She ground her teeth and mentally chastised herself for being such a control freak. Why hadn't she allowed Marcus to be the one with signing power? At the time of the initial organizing meeting, she was still so mad at Marcus for the whole Dara debacle, she didn't want him to have the lead on anything she was associated with. And now look . . .

"Obviously, this type of incident normally requires immediate disciplinary action," the principal continued. "But because of the wonderful fund-raising work you've accomplished in the past and your parents' generous donation history, I'm willing to give you some time. I will use the money in Brookhaven's emergency discretionary fund to cover this evening's events and presentation to the board. However, come Monday morning, I expect all fifteen thousand returned to the account. Otherwise, I *will* be notifying your parents and the authorities."

Sydney's chest tightened as if she were stuck in a vise. "What am I supposed to do?" Sydney questioned desperately. "I didn't take the money; I don't know how this even happened."

"Well, I'm not one for idle gossip, but the bank manager said that the last time something like this happened, it was a family member who was to blame," the principal hedged.

"Excuse me," Sydney said in total disbelief. "I don't know what you're implying, but Lauren is not a thief!"

"No? Well, then, how about your stepfather? I understand that he's been under a bit of a financial strain lately. Perhaps . . ."

Sydney could feel the vein in her temple throb. "Principal Trumbull, I don't know who stole this money, but I assure you, it was no one that I love or care about," Sydney snapped as she cut him off. "I appreciate you giving me the benefit of the doubt for the length of the weekend; you will have the fifteen thousand on Monday." And with that, Sydney disconnected the call.

"Are you sure you're okay, Syd?" Carmen asked gently as the trio finally left the spa an hour later. "I don't know what Principal Trumbull said or where you disappeared to, but ever since you came back you've been really quiet."

Mentally a million miles away, Sydney just nodded her head. "Uh-huh, I'm fine," she said as she repeated her conversation with Principal Trumbull over and over in her head. *A family member was to blame . . . how about your stepfather? I understand that he's been under a bit of a financial strain lately.* His thinly veiled indictment skipped through her thoughts like a DJ scratching a beat. Thankfully, she was certain Lauren would never steal money from her — clothes, maybe — but fifteen thousand dollars was absolutely ludicrous. However, if Altimus was capable of murder, stealing fifteen thousand to get the IRS off his back suddenly seemed like small potatoes.

"So are we still meeting up at Carmen's house at seven

to get dressed?" Rhea questioned as the girls waited for the valet to bring around their respective cars.

"That's the plan," Carmen said as her Land Rover came careening around the corner. She walked over and gave the driver a five-dollar tip. "I'm out of liquid eyeliner; do you guys want to roll with me to the M.A.C. store in Phipps right quick?"

Rhea shrugged her shoulders. "Sure, why not? We still have at least two hours to kill, right?" She turned and looked at Sydney as the drop-top Saab came up next. "Syd?"

"You know what?" Sydney said. "I actually need to run by my stepdad's dealership for a quick minute. I heard a weird noise by my front right tire the other day. And I want to bring it in for a quick check before the weekend," she said, lying.

Carmen and Rhea looked at her hesitantly but said nothing. They seemed to understand that whatever was on her mind, she wasn't ready to discuss it and there was no point in pushing the issue. "Okay, then," Carmen said finally. "We'll see you at my house at seven o'clock."

"Seven o'clock, I promise," Sydney said as she handed her valet a tip, pulled around Carmen's SUV, and took off.

A really cute African-American couple holding hands was walking around the showroom when Sydney finally walked through the door. They turned briefly at the sound of her entrance, and Sydney could see the beginnings of a baby bump on the woman. Sydney smiled momentarily before turning to scan the expansive room for her stepfather.

"My prayers have been answered! My long-lost love is here," a friendly voice called out from behind her left shoulder. Sydney spun around to face one of the dealership's salesmen, Donovan Sinclair. He immediately walked over and greeted Sydney with a hug and kiss on the cheek. "How are you, princess? I haven't seen you in a long time," the friendly giant of a man greeted Sydney. He stepped back to admire her striking updo and fresh manicure/pedicure. "Wow, don't you look pretty! Did I forget our wedding anniversary or something?" he teased good-naturedly.

"Hey, Mr. Sinclair," Sydney giggled in response. Donovan's flirty ways helped him remain one of the showroom's most popular salesmen over the course of his career. "How are you, sir?"

"Better, now that you're here. But enough about me, what brings you by today? For some reason, I'm guessing it's not my charming wit," he inquired kindly.

"Actually, I need to speak to my stepfather, sir," Sydney said, immediately sobering up.

The jovial look immediately disappeared from Donovan's eyes. "You just missed him, sweetie. He headed over to his lawyer's office to discuss more of this audit business," he explained in a lowered tone.

"Oh," Sydney said simply. "Well, in that case," she said as she turned toward the door.

"You know, it's really none of my business, but I have to say, I have a lot of respect for that man. And I think what this government is doing is just awful," Donovan confided as he put his arm around Sydney's shoulders and walked her toward the door. "He gave a chance to a lot of people others might have given up on. Thank God, he's got a good lawyer and a trusty accountant. The three of them have been holed up in his office till almost midnight every single night for the past three months preparing for this one," he said with a rueful shake of his head. "And he's serious about beating all the charges. It takes a confident person to take it to court."

"Is that so?" Sydney said carefully. "I didn't realize that the audit started three months ago."

"Not officially, but you know Altimus always has his ear to the ground," Donovan explained. "So when he heard a lot of the independently owned businesses in the area were getting audited, he started preparing. I'm surprised you didn't notice that he was out of the house a lot."

"Um, there's been a lot going on at school," Sydney mumbled. Donovan nodded understandingly as she paused by the front door. "It's okay, you don't have to walk me out," Sydney said as she turned to look at the couple who were now circling a hybrid Lexus SUV. "I think you've got some money to make over there."

Donovan smiled and kissed the top of Sydney's head. "Okay, princess. Let me go work my magic. I'll tell your dad, I mean stepdad, you came by. Take care," he said with a smile as he headed off to make another sale.

Sydney walked out to her car more confused than ever. From the sound of it, between working at the dealership and meeting with his defense team, Altimus barely had time to sleep over the last three months, let alone plot how to steal from Brookhaven's Sadie Hawkins account.

And if he was trying to fly completely under the radar to avoid getting caught for Rodney's brutal murder, why would he want to take the case with the IRS to trial? Add to that his recent decision to help bail Dice out of jail, and something in the milk just wasn't clean. There was no way her stepfather stole the fifteen thousand dollars. As she opened the driver's-side door of her Saab, an even graver realization hit her like a ton of bricks — maybe, just maybe, Altimus wasn't the one who killed Rodney.

14
LAUREN

Lauren pushed the tiny post onto the back of her diamond-studded hoop and then leaned into her bathroom mirror for a final check. She forced a smile, but it was a weak one — far from the usual dimple-inducing grin she gave herself when she knew she looked hot. Right about now, the only thing that was making her happy was the flutter her silky, one-shoulder, drape-sleeved top produced when she twirled from the sink to her bathroom door; it was like someone had cued a wind machine — movement that could only be produced by her absolute fave designer, Sonia Rykiel. Indeed, Lauren was absolutely convinced that Sonia was her secret fairy fashion godmother, holed away in a tiny room somewhere, thinking up ways to make Lauren Duke look like an absolute party stunner. For this outfit, Lauren was grateful;

she absolutely had to look like she owned Brookhaven Prep — not just because of the mess with the dance squad, but because of her questionable arm candy: Jermaine. She'd made the mistake of not only turning down his offer of a Friday night dinner and a movie, but of also telling him that she was hitting Sydney's latest Christmas event stag. She could have told him she was going out with her parents, could have told him she was on punishment, could have told him she was planning on sitting in her room and picking her toenails. But no. She just had to go blabbing about how hot the party and the DJ and the spread were going to be, and how all the girls had to invite their dates, and everybody was going to be there. And, of course, he had to go ahead and ask when he should expect his invitation. And she just had to say a really weak, tentative "Uh, okay, um, Jermaine, will you go with me to the dance?"

Needless to say, he didn't really appreciate the tepid response, but that didn't stop him from accepting the invitation anyway. Oh, joy.

Lauren's ponytail swung as she bounced over to her closet and tore through the piles of clothes and shoes looking for her silver Jimmy Choo stiletto sandals. They were nowhere to be found. Bending carefully to avoid splitting her *über*-tight black miniskirt, she checked under her bed, under her dresser, behind her chaise, on the chaise —

everywhere. But they were nowhere to be found. She glanced at her digital alarm clock: The chauffeur was going to be there any minute, and she was still barefoot, she hadn't packed her purse yet, and, most important, Jermaine still hadn't called to let her know if he was home from work yet and ready to go. "Damn it all to hell," Lauren said, struggling to her feet.

"Um, girls as pretty as you usually don't use those kinds of words — especially in front of their mothers," Keisha said, appearing in Lauren's doorway. Lauren jumped at the sound of her voice.

"Oh, hey, Mom, I didn't know you were up here," Lauren said. "Sorry."

"Uh-huh," Keisha smirked. "You look nice. What's the problem?"

"I can't find my shoes," Lauren said simply, putting her hands on her hips while she surveyed the room.

"Well, it's no wonder," Keisha said. "Your room is a hot mess. It's a wonder you can find the bed. There's only so much Edwina can do to clean it if you don't help her out, you know."

"Mom, I don't have time to clean my room right now — I just need to find my sandals."

"You want to be more specific?"

"Well, maybe I can try to pull it together sometime over

the weekend, like Sunday, after church, but really, I have a lot of homework this weekend and Donald wants to go out after church and . . ."

"I wasn't talking about schedule specifics," Keisha said. "I was talking about the sandals."

"Oh!" Lauren giggled. "Right, the sandals. My silver Jimmy Choos. I can't find them anywhere."

Keisha raised an eyebrow as she glanced around the room again. "And I assume you checked the closet, where expensive shoes should be arranged neatly and categorized by style, color, and . . . aw, hell, who am I talking to?" Keisha smirked again. "Did you ask your sister?"

Lauren rolled her eyes. "No," she said firmly.

Keisha folded her arms and wrinkled her brow. "What now?" Keisha asked.

"What?" Lauren asked innocently.

"Don't give me that — I know when my girls are at each other's throats. What's the problem?"

"There's no problem — she's just in her own world right now, and I don't feel like getting snapped at again," Lauren said. She kept details of the latest skirmish with her sister — the one over Dice — to herself.

"Well, unless you plan on going to the gala barefoot, or that boy you're going with is going to carry you all night, it doesn't seem like you have much of a choice — unless you thought about a backup pair."

Lauren looked at her mother and then walked past her into Sydney's room, where her sister was furiously stuffing her makeup bag into her oversized Louis Vuitton duffel bag.

"Syd, have you seen my silver Jimmy Choo sandals?" Lauren asked.

"Why would I know where your sandals are?" Sydney snapped.

Lauren took a deep breath and tried her best to keep her voice even-keeled. "I can't find them in my room."

"And you're surprised by this?" Sydney smirked.

"Look, I didn't come in here for your stank-ass attitude — I want my damn shoes, that's all. Then you can go on about your business, and I can go about mine."

"Lauren — watch your mouth!" Keisha demanded.

"Ma, I just want my shoes."

"I swear, you've got to be kidding me," Sydney shot back. "The last time I walked into that mess of a room of yours, I was on blank stare mode for a week. Why don't you check under the three-week pile of dirty clothes on your floor, or behind your junky couch, or . . ."

"Wow . . . just, wow," Lauren said softly, glaring as she walked over to Sydney's perfectly organized closet. She plucked her sandals off the second shelf.

"Whatever," Sydney said weakly. "I don't have time for this. I have to get over to Carm's to get dressed, and all this foolishness . . ."

205

Lauren shushed Sydney; she heard her phone in the other room — D'Angelo's "You're My Lady" ringtone was blasting. Jermaine. "Later, Syd," Lauren snapped, rolling her eyes. "Do me a favor, though. Next time you're thinking about wearing my stuff, don't."

Lauren disappeared into her bedroom and slammed the door before Keisha and Sydney could say another word, then she dove for the phone. "Hey! Where are you?" she demanded.

"Well, hello to you, too," Jermaine said slowly. "How are you? I'm fine."

"Come on, don't play with me," Lauren said, peeking out her window. The car was waiting for her in the circular driveway. "Are you ready?"

"My day was great. How about yours?" Jermaine continued.

"Jermaine!" Lauren yelled. "Now's not the time, seriously. The car is here. Are. You. Ready?"

"Lauren, it's me. Calm down."

"I am calm," she said, slipping on her sandals. "I'd be calmer if you gave me an ETA on when you'll be ready to go. I need you waiting outside."

"Are you at least going to let the car stop or am I going to have to hop on the bumper while you drive by?" Jermaine laughed.

"Blah, blah, blah — just be ready to go when I get there," Lauren insisted. "Your ex didn't exactly make me feel like I'm welcome in her neighborhood, so . . ."

"Who, Brandi?" he asked. "What, you think she's just going to be hanging outside my house waiting to see what I'm doing?"

"Who knows what Brandi's doing?" Lauren snapped. "I do know it just seems like she's always around. I hate to bring up old stuff, but . . . ahem."

"That's exactly what it is — old," Jermaine said, sounding annoyed.

"All of this is getting old," Lauren said. "Look, I'm leaving in the next five minutes. Are you going to be ready or not? Because I can just go by myself and we can hook up another time. . . ."

"I'll be ready," Jermaine snapped. "Seriously, what's wrong? What's going on, Lauren?"

"Nothing. Nothing's going on," Lauren said. She saw a shadow beneath the crack of her bedroom door. Keisha, for sure. "I'll see you in a few."

She didn't bother hearing his response — she just hung up.

"Damn, babe, if I'd have known you were going to look this good, I would have sprung for the disposable camera,"

Jermaine said, giving Lauren the once-over. He put his arm around her shoulder and tried to pull her closer to him, but she stiffly resisted.

"Yeah, um, thanks," she said, taking in Jermaine's shiny gold Sean John jacket and dark jeans. He was wearing a tie, which Lauren supposed was a good thing, but still, he had on sneakers. If he leaned in a little, he could have felt the fever she was giving him for dressing like he was going to his cousin's prom.

"You look nice, too, Jermaine," he mocked in a high voice. "I'm so glad to see you."

"Ha-ha, very funny," Lauren said, staring out the window.

"Yo, what's the problem, L?" Jermaine said. "You've been snapping at me all evening. What did I do?"

You actually showed up, and now I have to introduce you to my friends, Lauren screamed to herself. "Nothing, I just got into a little beef with my sister, is all," she said to him. "It's no biggie. I just need to be quiet for a minute — get my mind right."

"O-kaaay, then," Jermaine said, removing his arm from around Lauren's shoulders. "Well, you looking good, girl, don't sweat it. Besides, your man is here now. I went in to work late just so that I could buy this jacket, and we look good together fo' sho'. I'm ready to have a good time."

"Yeah, me, too," Lauren said weakly, leaning into Jermaine in hopes that her action would help mask her reticence.

"Well, do that, and I will love you long time," Jermaine joked, getting his first genuine giggle from Lauren. He smiled and gave her a peck on the cheek.

Just then, her phone rang; she grabbed it from her clutch to see who was calling, sure it was Donald checking up on her arrival status.

It wasn't Donald.

It was Dara.

"What the hell?" Lauren said, wrinkling her brow. "She can't be serious."

"Who is it?" Jermaine inquired.

Lauren sucked her teeth. "Nobody," she said, tapping IGNORE. Before she could get it back into her purse, the phone rang again. Lauren looked at the caller ID: Dara, again.

"Man, whoever that is, he sure is blowing up your phone. Should I be jealous?"

"First of all, it's not a 'he' calling me, it's a 'she,'" Lauren said. "And I don't know why she's calling me — she lost that right when she dissed my sister, although I'm starting to wonder why I'm cutting off my friends for her some-timey behind."

"Alrighty, then, sounds like you got a lot on your hands tonight," Jermaine said.

"Nothing at all," Lauren said, making a show of tapping IGNORE again and putting her phone on vibrate. Her nerves got worse as the car made its way up the block leading to the mile-long entrance to the school.

"Sir, could you turn on the radio, please?" Lauren called up to the driver. The music would calm her and, perhaps, would give Jermaine the signal to use his ears, not his mouth.

"What station?" he asked.

"107.9 would be great," she said.

"Yes, ma'am," the driver said, punching the buttons on his stereo. OutKast blasted through the speakers. Lauren nodded her head to the beat and kept staring out the window, each streetlight on their journey making her more nervous than the last. The school loomed in the distance, the searchlights beckoning them closer to what promised to be the gala of all galas if Sydney had anything to do with it. Lauren wasn't ready.

Her iPhone vibrated. It was Dara, this time, texting.

Lauren read the message once, then again. Now, why on earth would Dara be asking for her help? After everything that had gone down? Lauren frowned; she could feel Jermaine's eyes burning a hot hole into the side of her face.

"Let me call this girl and see what she wants," Lauren said, speed-dialing her former best friend. "Honestly, I'll put five on it that it's something dumb as hell."

The phone barely rang once before Dara picked it up. "Lauren?" she said, breathless.

"What's up, Dara?" Lauren said, clearly annoyed.

"Lauren, please, don't hang up," Dara insisted.

"Dara, why would I hang up on you — I called you, didn't I?" Lauren snipped. "What do you want anyway? I'm almost at the Benefit."

"I . . . I . . . oh, God," Dara screamed.

Lauren shot up straight. "Dara? Dara! What's going on?" Lauren shouted. Jermaine shifted in Lauren's direction and looked at her quizzically.

"Lauren, please, I need you to come to my house," Dara cried.

"Dara, what's wrong?" Lauren insisted as the car drew closer to the school. Lauren could make out glittery pockets of partygoers milling about the red-carpet entrance leading down the long stretch from the grassy, parklike island to the decked-out front door.

"Please, Lauren. I tried calling Marcus, but his phone is going straight to voice mail. He won't return my calls," she said.

The car drew closer. Lauren could make out Meghan and Caroline and Lexi. And there were Sydney and Jason with Carmen, Rhea, and their respective dates. YRT would be dripping with juice the next morning, for sure.

"Everything okay?" Jermaine asked, reacting to the look on Lauren's face.

"Sir? I need you to keep driving," Lauren said sternly.

"I'm sorry, ma'am?" the driver said quizzically.

"I said I need you to keep driving."

"But we're here, I don't underst —" Jermaine began.

"Just — just listen. We're not going to the party," Lauren insisted. "Keep driving!"

"What do you mean we're not going to the party?" Jermaine said, reeling back. "We're already here! I got dressed, I left work early, and we're here. Lauren, what's going on?"

"I need you to take us to 3241 Murray Street immediately," Lauren said, settling into the shadows of the car.

"Yes, ma'am," the driver said, practically screeching past the crowds.

Jermaine watched the crowds until he could see them no longer — well after the driver pulled the car out of the fortress that was Brookhaven Prep.

Not another word was exchanged between Lauren and Jermaine.

Not one.

* * *

Lauren's hand had barely touched the knob, but the heavy wooden door creaked open as if she'd pushed it. Just beyond the large, round mahogany foyer table decked with a fresh arrangement of bloodred poinsettias was Dara, posted up on the steps, bent over with her head in her lap. She lifted her head when she heard Lauren's heels click on the immaculate white marble floor.

"Lauren?" she asked weakly.

Lauren reeled back when she saw Dara's bloodshot, eyeliner-rimmed eyes. "Dara? What — what's going on?" Lauren asked, walking slowly toward her ex-BFF.

"I tried to call Marcus but he wouldn't answer his cell phone," she said, struggling to get the words out.

Lauren moved a little closer. "What were you calling Marcus for, sweetie? Dara? What . . ."

As wide open as Lauren's mouth was, the words refused to come. Dara had stood up, and all Lauren could see was the red on her hands and her winter-white Grecian mini-dress and the step she had just been sitting on.

"I think I need to go to the hospital," Dara said, bursting into tears.

"Omigod, omigod, omigod!" Lauren screamed, shaking her hands like she'd just touched something hot. "Oh, oh, we should call — we should call someone," she began.

"Call Marcus . . ." Dara said weakly.

Lauren rushed up to Dara — her arms outstretched; she could feel Dara's tears on her bare shoulder. "Baby, we don't have time to call Marcus," Lauren said gently, trying her best to sound calm, even as her heart thumped against her chest. "We have to get you to a hospital."

"But if I just wait a few more minutes, and he sees your phone number, he'll come. . . ." Dara cried.

"I'll call him, I promise," Lauren assured her. "But right now, we have to get out to the car."

"The car?" Dara asked, seemingly confused.

"Jermaine is outside waiting for us in the car. He'll help us, okay?"

"Oh, Jermaine is here? Oh, I ruined your date," Dara said.

"No, no, honey, it's fine," Lauren whispered. "Want to meet him? Come on, he's in the car," she said, putting Dara's arm around her shoulder. "It's a little cold, but it's warm in the car. I have a jacket there."

"Okay," Dara whimpered. "Lauren, I need you to know that I'm sorry. I miss you so much. . . ."

"Not now, honey, not now," Lauren said.

"But I need to hear you say you're okay with me — that we're good," she said, forcing each word through her lips.

"Dara, it's okay. Jermaine!" Lauren yelled as she ushered Dara down the stairs. "Jermaine! Help us!"

Jermaine opened the door and hopped out of the car in

one quick motion, followed by the driver. "Oh, shit, what happened?" he yelled.

"This is Dara," Lauren said, practically carrying her friend on her back down the stairs. "Don't just stand there, help us!"

Jermaine rushed up the stairs and put Dara's other arm over his shoulders, and together they dragged Dara down the staircase. When they got to the bottom, Jermaine took Dara into his arms and carried her to the car, where the driver was waiting with the door open. The three of them piled into the backseat.

"Please," Lauren said to the driver, "get us to Piedmont Hospital as fast as you can."

"Yes, ma'am," he said. "Right away."

No matter that he rushed through the stop signs, past the red lights, down the quickest side streets like a bullet in the night; to Lauren, it seemed like the driver could not make it to Piedmont fast enough.

15
SYDNEY

Sydney entered Principal Trumbull's dimly lit office hesitantly. "Have a seat, Ms. Duke," the imposing-looking man with thick glasses instructed brusquely from behind his desk. A strong wind blew the door closed with a loud slam as soon as Sydney sat down on the uncomfortable, brown pleather armchair. She almost jumped out of her skin with fright. "So do you have the money," the principal demanded as he leaned forward over the desk.

"I, um, I don't know where the money is," Sydney stammered.

"I didn't ask you that! I said, do you have the money?" Principal Trumbull now glowered. His eyes seemed to glow with a supernatural-looking, fiery red.

"No — no, sir, but I didn't take the money," Sydney stuttered as she tried to move back from the principal's burning eyes. She could feel her feet pushing against the cheap industrial carpet that covered his office floor, but for some reason the chair seemed to be moving closer and closer toward his desk. "I swear to you, I looked and I looked," Sydney insisted frantically, when out of nowhere handcuffs locked her into the seat.

"I *told* you what would happen if you didn't get me my money," the principal roared like a wild banshee as his entire face morphed into a werewolf-like creature and he leaped over the desk, mouth agape, at Sydney.

Completely terrified, Sydney struggled against the handcuffs and screamed for her life, "No, please, noooooo!" Sydney screamed so loud, she finally woke herself up.

"Omigod, omigod," she panted as her chest heaved in and out. Completely tangled in the sheets and dripping in sweat, she sat straight up in the bed. "It's just a dream, it's just a dream, Syd," she said, trying to talk herself off the ledge. Despite the reassuring words, her heart felt like it was going to explode at any moment. She slowly surveyed the semidark room as she tried to bring her heart rate down. When she was finally convinced that she was in her own bed and not about to be eaten alive by the angry werewolf Brookhaven principal, she allowed herself to lie back down on the mattress with an audible sigh of relief.

She turned her head and looked at the iHome clock. Its digital numbers read 10:45 A.M. There were still two hours before she was supposed to meet Jason and some of his boys from the football team for a post-party brunch at The Flying Biscuit. And considering she'd only gotten home at three A.M., her achy body could definitely stand another thirty minutes of rest. Sydney closed her eyes and tried to conjure up some of the deep-breathing techniques she learned in yoga class. "Om," she murmured to herself, desperately trying to erase all the scary flashes of the nightmare from her mind. The sound of her exhaling through her nose filled the room. And still, she just couldn't relax. Sydney flexed and wiggled her toes under her comforter. The balls of her feet throbbed from dancing the night away in her gold Christian Louboutin evening shoes. Despite the gel pad she'd inserted beforehand, it was obvious her little piggies were in need of some serious TLC. Finally, giving up all hopes of falling back to sleep, Sydney sat up and started massaging her right foot softly.

As she surveyed the room, her gaze fell on her dress hanging across the back of her desk chair. A small smile momentarily played on her lips. As expected, the Sadie Hawkins Benefit was a success — the decorations were lovely, the food was delicious, and DJ Kiss was on point from beginning to end. Aside from a couple of unfortunate wardrobe choices — China Hayworth's bedazzled sea-foam taffeta ball gown, which made the naturally curvy girl look a thousand pounds heavier — Brookhaven's young, rich, and sexy student body turned it out with their designer frocks and accessories. By the end of the night, everyone who was anyone had showed up with their boy of choice in tow. There was not a single thing amiss except the missing fifteen thousand dollars. And every time Sydney accidently made eye contact with Principal Trumbull, the searing side-eye he shot at her wouldn't let Sydney forget it. *It was probably those beady eyes that caused my nightmare,* she thought bitterly, switching feet.

Someone else that seemed a little shady to Sydney was Marcus. His phone had been off, and he hadn't returned any of the voice mail messages that she left before the party started. But she figured he was probably busy getting ready and reassuring Dara that she didn't look like a beached whale. And then, he had arrived late, alone, and looking extremely stressed out. Normally, Marcus made it a point to arrive on time to any school function where there was going to be a red-carpet arrival, especially when he had been a part of the planning process. Not to mention, while the entire student body couldn't seem to stop complimenting Sydney's appearance, Marcus said nothing.

Sydney had hoped she'd find a moment to pull him aside so that they could compare notes on the missing money, but it never happened. Sydney wasn't sure if it was because Jason was stuck to her side like glue or what, but Marcus went out of his way to make sure that he was never anywhere near Sydney all night. And to that effect, as soon as they had finished saying their official co-chair welcome to the guests, he disappeared into the crowd, not to be seen again for the rest of the night.

Sydney looked at the clock again; this time it read 11 A.M. There was no way she was going to be able to go to this post-party brunch if she didn't speak to Marcus and get this mess cleared up. She took a deep breath and stood up. Sydney padded over to her desk, where she had thrown her clutch when she finally came in earlier that morning. She fished her iPhone out of the bag and tried to turn it on. No juice. Sydney put it in the charger and waited a few seconds before turning it on. She immediately pulled up Marcus's number and pressed the dial icon.

"Come on, come on," Sydney muttered under her breath as she twirled a strand of hair around her right pointer finger and waited for the call to connect. The phone rang once and went directly to voice mail. "You've got to be kidding me," she cursed, ending the call without leaving a message.

Of course his selfish butt is still sleeping, she thought

bitterly, *he ain't the one about to be expelled from Brookhaven!* Sydney slammed down the phone with a thud. She started to pace the length of the room. Feeling absolutely frantic, she realized that she had no choice but to go to Marcus's house. Sure, Jason was going to have a fit when she canceled their plans, but there was no way Sydney Duke was about to wind up flipping Krystal burgers for a living because of somebody else's bullcrap.

She rushed into the closet and hurriedly pulled on her favorite pair of Citizens of Humanity jeans, a white Gap tank top, and a tangerine-colored Ralph Lauren cashmere sweater. She untied her head scarf and shook out her head full of two-strand twists. Then she grabbed her silver hoops and rushed into the bathroom. After washing her face, brushing her teeth, and applying some Dove deodorant, she was ready to roll. Grabbing her chocolate-colored Tod's tote from the handle of her bedroom door, she tossed in her wallet, phone, and a small makeup kit. She quickly glanced around the room and bounced.

"Where you going?" Lauren asked, coming out of the kitchen holding a huge cup of hot cocoa and still wearing her outfit from the night before.

Sydney stopped dead in her tracks at the sight of her sister. "What happened to you?" she asked, momentarily distracted by Lauren's disheveled appearance. "I didn't see you at all after you rushed out of my room last night. . . ."

Lauren sighed and looked at the floor. "It's a long story . . . Dara had . . . She called me last night when we were on our way to the party. She lost the baby," Lauren admitted quietly as she cradled the mug.

Sydney's mouth dropped open. "Oh, my God, I'm so sorry," she said in shock. "I don't even know what to say. Is she okay? Where was her mom?"

A million emotions rushed through Sydney's mind as she processed her sister's horrific words — shock, sorrow, pity, and as much as she hated to admit it, relief. While she could only imagine the devastation of losing a child, a small part of her knew neither Dara nor Marcus was ready to be an underage parent.

"There's nothing really to say," Lauren said with a shrug. "As usual, her mom was away. I think she's at the *SET* Magazine ski weekend event in Tahoe. I think calling me was really Dara's last option. But I do know that I'm just glad I didn't ignore her messages, and I'm even happier that you left Marcus. 'Cause trust me when I say, that boy ain't about nothing. Ya dig? As of this morning he still hasn't called her back. What a loser." Lauren struggled to stifle a yawn. She felt as if she'd aged at least ten years in one night.

Hearing the boy's name snapped Sydney back to reality. "Yeah, well, something tells me that what you know is just the tip of the iceberg," she said.

"Yeah, I'm sure," Lauren responded wearily. "Anyway, I'm going to get me some sleep. I told Dara I'd head back to the hospital later on this afternoon when I woke up." Sydney looked at her sister with raised eyebrows. "Try not to judge so quickly, Syd," Lauren said softly. "Everyone deserves the benefit of the doubt. And not for nothing, she's really alone right now."

"I hear ya," Sydney replied as she walked out the front door. She just hoped that Principal Trumbull would be as merciful to her come Monday morning if she didn't straighten this mess out.

"Morning, babe." Jason answered Sydney's call hoarsely. Sydney could hear him clear his throat several times.

"Morning, sunshine," Sydney replied as she switched lanes on Georgia 400. "How did you sleep?"

"Um, okay. How about you? You seem wide-awake considering I just dropped you off at three o'clock in the morning," Jason replied.

"So-so," Sydney admitted. "I had a really weird dream that woke me up."

"Oh, yeah? You think it was all the fried food we were

eating at Tim's after party?" Jason asked with concern. Sydney could hear his sheets rustling as he changed positions in his bed.

"Maybe," Sydney responded as she hit a stretch of bumper-to-bumper traffic. She sighed out of frustration.

"Where are you?" Jason questioned curiously. "Why do you sound like you're in the car?"

"Um, yeah," Sydney said hesitantly. "That's actually what I was calling you about. . . ." Jason remained silent. "I had to, ah, run out this morning. And I'm not sure that I'm going to make the brunch."

"What you mean?" Jason said sharply. "Where you running to on only a few hours' sleep?"

"There were some issues with the Sadie Hawkins account, and I need to take care of them before Monday," Sydney offered, bracing herself for the inevitable backlash.

"So you're on your way to the bank? To school? I'm confused, Sydney," Jason responded.

"No, not exactly. I'm on my way to Marcus's —"

"You're kidding, right? This is some type of joke. Because I know you're not canceling our plans with my friends to go hang out with your ex-boyfriend." Jason's voice started to rise.

"Jason, I am so sorry but there's nothing I can do," Sydney pleaded as she saw the exit sign for Marcus's house ahead. "Trust me, please."

"Trust you? Are you for real? How could I ever trust you? You're a liar! You're not over your ex, you're just playing me out so that he'll take you back!"

"Jason, I swear to God that's not true! The last thing I want is to cancel our plans but I have to take care of this," she insisted.

"Take care of what? You still haven't told me what is so important that you need to go see Marcus, at his house, on the first Saturday morning we've had planned to spend together since we started dating!"

"I can't discuss it." Sydney struggled to keep her voice steady. She knew Jason was going to be upset but hadn't expected this. She turned off the exit and made a right-hand turn. "If I could, I would, but I just can't." For a moment, the only sound coming from Jason was his breathing.

"I'm not doing this with you anymore, Sydney," he said finally. "It's either him or me. You can't have it both ways."

"But it's not —" Sydney tried to cut in, to no avail.

"Stop lying, Sydney," Jason insisted loudly. "I'm sick of you making excuses. You think I'm a fool or something? Well, I'm not. If you want to be with Marcus, then so be it. I'm done." And then Jason hung up the phone.

"Why, Sydney, what a surprise," Ms. Green exclaimed as she opened the front door. She opened her arms for a hug. Without a moment's hesitation, Sydney stepped right into them. "I am so happy to see you! Come in, come in," the attractive older woman said as she pulled Sydney into the foyer and closed the door.

"Hey, Ms. Green," Sydney said shyly, suddenly remembering everything that had happened the last time she showed up at her ex-boyfriend's house unannounced. "I'm good. How are you?"

"I'm making it," Ms. Greene replied as she pushed her reading glasses onto the top of her head. "I'm just going over some budgetary bills that I intend to introduce at the top of next year."

Sydney nodded and smiled. As one of the more powerful City Council members in Atlanta, Ms. Green was always championing a new cause. "Wait, where are the babies?" Sydney asked curiously about the councilwoman's two teacup Yorkies, Pork and Chop.

"Ha! Belinda took them to the groomers for their monthly bath," Ms. Green said with a smile. "Lord knows I can't deal with bad, stinky dogs. Bad dogs perhaps . . . but definitely not bad, stinky dogs."

Sydney chuckled because she knew how much Marcus's mom loved those two little terrors. "I hear ya," she said with a smile.

"So is everything okay?" Councilwoman Green asked curiously. "Like I said, I haven't seen you in a while. Every time I ask about you, Marcus makes up some lame excuse. I know the affairs of the heart can be a little tricky, but I certainly hope that it's nothing you two kids can't fix," she continued sweetly.

Sydney struggled to keep a straight face as she realized that Marcus had yet to tell his mother that the two of them had broken up, or worse, that Dara had been knocked up. "Yeah, uh, I guess we'll have to see," she finally croaked in response.

"Well, like I always say, where there's a will, there's a way," Ms. Green said matter-of-factly. Sydney swallowed the huge lump in her throat and smiled weakly. "Well, I won't keep you any longer. Marcus is in his room," she offered. "When you guys finish, please feel free to come down and have some breakfast. I don't think my son has left that room since he got home from the dance last night."

"Uh, okay, thanks," Sydney said, staring at a small scratch mark on the wooden floor. Ms. Green quickly hugged Sydney before heading back to her study. Sydney took a deep breath, made the sign of the cross, and headed upstairs.

As soon as Sydney reached the top of the stairs she could hear Marcus's muffled voice from behind his closed bedroom door at the end of the hall. Even though she couldn't make out the exact words, it sounded like he was involved in a heated discussion. Sydney tiptoed closer to get a better listen.

"I told you, I'm good for it," Marcus insisted passionately. Sydney could hear his footsteps as he paced the room. "Listen, didn't I get you the first half of the money, just like I said I would? I just need a little bit of an extension, that's all. I wasn't able to get the rest out in time," he replied to the unknown caller. Sydney glued her ear to the door and held her breath. "Listen, Sergio, I promise, you will have the other fifteen thousand. Please just leave my mother out of this. She had nothing to do with it," he pleaded. There was a brief pause. "Okay, okay, I understand. Thirty percent interest on the remaining fifteen for the extension; that's fine, I'll take it. Just give me until the end of the week, I'll figure it out. You have my word." Sydney's jaw dropped open. "Thank you, bye," Marcus said before slamming the cordless phone down on his desk.

Unable to wait a second longer, Sydney burst in the door. "It was you! You stole the fifteen thousand dollars from the account!!"

"Syd, Sydney, what are you doing here?" Marcus asked, his eyes as wide as saucers. He was now standing by his desk with the laptop open.

"Answer me, Marcus, goddamn it! Who the hell is Sergio? And why did you give him fifteen thousand dollars?" Sydney fumed as her eyes fell upon what looked like an online card game. She felt her adrenaline rush through every inch of her body at the thought of Marcus playing a damn video game while her future was going up in flames.

"Calm down, Sydney, just give me a second to explain." Marcus slammed the laptop closed and then rushed to close the door behind Sydney before her voice carried all the way down the hall.

"Well, you better hurry the hell up, because I'm going to go get your mother in about two seconds, Marcus Green!" Sydney retorted, crossing her arms over her chest defensively.

"I — I," Marcus stuttered as he hung his head in shame. "I messed up," he admitted quietly.

"What do you mean, you messed up?" Sydney spat back vehemently.

"I don't know. It started out as a game," he mumbled. "It just got out of control. I didn't mean for things to go this far, but I just couldn't stop."

"Marcus," Sydney said very slowly as she struggled to understand. "What are you talking about? What did you do?"

Marcus sighed heavily, headed over to his bed, and sat down. "Gambling. I've been gambling online. I started about three weeks ago and I was winning and then, and then I lost. I lost big," he said sorrowfully.

"How damn big?" Sydney pushed, needing to hear the whole truth.

"Twenty-five thousand before the interest," Marcus admitted meekly. Sydney's mouth dropped open. "So I didn't have a choice. I had to take the money."

Sydney felt the room start to spin around her. She grasped for the desk chair by her side. Marcus jumped up to help her down into it before her legs gave out. "Sydney, please," Marcus pleaded with tears in his eyes.

Regaining her bearings, Sydney immediately shooed him away. "When?" she asked. "How?"

"The very first time you sent me to do the deposit; I forged a copy of your signature on a withdrawal slip. I've been making small withdrawals all along just to keep me afloat. Which were the ones you didn't recognize on the statements. Then after you gave your final quote to Principal Trumbull, I went and took out the fifteen," he answered quietly.

"Oh, my God, who are you?" Sydney said, struggling to believe her own ears. "You set me up to be expelled?"

"No, no, it's not like that at all," Marcus rushed to reassure Sydney. "I figured that Principal Trumbull would just think you had done the addition incorrectly. I didn't expect him to look into it so carefully," Marcus insisted as he grabbed her hand. "And by the time you found out about it, I figured I would've won the money back again . . ." he trailed off miserably.

Sydney pulled back her hand and struggled to her feet. "Do you even hear yourself right now? You would've won the money back? What are you, some card shark?" she exclaimed. "Do you even understand what you've done?"

"Sydney, please, I'm so sorry," he pleaded.

"I'll bet you are . . . real sorry you got caught," Sydney said disdainfully. "But I'll tell you what; I'm not going down for this, Marcus. You better figure something out, because come Monday morning, it's a wrap!"

"Sydney, wait! You can't tell anyone, not Principal Trumbull, not my mom, not anyone. Please, you don't understand," Marcus begged as his voice cracked with desperation. "I turned off my cell phone yesterday to try and buy some time, and now they're calling on the landline. I don't care what happens to me, but they're threatening my mother, Syd. I don't want this to hurt my mom."

Sydney paused. She loved Ms. Green more than her own mother at times. The last thing she wanted to do was put her in harm's way. She felt completely torn. "Marcus, I can't be responsible for this. You've got to figure this out, 'cause, for real, the cheating thing sucked, but this, this is bad," Sydney said simply as she turned and walked back out the door. She paused. Behind her she could hear the sound of Marcus crying. "And not for nothing, I think you should pull yourself together and call Dara. She really needs you right now."

Sydney had barely pulled out of the Greens' driveway when her stomach staged a revolt. Quickly pulling over, she opened the car door and started dry heaving. When the spell finally passed, she sat back in her seat and closed her eyes.

"I cannot believe this," she murmured as the sound of cars rushing by filled her ears. Sydney had no idea what to do. If she didn't say something, she was going down for the count. The idea of being expelled and possibly prosecuted made her stomach twist in a huge knot. On the other hand, if she ratted Marcus out, it wasn't just him who would get hurt. It was clear that Ms. Green would suffer as well. And from the sound of it, these people weren't just talking about emotional pain. There was no way she could live with herself if something happened to Ms. Green.

Suddenly, her cell started ringing. She grabbed it out of her bag and looked at the caller ID. It was Jason. With a sigh, she sent the call to voice mail. She couldn't deal with more of his drama on top of everything else going on right now. Sydney tossed the phone back in the bag and started her car. There was only one person she could trust enough to talk to about this — her father. Even though Altimus and Keisha had issued strict orders for her to stay out of the West End, Sydney had no choice. She needed her dad. Now.

Sydney pulled out into traffic and stepped on the gas. Driving along, she thought about how surreal her life had become. Just hours ago she'd partied the night away with her boyfriend and two best friends, and now she'd been kicked to the curb over her gambling-addicted ex and was headed to the shadiest side of Atlanta in search of her father. Sydney shook her head as she jumped on I-85; she wondered if she'd ever have her old life back again. And if not, what was going to become of her?

Dipping in and out of traffic, Sydney reached her Aunt Lorraine's dilapidated house within fifteen minutes. As she pulled up into the driveway, she said a small prayer. *Dear God, please don't let my Aunt Lorraine be home today*, she thought to herself as she stepped out of the Saab and locked the doors behind her. She jumped over the decapitated head of a Barbie doll on her way to the front door, rang the bell twice, and stepped back to wait.

"Sydney? What are you doing here?" Dice questioned with concern from behind the screen when he finally opened the door. Sydney could see him looking past her into the street to see who was outside.

"I need to talk to you, Dad," Sydney pleaded as her father unlocked and opened the screen door. When Sydney stepped inside she could see the uncomfortable-looking electronic monitoring bracelet attached to his ankle. "Is Aunt Lorraine here?" she questioned apprehensively, even though the pungent odor of Newports was missing.

"Naw, she and her girlfriend Sylvia flew up to Atlantic City for the weekend," Dice said with sarcasm in his voice. "I guess getting back on your mother's good side has its benefits, huh?"

"I guess," Sydney mumbled as she followed him into the living room. Without her aunt chain-smoking and laying up in the E-Z chair, the room suddenly seemed more spacious to Sydney. "So, how you been?" Sydney asked hesitantly. With everything going on, she hadn't had a chance to come over and see her father since his release. And it seemed like whenever they spoke on the phone, he was really short with her.

"I've been making it," Dice answered truthfully as he stared intently at his elder daughter. Sydney met his gaze. "I have to tell you, at first I wasn't really feeling the whole get-out-of-jail-on-Altimus thing," he said slowly.

"Dad, I know but I —"

"Let me finish, young lady," Dice continued sharply. Sydney immediately closed her mouth. "But I've been praying, and I understand that it wasn't an easy decision for you to make. And I guess, ultimately, I'm grateful."

"Oh, Dad," Sydney exclaimed in relief as she hugged

her father's lean frame. "I just wanted you to be home. didn't mean to upset you or anything. I just figured that you might be able to find something out about Rodney's real killer if you were out. . . ."

"It's okay, Ladybug, you don't have to explain anything else," Dice reassured Sydney as he stroked the top of her head. "I know you love me and that's all I'm gonna focus on. The rest will fall into place." Sydney leaned her head on her father's shoulder and exhaled heavily. "So what brings you over here?" Dice asked after a moment. "You seem upset."

Sydney raised her head to look at her father. "I'm in trouble," she said plainly. Dice's eyes immediately narrowed.

"What kinda trouble, Syd?"

"I've been accused of something I didn't do," she continued. "And I know who did it. But if I tell, a lot of people that I care about will get hurt."

Dice nodded slowly. "I see," he responded with a bitter smile. "Sounds like déjà vu to me."

"There are going to be really serious consequences for whoever takes the fall, Dad. I just don't know if I can stand tall like you did," she admitted.

"Listen here," Dice said as he pulled away from Sydney slightly. "You are too young to get yourself involved in anyone else's drama. When I stood tall for that crime, it's because I knew my hands weren't clean. But you're not me. Ya hear? And you don't owe anybody anything . . . ever."

"I guess I just —" Sydney started when Dice put a gentle finger to her lips.

"Don't guess, know."

16
LAUREN

It was incredibly beautiful outside, particularly considering it was only a few days before Christmas. That's Atlanta in the wintertime — everywhere else, it's snowing or freezing, and in ATL, it's sixty-five and sunny. Still, standing in the shadows of the church bookstore and cultural center, Lauren pulled the collar of her white Bogner ski jacket tight around her neck to block the chill. Jermaine cupped his eyes as he peeked through the window — his breath steamed up a patch of the glass. "I know she's here," he said, checking his watch. "She always comes here after the Shrine service lets out."

"What is this place, anyway?" Lauren asked, stuffing her hands into her jacket and peering through the display window.

"It's someplace really special to me." He smiled, moving toward the door. "Here she is now."

Lauren and Jermaine stood back as a regal-looking woman with an Afro adorned with a colorful wrap opened the storefront door. Loud bells clanked against the glass, announcing the couple's entrance. "Come on in here, boy," she said. "How you been? And who's this lovely young lady?"

"Hey, Ewa," Jermaine said, meeting her embrace with open arms and an ear-to-ear grin. "Good to see you. This is my friend Lauren. Lauren, this is Ewa."

"Well, it's nice to meet you, Lauren," Ewa said, extending her arms to pull Lauren in for a hug.

"Likewise," Lauren said, awkwardly returning the gesture.

"Thanks for letting us in, Ewa," Jermaine said. "I wanted to show Lauren around — sit and talk for a while."

"Anything for you, Jermaine," she said.

"You wouldn't happen to have any leftovers from Sunday dinner, would you?"

"Already made two plates — they're sitting on the table near your favorite spot, sweetie," she smiled.

"Ah, good looking out," he said.

"You know I got your back," she said, walking around the register counter to grab her purse and keys. "Young lady, you sure must be someone special to be with someone so special," Ewa continued. "Jermaine doesn't just bring any ole body to the Shrine. He's a fine young man — a soldier — got a good head on his shoulders, he's about something. One of the good ones. But I'm sure you already knew this."

"Yes, ma'am." Lauren giggled, tossing a "yeah, right" side-glance in Jermaine's direction.

"Huh? Huh? What'd you say?" Jermaine said, cupping his ear. "Did you say you know I'm a good brother?"

"Whatev," Lauren laughed. "You can't just take the compliment, huh?"

"Aw, big head or not, he's still a good boy," Ewa sighed as she headed for the door. "Okay, baby, you know the drill: Lock up when you're done; leave the key in the mail drop at the sanctuary."

"Yes, ma'am," Jermaine said, extending for another hug.

"Nice meeting you, Lauren," Ewa said, stepping out onto the sidewalk. Again, the bells rang out as they smashed against the glass door pane.

"So, you going to tell me where I am and what we're doing here, or what?" Lauren insisted, tapping her fingers on the top of a beautifully carved African drum. She stood in the middle of the foyer and took in the place, part bookstore, part African market, with display after display of colorful mud cloth, elaborate masks, sculptures, walking sticks, and other trinkets. Lauren almost lost her breath when she caught sight of a beaded belt she instantly envisioned wrapped loosely around the waist of her Joe's jeans.

"This is the bookstore at the Shrine of the Black Madonna," Jermaine said. "The church is next door, and this is where they sell all kinds of stuff imported from different countries in Africa. I come here sometimes, mostly on Sundays, though. Ewa lets me come in and read. They got a lot of books you can't really find in the mainstream bookstores — stuff on black leaders, African-American history, theory, religion, science. They got novels, too, a nice teen selection. Sometimes I buy my moms jewelry from here, on special occasions. Actually, I was hoping you could help me pick out a Christmas gift for ma dukes."

Lauren walked toward a shelf of books and flipped through the pages of a paperback with a cartoon character of a little African-American girl named Ruby. "Wow, I've never seen this many books about black people all in one place," Lauren said, her eyes taking them in as if she were gazing at a feast.

"Yeah, Ewa does a great job making sure all the bookshelves stay full," Jermaine said, following behind Lauren.

"How do you know her?"

"Who, Ewa? Her son plays ball down at the community center where I work. I guess I'm his mentor, or at least that's what Ewa says. He was in a little trouble a while back, and I helped him get out of a jam, so let's just say she's grateful."

"Must be, hooking you up with Sunday dinner and everything," Lauren said as she came upon the table where Ewa had laid out two plates, each piled high with mac & cheese, roast chicken, fried fish, collards, candied yams, and corn bread.

"Oh, yeah, well, when she's not running the bookstore, she helps out in the kitchen when they have special after-service events at the Shrine," he said. "I just give her a call and let her know if I'm coming through, and she puts a little something aside for me."

"You called for both of us?" Lauren asked, peeling off a piece of the crispy fish and popping it into her mouth. "This fish is crazy!"

"Mos def," Jermaine said. "They hooks it up. And, yes, I told her I'd be bringing you here because I wanted to show you where I like to hang. Pride ain't the only spot in town."

"I wouldn't go to Pride if you beat me all the way there with one of those walking sticks," Lauren said, tossing in a halfhearted laugh.

"Yeah, um, about Brandi and them . . ."

"No, no, it's cool — it's cool. I've just decided that when I come here it's best to wear my running sneakers, 'cause I never know when I'm going to run into the ex."

"Running shoes, huh?" Jermaine said, looking down at Lauren's feet. "So then what's with the tight, high boots?"

"Oh, well, who needs sneakers when I'm with you?" Lauren said, walking up to Jermaine and wrapping her arms around his waist. She kissed his lips once, and then again. He returned her affection with a kiss of his own, this one more passionate, deeper. Tongues were definitely involved.

"Hmm, how about those candied yams?" Lauren said nervously, pulling away and wiping the corner of her lips.

"Yeah, yeah," Jermaine said, laughing and pulling out Lauren's chair. "Let's eat."

"Good idea," Lauren said, rubbing her hands together.

Jermaine took his seat, bowed his head for a quick prayer, and got to grubbing. "So, what's up with your girl Dara? She all right?"

Lauren swallowed hard and let her fork linger in the greens. She'd talked to her just moments before Jermaine came to Grace Temple AME to pick up Lauren for their Sunday afternoon date; Dara was home resting — still too weak and, moreover, upset to be around anyone other than her mom. She'd asked Lauren to come by her house, but she'd already committed to hanging with Jermaine and decided, after all of the drama of Friday night, she really had some making up to do. But Lauren promised to check up on her when she got back in.

"Dara's getting better, but it's not easy. She didn't go into the eleventh grade wanting to be somebody's mother, but she's pretty hurt that she lost the baby," Lauren told Jermaine.

"Damn, that's rough," Jermaine said, biting into his chicken.

"Yeah, and then Marcus isn't helping any," Lauren continued. "Even though he called, he still hasn't gone to visit her. I swear, I always knew he wasn't nothin', but this mess right here? I have no words. But you know what? That's Marcus. Acceptance is the first step."

"Sounds pretty trife," Jermaine offered.

"Not as trife as what was on YRT," Lauren said. "I refuse to even repeat some of the mess they were saying about her. I swear somebody ought to just hire a private detective to see who keeps making up that mess and then send a secret bat signal to her computer that'll blow it to smithereens. That would make a lot of people happy."

"You included, huh?" Jermaine said, between crunching on his fish.

"Hell, yeah," she said without hesitation. "Down with YRT. I'm printing that on a sheet of iron transfer paper as we speak."

"'Cause you really care about what they say about you on there, huh?"

"Who wouldn't?" Lauren demanded. "Some random person is dissecting your life, making up half-truths and big lies, and putting it on the Internet for the entire world to see?"

"They ever put anything on there about me?" Jermaine asked. "Wait, that would be impossible, because none of your friends or enemies know I exist."

Lauren put the piece of fish she was about to pop into her mouth back down on her plate and wiped her fingers on the napkin resting in her lap. She seriously contemplated whether to take the bait or just go on ahead and change the subject — move on. She chose the former. "What's that supposed to mean, Jermaine?"

"It's exactly what you think it means," Jermaine said without hesitation. "None of your friends would know who I was, even if I showed up in the clubhouse parking lot with a front seat full of flowers, looking for you."

"You know, for the record, you shouldn't just pop in on people unannounced and then expect somebody to drop what she's doing to follow behind you," Lauren snapped.

"Follow behind me, huh?" Jermaine said, frowning. "Well, for the record, I wasn't planning on asking you to follow behind me — I was going to ask you, my girlfriend, to come out with her man."

"I was with my friends," Lauren said simply. "Unannounced can be cute sometimes, but mostly it's rude."

"You weren't with your friends," Jermaine said, leaning back in his chair.

Lauren wrinkled her brow. Did he know something? "Yes, I was. It was after squad practice, and we were leaving when you called."

"You were all leaving, yes, but you were alone. I saw you."

Lauren's heart skipped a beat. *Damn, he saw me*, she said to herself. She didn't know what to say, but that, of course, didn't stop Jermaine from continuing his inquiry. "So what happened? You were afraid we'd end up on YRT? What, me with my beat-up car, in my baggy jeans and tennis shoes — I threw you off or something?"

"That's not it, Jermaine. It's just that . . ."

"Your friends are expecting more, and here I come — ole boy from the SWATS. I get it."

"You get what, Jermaine? What? You don't know what it's like to be in my shoes — you have no idea. People running all around Brookhaven Prep thinking my stepfather's freakin' Marlo Stansfield from *The Wire*, and my real dad is some kind of low-life prison rat, or that Altimus is a thief who doesn't pay his taxes, and my mom is a ghetto queen who just happened to marry into money, and, oh — don't let me leave out that I'm some wannabe video ho well on her way to becoming the next Karrine Steffans. What do you know about all that?"

"I know that when you have something real in front of you, you don't dis it for fake-ass people who don't give a shit about you!" Jermaine shouted. "The same people you were too afraid to introduce me to — the same people you damn near had the driver run over rather than get out of the car with me on your arm at the gala — are the same people who talk about you and your family behind your back. That's real, Lauren — open your eyes."

Lauren shook her head and pushed herself away from the table. She grabbed her purse and jacket and headed for the door. "I don't have to listen to this, and I'm sure not going to let you stand here yelling at me like I'm a five-year-old who needs to be checked," she said, stomping toward the door.

Jermaine looked down at his plate and took in a deep breath. "Damn," he said softly. Then louder, "Lauren, wait up — I'm sorry."

The bells slamming against the door made clear Lauren was waiting for no one. She ran out onto the sidewalk, pulling her jacket on and shoving her purse tightly under her shoulder while she tried to figure out exactly where she was. Because Jermaine had driven her here and she was so busy riding she didn't really pay attention to the directions he had taken to get them there, she hadn't a clue about even what the name of the street was that they were on. His car was in the back parking lot — that's about all Lauren could remember.

Jermaine burst through the door and ran out onto the sidewalk. "Come on, Lauren, I didn't mean to get you upset," he shouted.

"Well, you did, and you know what? I'm not going to stand around being ridiculed and judged by my boyfriend," she yelled. "No, wait, as a matter of fact, ex-boyfriend. Why don't you go box with Brandi since you're in the mood to fight."

"Come on, Lauren," Jermaine said, grabbing her shoulder. "Can't we just talk about this?"

Lauren snatched her arm away and stomped down the sidewalk. "We just talked. I'm done."

"Yo, wait up, Lauren — where you going?"

"Somewhere away from you," Lauren insisted. "I just need to get out of here."

Lauren rushed into the street, walking against the light; a car speeding through narrowly missed her. The driver honked. "Get yo' ass out the damn street!" he yelled, practically hanging out of the driver's side window.

Startled, Lauren lurched back and ran down the sidewalk to her left, past a series of small storefronts and then houses, Jermaine on her heels. "Leave me alone, Jermaine!" she yelled, not at all concerned about the Negro theater she was performing for the various homeowners who, having just returned from church, were making their way from their cars to their houses with one wary eye on the couple running and screaming down their street. Indeed, there was drama to be had in the West End, but on a Sunday afternoon — the Lord's Day? It was much too much. A few of the ladies shook their heads and grabbed their children's hands and stared as they shut their gates and front doors. Lauren could practically bite into the shade they were throwing, it was so thick. She tried her best to avoid their gazes — walked a little faster to get away from it all. She got to the end of the block and, after looking up and down the street for cars, went left. Still, she had no idea where she was, but that didn't stop her.

"Come on, Lauren, I didn't mean to upset you," Jermaine said as softly as he could so that Lauren wouldn't think he was still yelling.

Lauren didn't bother answering — just kept run-walking. She made a left — more houses.

"Lauren!" Jermaine called.

For some reason, this street looked familiar — really familiar. But what would Lauren know about it? Almost every time she'd been in the West End, it was in the dark, via MARTA or in a car with her navigation system and a prayer. Still, she recognized the pink shotgun house with the wooden fence, and the blue house next to that, lined with green shrubs that flowered well into December. She kept walking but looked back at the corner, her eyes searching for a road sign. She was on Peeples Street, near Uncle Larry's house.

"Yo, what up ma — what's the rush?" she heard the voice say just before she crashed into the body from whom the voice came. "Whoa, whoa, easy there."

Lauren reeled back and her eyes focused on the man, a young twenty-something dripping in goose down, his hood obscuring almost every inch of his face. Lauren was so distracted that she'd seen neither him, holding court in the middle of the sidewalk, nor his friends, three guys, similarly dressed, lounging on and standing next to an old sky-blue Cutty with the motor running and music blasting from the speakers. "Oh, God, my bad — I'm sorry. I didn't see you."

"It's cool, don't sweat it, shorty. What's —"

"I'm sorry," Lauren said, cutting off the man with a raised hand. "I'm really in a rush. I have to —"

"She has to get to her uncle's house, right over there," Jermaine finished, taking Lauren's hand into his. He stood taller than the man in the goose down, cutting an imposing figure, but the man didn't seem the least bit fazed.

"My bad, bruh, she with you?" the man asked.

"Yeah, man," Jermaine said, pulling Lauren along. "It's cool. Let's go, L."

"Yeah, run along, L. Enjoy your Sunday," the man said, moving out of the way just in time to avoid a shoulder brush from Jermaine. "Oh, and, um, Jermaine, right?"

Jermaine looked back at the man quizzically but kept moving.

"Tell Uncle Larry I said whassup," the man said.

In Lauren's ears, he was snarling.

"Come on, Lauren," Jermaine said, giving Lauren's hand a little tug.

She held on, but the moment they got to the foot of Uncle Larry's driveway, she snatched her hand away. "You can leave now," she said. "I don't need an escort."

"I know you don't, Lauren, just listen to me —"

"I've heard enough, Jermaine," she said, climbing the front steps. She pushed the doorbell. As if he had already been standing there waiting for the bell to sound, Uncle Larry snatched open his front door.

"You two get in here right now!" he demanded, opening the screen door so that the couple could push past him. He glared at them as they passed by. "What in the world are you two doing stomping up my stoop hollering and screaming and cackling like you're crazy?"

"Jermaine was just leaving," Lauren insisted.

"Oh, no, he's not," Uncle Larry said, pushing the two of them out of the way so he could close his front door. He rushed over to his window and looked out in the direction of where the man and his friends were standing. And then he quickly lowered his blinds. "You're going to stay right here until I say it's okay to leave."

Lauren frowned. Jermaine folded his arms. "What's up — something going on we should know about?" Jermaine asked.

"All you need to know is that neither one of y'all need to be out there on that street right now," Uncle Larry said.

"What, you think I'm afraid of some dough boy?" Jermaine asked, squaring his shoulder. "Ain't nobody studying them."

Uncle Larry glared at Jermaine and sucked his teeth. "You know what? Sit y'all's behinds down," he snarled. Lauren hopped to it. Jermaine — not so much.

"I'm good," he said.

"You good, huh?" Uncle Larry asked. "Well, I'm not, youngblood. I'm not at all. I told y'all to leave that drama for somebody else. And now here y'all are up in my living room with him right there on the corner."

"Who is he?" Lauren asked. "I don't understand."

"Somebody you do not want to know, Lauren. You don't want no part of him."

"Well, if he's so bad, how you know him?" Jermaine asked.

Uncle Larry wrung his hands and started pacing.

"How you know him?" Jermaine demanded forcefully.

"His name is Richard," Uncle Larry finally said after sitting and holding his head in his hands. "His mama calls him Ricky, but on the streets, they call him . . ."

"Smoke," Jermaine said. "I've seen him around."

"I figured you had," Uncle Larry continued. Jermaine cocked an eyebrow; Lauren folded her arms. "I mean, not because I think you've got any dealings with him. He knew your brother."

"Rodney? How he know him?" Jermaine inquired.

"I don't know, youngblood. But I reckon you can take a guess. You knew your brother better than anybody else — figure it out."

"You still haven't told us how you know him, and why you're so afraid right now."

Lauren's eyes danced between Jermaine's and Uncle Larry's; she was confused and couldn't quite follow just what in the hell the two were talking about.

Uncle Larry took a deep breath and sighed. "I know Ricky because I damn near raised the boy," he said. "His mother is my ex-girlfriend. She lived with me for a few years, and Ricky stayed between here and his aunt's house."

"Go on," Jermaine urged.

"Look, Ricky's got a big mouth and a bad temper, and ain't too much that goes down around here without his dumb behind mixed up in it. That's why they call him

Smoke, because wherever he goes, there's usually a fire not too far behind," Uncle Larry continued. "I thought he would calm down a little when Chere had his baby, but fatherhood ain't changed him none."

"Chere?" Jermaine asked, wincing.

"Yeah," Uncle Larry said. "Chere."

The two men locked eyes. Lauren didn't understand what was going on, but now Uncle Larry and Jermaine were on the same page, the same paragraph, the exact same sentence.

"Chere Wilkins?" Jermaine asked slowly.

"Yes," Uncle Larry whispered.

"That was my brother's . . ."

"That was your brother's girlfriend," Uncle Larry said. "Now you see why I don't need you here? With my niece? Shoot, Keisha finds out she's here, or, God forbid, I let something happen to Lauren here at my house knowing what that boy Smoke is capable of, that's my ass, don't you see? I'm all in the middle of this mess, and y'all keep coming around here pouring more hot sauce on the stew."

Uncle Larry's words pierced Lauren's heart — each one like a cut from a highly sharpened blade that sliced with a surgeon's precision. Everything she'd thought about Jermaine's brother, her stepfather, her mom, Dice — it was all wrong, all of it. Or maybe it wasn't? Uncle Larry was practically raising his hand and giving an oath to say that none of them had anything to do with Rodney's murder. But it was because of his murder that she'd learned all of her family's dirty secrets, and even the truth about her real dad — that perhaps he wasn't the bad guy she'd made him out to be all these years. And could it be that she'd just had a run-in with a stone-cold murderer? And he was standing right there outside Uncle Larry's door? Possibly waiting for her and Jermaine?

Jermaine looked at Lauren; she was hugging herself and rocking back and forth. "I need to get out of here," she yelled, standing suddenly, a move that made both Jermaine and Uncle Larry reel back.

"You're right about that," Uncle Larry said. He walked over to the window and peeked outside. Smoke was still holding court. "But he's still outside, and I really would prefer you not walk through that crowd again. He knows full well who you are."

"Well, if he knows who I am, then he knows who my stepfather is, right?" Lauren said, wiping a tear from her eye. She squared her shoulders. She had no time for a weak-kneed approach. For the first time, Lauren was recognizing — and acknowledging — the power that came with being a Duke. "He is aware that I'm Altimus's daughter."

"I'm sure he does, but . . ."

"But, then, there shouldn't be any problems. My real

father is not too far away from here. I can call him and ask him to pick me up, or I can get Altimus on the phone."

"Wait, Dice is out of jail?" Jermaine asked. "You didn't tell me."

"As I recall, you were too busy wondering about my friends to be concerned about my father," Lauren snapped. "But he's out on bail — you have my sister and Altimus to thank for that."

"Altimus?" Jermaine asked.

"Yes, Altimus and Sydney. Now, I don't know what this Smoke guy has to do with all of this, but I'll bet he's not crazy enough to raise his hand to my stepfather. Neither one of them." Lauren reached into her purse and pulled out her phone.

"No, no — don't call, Lauren, please," Uncle Larry implored. "We'll go through the garage; I'll drive."

17
SYDNEY

Sydney sat in her car and watched the students make a break for the school building as the first warning bell sounded before the Brookhaven Monday-morning announcements. With a sigh, she leaned over and grabbed her black Gucci-logo tote full of books that she should've been studying over the weekend. "You can do it, you can do it," Sydney muttered repeatedly to herself as she took a last look in the vanity mirror, popped the trunk, and hopped out of her car. After closing the door, she headed around to open the trunk and grabbed her dirty pink Nike gym bag. With a firm slam, she was on her way.

There are eighty-three steps from the front entrance to the principal's office. Sydney made a mental note as she stood in front of the open door, willing her stiff limbs to take another step forward. A gaggle of freshman boys rushing down the hall on their way to class almost knocked her over. "Hey, my bad," the pimply faced one on the end apologized over his shoulder as the group kept moving. *That was just God's way of pushing me*, Sydney thought as she squared her shoulders and finally stepped inside the receptionist's area.

"Good morning, Mrs. Tisdale, I'd like to speak with Principal Trumbull," Sydney greeted the elderly woman with a determined look on her face.

"Good morning, Sydney. Principal Trumbull is speaking with another student right now. Would you like to have a seat?" Mrs. Tisdale responded, motioning toward the stiff, overstuffed, burgundy leather couch behind Sydney.

"Yes, ma'am," Sydney said as her heart pounded in her ears. When she sat down, her foot tapped nervously on the floor. She twisted the diamond stud in her right ear and looked out the door at all the students hurrying to get to class before the final warning bell sounded. More than anything, she wished she was one of them. Sydney closed her eyes and tried to envision the look of confidence on Dice's face when he assured her that she was in the right. "Yes, I can. Yes, I can," she murmured softly. Her eyes snapped open at the sound of the principal's inner office door opening.

"You should go clear out your locker immediately," Principal Trumbull instructed gravely as he rested his right hand on Marcus's left shoulder.

Marcus nodded sadly in response. "Yes, sir, I will." Sydney finally stood up from her seat. For a moment, Marcus made direct eye contact and then cast his gaze downward.

"Good morning, Ms. Duke," Principal Trumbull said. "Step into my office, please."

"Yes, sir," Sydney replied immediately as she picked up her bags and walked toward the inner office.

As Marcus stepped aside to let her pass, he reached out and touched the sleeve of her black Calvin Klein button-up. "I'm so sorry, Sydney," he whispered softly. "And thanks for telling me about Dara. I really appreciate it."

Sydney didn't respond for fear of falling apart. Instead, she rushed inside the inner office and sat down without a backward glance. Principal Trumbull closed the door behind them and headed over to his desk. Sydney placed her tote on top of her gym bag, and sat back in the chair anxiously.

"Well, Ms. Duke, I'm happy to inform you that the missing money has been located," he said quietly. "Under normal circumstances, I wouldn't discuss the details of the return with you, but as the co-chairwoman you have a right to know."

"Don't you mean, since I was being accused?" Sydney corrected.

Principal Trumbull raised his eyebrows. "Well, yes, and as I'm sure you can understand, I apologize for my hasty misjudgment. But as I said, the good news is that the money has been located. Apparently, your co-chair has developed some bad habits and personal issues that compromised his integrity. And in light of this, his mother will be returning all the missing money as well as making a generous donation to the teachers' retirement fund." Principal Trumbull stopped to take a swig of water from the Crystal Springs bottle on his desk before continuing. "Since the nature of the issue is so personal, we think it's in his best interest for Marcus to take the next semester off and spend some time at a rehabilitation facility."

"Wait, you're sending Marcus to rehab?" Sydney asked incredulously. "Are there actually rehabs for thieves or isn't that just jail?"

The principal cleared his throat and tugged uncomfortably at his Hermès tie. "Again, because of the nature of the illness and out of respect for Councilwoman Green, we have decided not to press charges."

Sydney shook her head in disbelief. "Wow, okay," she said softly. She bent over to pick up her tote and gym bag.

"I appreciate your understanding the delicacy of this matter, Ms. Duke. And it goes without saying that none of the details of this conversation should leave this room," Principal Trumbull stated solemnly. "And again, I apologize for any unnecessary anxiety this may have caused you over the weekend."

Sydney stood up. "Understood," she said as she turned and headed toward the closed door.

"You may leave the door open," Principal Trumbull requested gently.

"Yes, sir," Sydney mumbled as she walked out.

"Do you need a pass to go back to class?" Mrs. Tisdale asked as Sydney passed her desk, heading for the hallway. "We wouldn't want you to get into any unnecessary trouble now, would we?"

"No, no, we wouldn't," Sydney confirmed.

Sydney stood in front of her open locker facing her books. For the life of her, she couldn't remember what class she was supposed to be going to at the moment. In fact, the only thing she could think about was that Marcus was being sent away to rehab. Principal Trumbull's words echoed in her mind: "We think it's in his best interest for Marcus to take the next semester off and spend some time at a rehabilitation facility." Sydney shook her head; life was becoming more surreal than Mariah Carey and Nick Cannon's crazy wedding.

Finally, Sydney grabbed her Global History text and

shut the locker. She checked her Cartier tank watch; there were still twenty minutes left in the period. As she opened her tote to drop in the book, her phone vibrated twice, signaling the arrival of a new text message. Wondering if the news about Marcus had already hit YRT, she nervously pulled out her cell. Thankfully, the text was from Lauren: FYI, talked to Uncle L. OMG, U R so not going 2 believe this — Rodney got killed by some wack corner boy. L

Completely stunned, Sydney stopped dead in her tracks. She punched in her reply as fast as she could: Whaaat? Dish! She leaned up against the nearest locker to wait for a response. Finally, her phone buzzed again. To her dismay, Lauren's response was far from informative: Can't. Got the crazy Chem teacher breathin down my neck, we'll talk at home later. L

"May I see your pass?" the heavyset hall monitor with a head full of blond-and-black microbraids asked from down the hall. Sydney quickly dropped her phone back in her bag before the monitor saw it and gave her a detention. She pulled the pass out of her back pocket and waved it in the air. "Alrighty, then, perhaps it's time for you to keep it moving," the monitor suggested.

"You're absolutely right; it's time for me to keep it moving," Sydney replied and walked away.

* * *

261

"Great job this morning, Ms. Duke." Sydney's riding instructor, Jackson Harper, complimented her as they led their horses back to the stables. "Your form has really improved. This upcoming spring season should be very promising for you," the tiny, green-eyed man continued as they reached the entrance to the stall of Sydney's filly, Thunder.

"Thanks," Sydney said simply as she gave Thunder one last rub before the stable boy took her away. Still a little shell-shocked from the early morning double drama, she found it hard to process the praise. "I know I kinda slacked off for a while . . ." Sydney admitted as she removed her riding helmet and tucked it under her arm.

"Well, as I've explained to the athletic director numerous times, sometimes having the lessons first thing in the morning is difficult for the busier students. Luckily for you, your schedule includes a double study twice a week. So we were able to insert your lessons."

"Yeah, it totally made a difference," Sydney agreed with a nod. "My days feel much shorter now that I'm not waking up at five o'clock for our workouts."

"And as long as you stay on top of things from here on in," Jackson replied as he stroked his own mare, "you should be more than ready for competition." Another non-descript stable boy headed over to retrieve Jackson's reins.

"Speaking of getting ready, will you continue riding over the break or is your family headed out of town?"

Memories of past Christmas breaks spent sunning on the white sand beaches in St. Lucia or hitting the powder slopes at Tahoe immediately flooded Sydney's mind before she remembered Altimus's upcoming tax-evasion trial. "No, unfortunately we're not going anywhere this year," she said somewhat bitterly as she kicked at a pile of loose hay.

"Well, then, I certainly hope to see you for at least two or three lessons over the week," Jackson responded with an enthusiastic smile. "We'll dedicate an entire day to your jumps."

"Sure, sounds like a plan," she responded flatly. For the first time, it occurred to Sydney that both of her BFFs were leaving Atlanta with their respective families for the holidays and she'd have absolutely nothing to do but feel bad about getting dumped by Jason — for a second time.

"Well, I'll let you go so you have time to shower before your next class," Instructor Jackson said as he patted her on the shoulder. "Again, great job today."

Sydney had just finished throwing the last of her dirty riding gear into her gym bag when Jason's cryptic text message arrived: I think we should talk. Meet me behind the gym before next period. J. Completely caught off guard, Sydney hesitated. More than anything, she wanted to clear the air about everything that happened on Saturday, but today had been bizarre enough. The last thing her nerves needed now was an argument. Sydney started to toss the cell back in her bag but stopped. "Oh, what the hell," she muttered with a small grin. Throwing caution to the wind, she sent her BFFs a quick text: Gotta meet J behind the gym 4 a sec. Might be a couple mins late for Spanish, so cover for me, por favor? Taking a deep breath, Sydney checked her tote for her Spanish notebook, slipped into her coat, and slammed her gym locker closed. After a quick spin of the lock's dial, she grabbed her stuff and hurried out of the girls' locker room.

As she rounded the corner, Sydney could see Jason leaning against the back of the building, looking at his cell phone. *Wow, he is so cute*, she thought as she watched the sunbeams play off his chiseled profile. The butterscotch trim on his Louis Vuitton leather jacket complemented his complexion perfectly. Sydney paused to smooth down the front of her hair before walking over. She was almost in front of him before he noticed her approaching.

Jason immediately straightened up to greet her, "Hey! I wasn't sure you got my message in time."

"Yeah," Sydney replied softly. "I, um, didn't bother to reply since I was already down here."

"That's cool," Jason nodded. "You look nice."

"Thanks," Sydney responded as she looked down at the black-and-white Calvin Klein swing coat she was wearing. She shifted from foot to foot as a million emotions ran through her. She felt like she should say something, but she just couldn't figure out where to start. "So, um, how was your weekend?" she asked lamely.

"Let's just say I've had better," Jason laughed bitterly as he tugged at his navy Yankees cap.

"Yeah, me, too," Sydney admitted. She started twisting her right earring as the uncomfortable tension hung between them. She looked both ways at the deserted parking lot.

Finally, Jason cleared his throat. "I called you back, you know, after everything," his voice faded away.

"Yeah, I guess I was driving and missed the call," Sydney responded as she switched the bag to her other shoulder. "You didn't leave a message, so I wasn't really sure you wanted me to call you back."

Jason sighed as he scuffed the bottom of one of his all-brown Nike Air Force Ones against the pavement. The thumping sound pierced the air. "I guess I called to apologize," he mumbled as his eyes remained downcast. "I didn't mean for things to go so far. But when my call went straight to your voice mail, I just assumed that you were still with Marcus and I just hung up."

Sydney was surprised how little his words did to make her feel better. Maybe it was the whole Marcus drama, but for some reason, she just wasn't in the mood for another sorry apology. "Yeah, well, I wasn't," Sydney said with a shrug. "But it's cool."

"Is it?" Jason questioned, his voice rising just a tad. "'Cause I'm really messed up about this whole thing and, I don't know, you seem pretty okay."

Sydney tried to conjure something really reassuring and positive to say to get the two of them back on track, but she drew a complete blank. "It's not that I'm okay, J, it's just that it's a lot," Sydney answered slowly and truthfully. "There's so much going on with me. And I want to tell you. But I never really know what I can and can't say, because I never know how you'll react."

Jason's head snapped back slightly as an expression of disbelief clouded his face. "What are you talking about? You can tell me anything," he retorted, clearly offended. "You make me sound like some kind of . . . I don't know, some kind of monster!"

"Can I tell you anything, Jason? I don't know what it is, but I feel like no matter what I say or do, you won't ever really trust me. And seriously," Sydney paused and took a deep breath before she blurted out the question that'd been on her mind since Saturday. "What is the point of *us* if you don't trust me?"

"You don't know what it is?" Jason snapped as he pushed off the wall and stood over Sydney menacingly.

"Weren't you the same broad who went behind my back and had a date with Marcus the last time we were dating?"

"And I said I was sorry," Sydney responded nervously as she reflexively took a step back. "I know what I did was wrong, but it was only one time."

"Do you know? Or are you just playing some type of game with me?" Jason growled.

Sydney's heart started pounding in her chest. She was not feeling Jason's tone or the sinister look in his eye. She snuck another look at the deserted parking lot and regretted her decision to meet him so far away from where anyone might hear them. "You know what, Jason?" Sydney said hesitantly as she nervously fingered the Cartier bracelet. "I don't think this is working for either of us right now. I think that we may have taken things a little too fast. . . ."

Sydney didn't have a chance to finish her sentence before Jason grabbed her by the right arm and twisted it. "Oh, you think you can just make a fool of me and get away with it?"

Sydney whimpered as tears filled her eyes. "Jason, please. Please stop," she begged. "I'm not trying —"

"You're not trying to what?" he demanded as he shook her forcefully. Sydney tried to yank her arm away but his grip only got tighter. "You're not leaving me." Jason threw Sydney against the wall.

"Ouch, please, Jason," Sydney sobbed from the sharp pain where her shoulder hit the concrete. Her bags and personal items were scattered around her. She cowered fearfully. "Please stop. I'm sorry. Please!"

"Oh, you ain't sorry yet, you selfish, conniving brat," he threatened as he raised his hand. Sydney closed her eyes in anticipation of the impending blow.

"Hey! What are you doing?" Carmen suddenly shrieked from out of nowhere.

"Get the hell away from her, you asshole," Rhea yelled as the two came hurtling around the corner.

Jason looked up at the two girls running at him and stepped back from Sydney. He shook his head and looked completely bewildered, almost as if he didn't know how he'd gotten there. "She started this . . . she made me," he stuttered as Rhea's oversized lavender quilted Marc Jacobs bag connected with his right shoulder.

"Help! Somebody help us!" Carmen screamed at the top of her lungs as she raced to her friend's side. She helped Sydney scramble a few feet away.

"Omigod, you freak! Get the hell away from her!" Rhea screamed as she connected with the side of Jason's head. She knocked his Yankees cap to the ground.

"Rhea, it's enough," Carmen called out. "He's not worth it!"

"You crazy bitches! You all deserve one another," Jason hissed from between his arms as he blocked the blows. He stooped down to make a quick grab for his cap and turned to run away.

"I got your bitch," Rhea yelled from behind him when she finally stopped brandishing her bag like a lethal weapon. She walked over to where Carmen was holding Sydney.

"Omigod, thank you so much," Sydney sobbed. "How did you know?"

"Shh, it's okay, calm down," Carmen soothed her. "It's okay, we're here. It's okay."

"Girl, what in the world? Is that fool crazy?" Rhea exclaimed in disbelief as she looked at her friend sitting on the ground crying. She started picking up Sydney's scattered belongings.

"I don't even know what happened," Sydney said, shaking her head. Tears continued to streak down her face. "I just told him that it wasn't working out, and the next thing I know he snapped."

"Wow! You are so lucky we had a substitute teacher today! That's the only reason Carmen and I came out behind you. We wanted to tell you not to rush back to class," Rhea explained as she walked over and held Sydney's hands tightly. Sydney just shook her head as her sobs and tears finally started to subside. She slowly rubbed her bruised shoulder.

"Did he hurt you?" Carmen asked with concern when she saw Sydney wincing in pain. "Honestly, I think we should go to the principal's office right now."

"Absolutely, Syd," Rhea co-signed.

"But what will people say — it's his word against ours? Who's gonna believe us?" Sydney asked, suddenly uncertain as she thought about how crazy the incident might sound to anyone who hadn't witnessed the altercation.

"Damn what people say. You're Sydney Duke," Carmen said vehemently.

"We got you, Sydney," Rhea swore truthfully. "We got you."

Sydney sat silently thinking about Carmen's words before finally standing up and straightening out her clothes. "You're right. I'm Sydney Duke and I'm better than this," she said determinedly as she reached for her things. "And no one is going to hurt me and get away with it ever again."

18
LAUREN

She'd seen the "Crime Stoppers" billboard hanging on the side of a hair-braiding salon at the end of a row of stores near Pride and actually considered that she might just have to use the number that time she went looking for Jermaine and, instead, got her first verbal smackdown from Brandi. On her train ride home that day, Lauren even gave a nervous giggle as she fingered the number on her cell and zoned out, imagining how the police cars, lights and sirens ablaze and the "Bad Boys" theme song blaring from giant speakers, would speed up to the tiny storefront with cops and K-9s swarming from every which way, looking to drag Brandi away to the pokey. But then she dismissed the billboard, the number, and the Brandi-goes-to-jail fantasy as quickly as she'd conjured it, recognizing that once she stepped just one of her pretty pedicured toes back over the Buckhead line, there would be absolutely no need to call the snitch hotline. Wasn't nobody coming to the Duke estate.

But the West End was a whole 'nother story, and Lauren had come to recognize one true thing: As long as Smoke was running around the West End, no one — not Lauren, not Sydney, not Jermaine, not Uncle Larry, not Dice, not even Altimus and Keisha — was safe. This was on Lauren's mind when she tiptoed into Sydney's room, laptop in tow, looking for some help dropping dime on the guy who was threatening to single-handedly dig up all the Duke family secrets and ruin life as Lauren knew it. Sydney's light was on, but her eyes were closed.

"Syd, wake up," Lauren whispered, shaking her sister's arm. It was a little after midnight. Altimus, keeping another late night holed up in his lawyer's office strategizing over his ominous tax situation, had come in only a few minutes earlier and already had eased into a closed-door nightcap in the library, while Keisha was about two hours into dreamland. "Syd! Come on, wake up — it's important. I need your help!" Lauren whisper-shouted.

"I'm not asleep," Sydney said, turning over to face her sister. Her mascara and thick black eyeliner were making dried tracks all the way down her face; pink lipstick smudged her cheek and pillow. Sydney swiped her hand under her eye; Lauren saw moisture.

"Um, what's going on, Syd? Why are you crying? Is everything okay?" Lauren asked, leaning in for a close-up view.

"Everything is fine. There was an eyelash in my eye, that's all," Sydney insisted halfheartedly. Lauren looked at her twin with a knowing eye but held her tongue. Something was up.

"Look," Sydney insisted, deciding to just tell the truth. "I'm okay, really. Some stuff with Jason went down and I'm a little upset, but I'll be over it by morning — no biggie," she reassured, sitting up in her bed. "What's up?"

"Well, um, I think I may have found out what happened to Rodney," Lauren said, skepticism rimming her voice. "Or at least I think I found a way to get the heat off everyone."

"What?" Sydney asked. "What are you talking about, Lauren?"

"Don't you remember that text I sent you? Seriously, I think I might have figured out how to get everybody off the hook," Lauren said.

"Wait, so that was for real? I mean, you don't get people 'off the hook' for murder," Sydney said. "You find the person who actually did it so innocent people don't have to go down for something they didn't do."

"Well, then, let me be the first to say to you that I don't think our dad has to go down for Rodney's murder," Lauren said simply.

Sydney squinted, unsure whether she'd heard her sister correctly. "You're saying you don't think Dice did this? Or are you saying that you don't want him to go to jail over it? Because if you're suggesting either one of those, I would almost be forced to think you actually care what happens to my father," Sydney said.

"I do care about *our* father, Sydney," Lauren said, annoyed. "It's just that —"

"That's news to me," Sydney interrupted sarcastically.

"Look, I didn't come in here to get into a debate over whether or not I love my father," Lauren snapped. "And blog bulletin: Lauren has feelings, and she happens to be capable of caring about other people. But just because we're twins doesn't mean we have to think alike. You of all people should know —"

Sydney raised her hand, motioning that she didn't need to hear any more of her sister's soliloquy. "I get it, I get it," Sydney said. "I don't want to argue about it."

"I wasn't trying to argue. I came in here to tell you that Dice didn't kill Rodney, and Altimus and Mom probably didn't have anything to do with it, either. He didn't come right out and say it, but Uncle Larry thinks a drug dealer named Smoke killed Rodney over some girl."

"A girl? What kind of girl do you kill somebody over?" Sydney asked, confused.

"Maybe she has some extra grease in her pork chops or pearls in her na na — how in the hell would I know that?" Lauren retorted. "Uncle Larry said something about how she had this guy's baby and Rodney was messing around with her and the drug dealer doesn't play that with his girl. It sounded like a lot of things, but none a reason to beat someone to death. But what do I know about all of that? What I do know is this means we're all off the hook over this."

"And exactly how is that possible if everybody thinks one of our dads did it?" Sydney demanded.

"That's where this comes in," Lauren said, turning her laptop so Sydney could see it.

"Crime Stoppers?" Sydney asked. "That's your big idea? You're going to call Crime Stoppers and do what? Tell them you found the real killer? Okay, O.J.," Sydney said skeptically.

"Come on, Syd, it can't be that bad an idea. People really do get caught behind this Crime Stoppers thing."

"Methinks you've been watching too many episodes of *Law & Order*," Sydney laughed, shaking her head.

"Seriously, come on, Sydney, hear me out," Lauren said. "I just Googled it, and there was a story I read that said that here in Atlanta they've used it to solve a bunch of crimes, and you don't even have to testify in court or anything, you're just giving them a tip and the police follow up."

Sydney rubbed her temples and winced. "I have a serious headache," she said. "All of this is just too much."

"Yeah, well, tell that to Dice when he goes down for a murder he didn't commit," Lauren sighed.

"You know he really loves you, right?" Sydney said quietly.

Lauren cracked her neck and held on tighter to her laptop; she wanted to acknowledge what her sister said, but she wasn't really ready to deal with the implications.

"I'm just saying, it wouldn't be a bad thing if he knew that the one girl he loves as much as me acknowledged him," Sydney said.

"First things first," Lauren said. "He may be happy to hear those three words, but I'm thinking he'll be even happier to get the monitoring bracelet off his ankle. And that can't happen until I make the call."

Sydney reached for her cell and handed it to Lauren. "Do your thing," she said.

Lauren stared at the phone and slowly pulled it from Sydney's fingers. "Well, um, let me just see what else it says about making this anonymous. Do you think they'll trace it back to your phone?" she asked, staring at the numbers.

"You have a point," Sydney said. "What does the Web site say?"

Lauren pushed the space bar on her MacBook, which had gone to screen-saver mode. When the Atlanta Crime Stoppers page popped back up, she focused on the dark blue line that read "Submit a tip online." "Look, I don't have to call," she said to Sydney. "All I have to do is fill out this page and send it in. It says you don't have to give your name or anything."

Sydney sat up and peeked at the screen for herself. Satisfied her sister knew what she was talking about, she said, simply, "Well? Get to it."

And Lauren did, typing in as much information as she could about the man she was certain was going to get her father and her boyfriend off the hook for a crime she was now sure neither had committed. "Now, how in the hell am I supposed to know how tall he is and how much he weighs?" Lauren questioned.

"Can you give a guess?"

"I mean, if I get it wrong, won't that keep them from finding him?" Lauren questioned.

"You can still estimate, though. Think about it: Is he as big and tall as Altimus?"

"No, he's smaller — much smaller. Like Marcus's height."

"Marcus isn't that small," Sydney said, frowning.

"Well, he ain't as big as Altimus, that much I know," Lauren said.

"Whatev, Lauren," Sydney snapped. "If he's Marcus's height, he's about five-nine."

Lauren scrolled down and clicked on 5'9". "He's about Marcus's weight, too. How much does Marcus weigh?"

"I don't know — I wasn't at his last physical."

"Come on, Syd, work with me, not against me," Lauren insisted, rolling her eyes for emphasis.

"Okay, okay — he's about one seventy-five, one eighty," Sydney said.

Lauren scrolled down some more. "Dang, they want his cell phone, his addy, they want to know what scars and tats he has, what kind of dogs he has, his weapons. How in the hell am I supposed to know all of that?" Lauren asked, exasperated. "Like, maybe, I don't know as much as I think I know. Maybe," she added, "this isn't a good idea."

Sydney touched her sister's shoulder to calm her. "Come on, Lauren," she said gently. "You can do this. I know you can. You can just put as much of the info in there as you can, and let the police sort out the rest. If you don't say anything, though, then you're leaving it up to the police to figure it out, and you see what that's got us."

Lauren sighed and stared at the screen. Of course,

Sydney was right; she had to do what she had to do. She scrolled down the screen some more, until she got to an entry she could handle: Where did you last see this suspect, the form questioned.

Lauren typed in, Peeples Street, the West End, and then scrolled down some more, past the "vehicle information" and on to the "crime notes" section. Under "type of offense," she slowly typed the word "murder," her fingers trembling with each tap of the button. Then she hesitated, if only for a moment, struggling to find the words to describe what little details she knew. She looked at Sydney, who was busily twirling the earring in her right ear, and then poured out all she could.

This guy Smoke beat up Rodney Watson because Rodney was dating his baby's mother. The baby's mother's name is Chere, and I think she lives in the West End, too, and should know where Smoke lives. It happened in the West End, and Smoke left Rodney to die on his front lawn, on Hopewell Street. I know this because it's what I heard.

Lauren read her statement aloud so Sydney could hear it, and, after they went over it a few more times, Lauren scrolled down some more, entered a password so that she could, as the site stated, check back and add more details if she wished. Then she carefully read the privacy policy, said a quick silent prayer that what she was doing was the right thing and most of all, that nobody would find out she was snitching, and then gave a final look to Sydney.

"Go ahead, do it, Lauren," Sydney coaxed. "It's going to be all right. I promise."

She wasn't really sure she believed it, but there was something in her sister's eyes that made her push those negative thoughts to the recesses of her mind.

And with Jermaine's face dancing in her head, Lauren did it: She clicked on the button that said SUBMIT TIP.

Lauren walked gingerly up the walkway and then the steps, each inch she took feeling like a mile in quicksand. She couldn't quite put her finger on why she was so nervous; it was him, after all, who had wanted this for so very long — she who had resisted with all her might this reunion, this coming home. In the car on the way over, she'd imagined him opening the door, taking one look at her, and slamming said door in her face — a pittance of the fitting retribution she deserved for all the drama and anguish she'd brought into his life. A face full of wood? She deserved at least that much.

But really, what Lauren was looking for was forgiveness.

She yanked at her jacket and pulled her purse up onto her shoulder, using her underarm to grip it a little tighter. And then she did it: She rang the bell.

The shuffling of feet in the room just beyond the door was audible and instantaneous, but it took an eternity for the door to open. His eyes immediately locked with hers, even as she shifted from one foot to the other.

"Hey, Ladybug — fancy seeing you here! I like the new hairdo," Dice laughed, pulling her into his embrace. "Wait, I thought you had riding lessons today."

"Um," Lauren hesitated, awkwardly hugging her father back, "I don't take riding lessons. That's Sydney."

Dice went still for a moment, even as his long arms remained wrapped around Lauren's shoulder. Slowly, he pushed her back so he could get a good look at his daughter. "Lauren?" he questioned.

"H-hi, Dice," she said, looking into his eyes again. He looked just like he did in the pictures Sydney had showed her in the photo album, except with less hair on top of his head and more gray everywhere else. His arms were muscular, like she'd imagined; she wondered if they'd gotten that way from lifting in the prison yard, or if his arms always felt that way. Looking into his eyes was like looking into Sydney's and her own; all these years, she never realized they'd gotten those almond-shaped browns from their father — their birth father.

"Lauren?" he asked, slightly bewildered. "Baby, that's you, for real? Oh, my God, I can't believe you're here!" he said, pulling her back into his arms. "What? Why? How?"

"Hey," Lauren said, patting him on the back. "It's me, live and in the flesh."

Dice pushed Lauren back to get another look at her. "I can't believe you're here! Come on in, come on in," he demanded, taking her hand and pulling her into the humble house. He closed the door behind her and stared some more. "I'll be damned, look at you!" he laughed. "All these years I told myself that I would be able to tell the difference between my own daughters. You know, when you two were little, I could tell you apart so easy. I guess I'm a little rusty."

"Yeah, people usually tell us apart by our hair and I guess our voices," Lauren said, forcing a smile to her face. "Mom's pretty good at it, though. I think maybe because she can tell our different personalities."

"Yeah, I can see that," Dice said. "A mother knows. Usually, so does a father. I guess I kinda missed out on that, though. I'll work on it — promise."

"No, no — it's cool," Lauren reassured.

Silence pierced the air — hung thick between them as they searched each other's eyes. Finally, Lauren spoke again. "Can I, um, sit down?"

"Oh, yeah, sure, sure — where are my manners? Come on in, have a seat over here on the couch," Dice said, rushing to move the newspaper, his reading glasses, and a tattered blanket he'd been using as a pillow. He tossed all three on the coffee table, swiped at the sofa cushion, and then patted it — an invitation for Lauren to sit. She obliged, albeit hesitantly. "Can I get you something to drink — some water? Soda? I think Lorraine has some orange juice in here somewhere. . . ."

"I'm fine, Dice — I'm good," Lauren said. "Thanks, though."

"Yeah, okay," he said, unsure of what to say next.

They were quiet again; for the first time, she noticed music softly playing on a small stereo system sitting on a wooden console next to the TV. Lauren had never heard the song before, but she thought she recognized the voice. "Who's that singing?" she inquired.

"Who, that playing right there?" Dice asked. "That's Donny Hathaway, baby. The one and only. I was at this record shop down in Little Five Points the other day and I found this CD," he said, hopping up and rushing over to the stereo to find the case. "That's him in concert. 'Sack Full of Dreams' is what's playing now. One of my favorites."

"Cool," Lauren said. "He sang that Christina Aguilera song 'A Song for You,' right?"

"Uh, correction, Dewdrop. Christie Alera or whatever her name is sang Donny's song," he laughed. "I think I might have heard her version while I was in the pen. Ol' girl can blow, that's for sure, but she ain't Donny."

Lauren shifted in her seat at the mention of "the pen," a movement that was neither lost on nor new to Dice. Most everyone, save cons, were nervous around ex-cons.

Dice smiled nervously. "Hey, hey — I want you to hear something," he said, leaning in to the stereo. He punched a button a few times, then twisted the volume knob. A slow, melancholy, almost funereal beat struggled through the speakers; Dice closed his eyes and stood, trancelike, as Donny's soul-drenched voice danced atop the organ and drum. Lauren watched her father mouth the words, each of them written decades before she was born but relevant to their circumstance all the same:

I'm not trying to be/just any kind of man/I'm just trying to be somebody/You can love, trust, and understand . . .

Finally, he opened his eyes and smiled, almost embarrassed by the way he was carrying on. "That song right there, it's called 'I Love You More Than You'll Ever Know,'" Dice said quietly. "When I was locked up, I played it over and over again in my mind, you know, 'cause we weren't allowed to have any music of our own. I mostly heard the popular stuff when the guards played their radios at night while they were on post. But none of those songs could touch Donny, and especially this song right here. That song? Baby, *that's* our song."

"It's a beautiful song," Lauren said simply as her father walked across the room and sat next to her.

"You're beautiful, Lauren, and I do love you more than you'll ever know," he said. "You and Sydney, y'all are the only ones on this earth besides my sister who I would die for. Shoot, all them years in prison, I was dead. Only somebody who kept me alive was your sister — her and the hope I held in my heart that one day you would understand why your daddy went to prison. I didn't go away because I didn't love you, Lauren. I loved you too much to stay. Please try to understand that, darling. I'm not asking you for anything but to understand."

Lauren wrung her hands, unsure of how to respond to her father without bursting into tears. She bit her bottom lip and grabbed her purse. "I have something for you," she said, rummaging through it, hoping that her father didn't notice the moisture in the well of her eyes. She pulled out a small photo and looked at it admiringly before handing it to Dice. "It's you, Sydney, and me at our fourth birthday party at —"

"Piedmont Park," Dice said, holding the picture gingerly. In it, Dice was holding both of his girls on his waist; Sydney was smiling at their dad, while Lauren, laughing, was staring at a blue balloon she was clutching between her tiny fingers. "Your mother snapped that picture right before I kissed you on those fat cheeks. You were giggling so, you let go of that balloon and it floated right on up into the sky. And then came the tears."

"It's funny, but I didn't remember that day until I came across this picture," Lauren said. She'd found it in the photo album Sydney had hidden behind the toilet in her bathroom for weeks before she could sneak it back downstairs into Keisha's old boxes. "Mommy threatened to beat my behind if I didn't stop crying over it, but you held me in your arms and wouldn't let go until I settled down."

"I told Keisha she better not lay a finger on you, either, or she was going to have to box me," Dice laughed.

"Yeah, you were always protective of me and Sydney, huh?"

"Y'all are my daughters," he said. "I would die for you."

Lauren put her hand across her mouth in hopes that it would keep her sobs from escaping, but it was no use. "I . . . I . . . know," Lauren stuttered. "All this time I hated you for leaving me, for leaving us, but these past few weeks I've found out a lot about you and Mom and Altimus and even myself. I just didn't know, Dad — I didn't know what they were capable of, and how much they hurt you."

"Why would you know, Dewdrop? It wasn't for you to know."

"But . . ."

"But nothing," Dice said sternly. "You didn't have any business being mixed up in grown folks' business to begin with, and I don't want you to worry about it now. Only thing that matters to me is that you're here. Right here — with me. I ain't going nowhere if you don't."

Dice pulled Lauren into his arms, and this time, she didn't fight it. She closed her eyes and melted into his embrace; for the first time in a long time, she actually felt, well, safe. They sat that way for quite a while, the rhythm of her breathing locking in sync with his. They stayed that way until Donny stopped singing. When Lauren opened her eyes, they focused on the newspaper sitting on the table.

Lauren sat bolt upright and her eyes got wide as saucers as they focused on the title of a small article in the local section: "Suspect in West End Murder Found Dead." She practically pushed Dice off to get at the newspaper and brought it up close to her face to make sure she was reading it right.

"What's wrong, Dewdrop?" Dice asked, concerned.

Lauren didn't answer at first — just kept reading the short article. "He's dead," she said. "Omigod, who?"

"Who's dead?" Dice asked. "What's wrong?"

"They found him dead?"

"Who?" Dice asked a little more sternly.

"Smoke — somebody killed him. The police found him dead," she said, still reading the article. "The police went looking for him, and they found him dead."

"Humph, dead, huh?" Dice said. "Smoke?"

Lauren looked up from the paper; her father was looking at her just as cool as you please.

"You know Smoke, don't you?" she asked quietly.

"I know of him," Dice said simply.

"You mean you knew him. He's dead," Lauren said.

"Okay, and? Hazards of the job."

"Well, the paper says he was the chief suspect in Rodney's death," Lauren said, pointing to the sentence in the paper and shoving it in Dice's face. "They were going to take him in for questioning when they found him."

"I still don't understand your fascination . . ."

"The police were supposed to arrest him for Rodney's murder — I made sure of it. I notified the Crime Stoppers Web site to tell them they should question Smoke's girlfriend. The only somebody who knew I was doing it was Sydney. And now he's dead . . ."

"Rodney's brother, I know," Dice said.

"So now he's dead?"

"Hell, Dewdrop, if the police think he killed Rodney, and he ain't around to say otherwise, that's a good thing!" Dice exclaimed.

"Wha — what?"

"It means this ankle bracelet is about to come off, baby!" Dice said, jumping up from the couch. "Means the police don't have any reason to keep coming for me if they think somebody else killed Rodney. Damn, baby, you saved the day!"

"I . . . but . . . who killed Smoke?" Lauren said, still confused.

"Don't matter," Dice said. "Don't matter at all. Look here, baby, sit right there and don't you move — I gotta call my lawyer. Don't move, okay? Stay right there. I don't want you to leave — we got a lot to talk about."

"Um, okay," Lauren said, fingering the newspaper in her hands.

She wondered if Jermaine read the *Atlanta Journal-Constitution*.

And if he did, he, too, knew that Smoke had sparked his last fire.

19
SYDNEY

"We got this. Don't you worry about a thing, you hear me," Keisha whispered loudly as she leaned forward in her seat to give Altimus a kiss on the cheek. Altimus gave her a small smile in return and turned back to face the front of the courtroom. Keisha cut the prosecuting attorney a mean side-eye, sat back in her seat, and smoothed out her black Donna Karan suit. She closed her eyes and started whispering a prayer.

Sydney turned to her right and looked to see if Lauren had just witnessed their mother's antics. However, instead of rolling her eyes in annoyance, Lauren was looking at the floor, mumbling her own little prayer. In the past four months, the younger Duke twin had matured so much, Sydney sometimes felt she almost didn't recognize her anymore. "It's really going to be fine, Lauren," she said softly as she reached out and rubbed Lauren's tightly clenched fists.

"I know, I know, I just wish someone could convince the butterflies in my stomach," Lauren responded with a rueful grin.

The small side door opened and the bailiff finally walked in. "All rise," he announced as the jury filed back into the room. As soon as the twelve Atlanta residents were back in the jury box, he announced, "The Honorable Emmanuel D. Highwater."

The stern-looking white man in a long black robe entered the room and walked up to his seat overlooking the courtroom. "Ladies and gentlemen of the jury, have you reached a verdict?" he asked in a gravelly voice.

The foreman stood up holding a piece of paper. "We have, Your Honor."

"And what say you?" the judge queried. The deafening silence in the room pounded in Sydney's ears. She struggled to swallow the huge lump in her throat.

"After careful deliberation, we, the jury, find Altimus Duke neither negligent nor culpable for the unpaid taxes and, therefore, not guilty of tax evasion," the foreperson announced solemnly.

"Woo-hoo! That's what I'm talking about!" Keisha screamed as she leaped over the wooden barrier and into

Altimus's arms, Whitney Houston style. "Give us free, give us free!!!" Altimus laughed and hugged her back while his legal team struggled to keep a straight face.

The judge banged his gavel several times before Keisha stopped whooping and hollering. "Order in the court! Order in the court! Mrs. Duke, please get off your husband!" The local press immediately started taking pictures and then rushed out of the room to jockey for position at the press conference Altimus's lawyers had called.

Lauren looked at Sydney and shook her head. "Um, can you please get your mother," she giggled, obviously relieved by the way things had turned out.

"I'm convinced there's nothing anyone can do to stop Keisha Duke," Sydney responded as she stood up and smoothed out her gray Nanette Lepore baby-doll frock. "Do you want to wait outside while they pull themselves together?" she asked.

"Hell, yeah," Lauren responded, grabbing the new cobalt-blue Chloé bag Keisha had given her for Christmas. "After you," she then offered to Sydney as she fished out her favorite oversized Chanel sunglasses and put them on.

"Why, thank you, my dear," Sydney replied as she picked up her own Christmas gift from Keisha, a navy Hermès Kelly bag, and turned to lead the way out of the courtroom. Busy celebrating with the legal team, neither Keisha nor Altimus noticed when the two sisters pushed their way out of the heavy swinging doors, down the long hallway, and walked side by side out into the sunshine.

"This is so crazy, right, Syd?" Lauren was the first to speak when the girls reached the curb across the street from the courthouse. They both turned to face the mob of press waiting for Altimus to come out and make a statement.

"Who are you telling," Sydney retorted as she started digging through her own bag for her sunglasses. "And forget about today. I can't believe the last few months. It's, like, is this really my life?"

"Yeah, there have been way too many ups and downs. . . ." Lauren's voice trailed off a bit. She pointed to Sydney's wrist where the Cartier bracelet used to be. "Speaking of downs, are you going to tell me what was the matter with you that night when I came in the room and found you all upset? I know you said you were okay but . . ."

Sydney slowly rubbed her shoulder and shook her head. "Long story short, I should've taken your advice," Sydney started out slowly.

"Oh, well, I could've told you that," Lauren teased gently. "Tell me something I don't know. What's the long story?"

Sydney smiled wryly at her sister. "Yeah, well, I'll bet you didn't know that Jason was going to flip out on me and literally shove me against a wall. Or call me the b-word."

Lauren's jaw dropped open. "What the hell?" she demanded as she tore off her sunglasses to look directly at her twin. "He did what? Are you freaking kidding me right now?" Lauren questioned angrily.

"I wish I was," Sydney continued. "We got into an argument because I had to go to Marcus's house to see about the missing Sadie Hawkins money —"

"Eww, I read about that mess on YRT," Lauren said with a little frown. "Rehab for a gambling problem? So déclassé!"

"You ain't never lied," Sydney agreed with a wry smile. "But anyhoo, that Monday Jason shoots me a text saying he wants to talk. And I'm thinking he wants to apologize for blowing things out of proportion and make up. But when I get there, I realize that I'm really tired of having to explain myself to anyone — to Mom, to Altimus, to Marcus, to Jason, to any damn body. And I really need some time to figure out what I want for myself. I've been in a relationship for the past four years; I need some time to get my sexy back."

"Okay, okay, I hear ya, superstar! And honestly, that all makes sense . . . so when does the ass whupping commence?" Lauren asked as she unbuttoned the top button on her black-and-gray Betsey Johnson three-quarter-length swing jacket.

"Well, as soon as I said that I didn't think the relationship was working out, he flipped. Grabbed me up, threw me against the wall, called me all kinds of names — it was a mess! Luckily for me, Carmen and Rhea happened to come looking for me and literally saved my life," Sydney said emphatically. "I swear . . ." Sydney started as she began to get choked up, "I don't know what might've happened if they hadn't come along."

"My God, I'm so sorry, Syd," Lauren said softly as she hugged her sister. "I can't believe that happened to you of all people."

Sydney rested her head on Lauren's shoulder. "You told me, you told me to listen to my gut. But I was too worried I was overthinking it."

"Why didn't you tell me sooner," Lauren demanded suddenly.

After a moment, Sydney slowly straightened up. "'Cause you're the little sister. Remember?" Sydney said with a teasing smile.

Lauren crossed her arms and rolled her eyes. "Whatever, Sydney, three minutes *so* doesn't count," she pouted playfully.

"Seriously, though, I know how much you've been dealing with yourself. And even though you may be a little faster on the draw, deep down inside, I'm very capable of kicking butt and taking no prisoners when needed," Sydney responded with a steely gleam in her eye. "But it's gonna be fine. Carmen and Rhea took me to the principal's office to report the attack. So let's just say, Marcus isn't the only one not returning to Brookhaven next semester."

"Humph, I know that's right," Lauren co-signed. "On the positive side, at least you're going to have that fresh start you wanted, huh?"

"Yeah, I guess I will, won't I?" Sydney said contemplatively as she tucked a stray curl behind her ear.

"Well, if it makes you feel any better, I broke up with Jermaine, too," Lauren hedged as she looked down at her blue Chloé knee-high boots.

"Wait? What?" Sydney exclaimed, completely shocked. "What happened? Jermaine is such a great guy! Please don't tell me he cheated on you!"

"Ha! The girls around his way just wish," Lauren laughed bitterly. "It's actually not something he did. I just . . . I don't know. Jermaine is amazing, but he really doesn't fit in with my crowd. His whole 'I'm from the wrong side of the tracks' thing is fine when it's just the two of us, but the kids at school are talking —"

"So? Since when do you give a damn if people are talking about you?" Sydney demanded. "Lauren, I'm definitely not in a position to give anyone relationship advice. But I will say this: Jermaine brings out the best in you. I have never seen you so in love with anyone . . . besides yourself, of course," Sydney said with a smile. "And at the end of the day, that's the important thing. Not what the trifling kids from Brookhaven or even Mom and Altimus have to say."

"You're always right," Lauren pouted.

"I know," Sydney responded playfully. She looked over and noticed her parents coming down the steps to the waiting crowd. She could see Keisha scanning the throng of onlookers. When her mom made eye contact with her, she gave Sydney the come-hither nod. "Uh-oh, I think Mom wants us to pose for the shiny happy-family photos. You ready?"

"To take pictures? Absolutely," Lauren said with her signature diva grin as she fluffed up her new sandy-blond-colored weave. Then she hesitated, "But, Syd, seriously, do you think we're going to be all right? I mean, our family? You, me, Dice . . ."

Sydney paused and considered her answer. "I can't really say. But no matter what, I'm by your side," she said, extending her hand. And hand in hand, the two girls walked back into the fray together.

20
LAUREN

Lauren peered into the rearview mirror yet again, slathered on a bit more lip gloss, and then slumped back into the driver's seat. The phone was practically burning a hot hole in her lap, but for the past fifteen minutes, she just couldn't will herself to do much more than roll it around in her fingers and stare at Jermaine's digits. She wanted to call him — really she did — but she was afraid of what he would say, and what she would say, too. They hadn't talked, after all, since the big breakup at Uncle Larry's place, and it seemed like an eternity had passed since the two of them found out about Smoke's connection to Rodney. So much had happened: Altimus was off the hook on the tax evasion mess (though the scandal, buoyed by a front page *Atlanta Journal-Constitution* story about Altimus's shrewd-but-questionable business practices, lived on . . . and on . . . and on . . . on YRT); Dice, though still a "person of interest" in Rodney's murder, was free and no longer had to wear the Fulton County ankle jewelry; and Smoke, considered the chief suspect in Rodney's death, was officially six feet under, though no one knew who was responsible for putting him there — which meant that Jermaine was probably somewhere popping bottles with glee. Lauren wouldn't know about that, though; she'd been ducking his phone calls, and then, later, was too caught up in the drama of final grades, Christmas, court dates, back-to-school anxiety, and the battle for her title as captain of the dance squad to think too hard about it.

But the electronic reminder on her computer earlier that morning snapped her out of her if-you-don't-think-about-him-he'll-go-away numbness: Today was Jermaine's birthday. And despite everything that had gone down, she wanted to wish him a happy one. And maybe tell him that she missed him a little. Okay, a lot.

She ran her fingers over his name in her phone's contacts queue and tested out what she'd say if she followed through and called the boy. *What's up — how you doing? How you been? What's going on, birthday boy?* She shook her head and looked at herself in the mirror again. She had nothing.

"Hello?" she heard a small, tinny voice screaming through her phone. "Lauren? Lauren!"

She looked quizzically at her phone, unsure why it was screaming at her until she realized Jermaine's picture was staring back at her. She'd accidentally dialed his number. Lauren was tempted to hang up on him, but then how foul would that be? She bit her lip as she lifted the phone to her ear. "Happy birthday to ya, happy birthday to ya, happy birth-day!" she crooned into the phone, singing the Stevie Wonder b-day song off-key.

"Whoa, whoa, Beyoncé, who sings that song?" Jermaine asked, laughing.

"Wait, you're not serious, are you?" Lauren said, shocked Jermaine had even fixed his mouth to ask such a silly question. "Kang Stevie, baby. I might have to revoke your black papers for not knowing."

"I might have to revoke yours for butchering the international black people's happy birthday song," Jermaine laughed. "Next time, maybe you should just send a card."

"I would have," Lauren said quietly, "but I was afraid you might send it back."

"I would have kept it if you put some Benjamins in it," Jermaine deadpanned.

"Oh, that's it, huh? I have to pay you off to get back in your good graces?"

"You never fell out of my good graces," he said, coaxing a smile from Lauren. They were silent for a moment, the many words they wanted to say to each other floating between them in that quiet space.

"So, what's going down for the b-day?" Lauren asked as she watched a group of her dance squad members climb out of Lexi's car and tumble into the Duke House, a sound track of giggles announcing their arrival. "You have a Super Sweet Seventeen party somewhere sexy?"

"Nah," Jermaine chuckled. "Won't be no million-dollar party with the cameras rolling and the Range parked outside. Besides, you probably did enough celebrating over the past few weeks for both of us, what with both your fathers beating the charges and all."

"Well, Keisha did throw a little somethin'-somethin' together for Altimus," Lauren said. "You would have thought he was coming off a twenty-year bid."

"Yeah, well, you can't blame her for celebrating. I know I wanted to do a little celebrating of my own over Smoke," Jermaine said.

"I guess, if one can celebrate someone's death," said Lauren, apprehension rimming her words.

"I'm not saying we were setting off fireworks and pouring champagne, but at least my family's happy Smoke got what was coming to him. I know my brother's resting in peace now, and my moms is sleeping a lot better because of it."

"I guess," Lauren said. "I've been checking the papers to see if they've found the person who took him out, but I haven't seen anything on —"

"It's not important who killed him," Jermaine said. "The only thing that matters is that he's gone from here. Look, why we talking about him anyway? It's my birthday, it's a new year, and things are looking up. My girl is on the phone, it's all good. What's up with you?"

"Nothing, really," Lauren said, glad to change the subject. "I'm about to head in to dance squad practice. Today's the day they're going to announce who's dance captain."

"Like there's any question?"

"One would think this one was a no-brainer, but they got me working hard for my position," Lauren said, smoothing her eyebrows in the mirror. "Seriously, some of these girls are running around here thinking I'm going to take a backseat just because of what's been going on with my stepdad, but they got another thing coming if they think it's that easy to push me aside."

"Well, go get 'em, tiger!" Jermaine laughed.

"Oh, snap, you're clowning me, aren't you?" she said. "That's cold."

"No, what's cold is you taking so long to call me."

"I — I know," Lauren stuttered. "I really don't have any excuses. There was a lot going on, and I was being such a brat, I just thought you'd moved on."

"Um, in case you forgot, you were the one who ran away, not me," he said.

"Yeah, I was wrong and I apolo —"

"You and me?" Jermaine said, cutting her off. "We're the same. You got another thing coming if you think it's that easy to push *me* aside."

Lauren closed her eyes, sat back in her seat, and smiled.

"So, you saying you're still the captain on my team?"

"Does a hog wallow in mud?"

"Wow, that was so not the image I was looking for," Lauren said.

"Okay, okay, does a bear pee in the woods?"

"Um, ewwa — that wasn't much better."

"Are you the captain of the Brookhaven Prep dance squad?"

"Hell, yeah," she said. "That's much better."

"Well, then, Captain Duke, get to it. Go in there and play your position — holla at your boy when you're finished showing them who's boss."

"I'm on it. You gonna be around later?"

"You know it," he said.

"I'll holla," she said. "Bye, Jermaine."

"Bye, Ms. Duke."

Anyone who could see Lauren in her car probably thought her a madwoman, seeing as she was hitting the steering wheel and hooting and hollering and giggling wildly. She even let out a little scream but quickly stifled it when she caught sight of Coach Maddie staring at Lauren from her car, which she'd pulled up a few spaces away from the Saab. The coach tossed an awkward wave and started gathering her belongings — a stack of folders, her briefcase, a bag of pom-poms, a Diet Sprite. Lauren hurriedly tossed her lip gloss and phone into her gym bag, checked her hair in her rearview mirror one last time, then got out of her car, smiling hard enough to make her dimples produce a deeper-than-usual dent in her cheeks. "Here, let me help you with that," she said, grabbing the pom-poms and folders out of the coach's hands. "I'm glad I caught up with you before practice; I wanted to tell you all about the Candy Crave fund-raiser. It was a smash," she continued, walking in lockstep with Coach Maddie, right past Lexi's car, right past a crowd of squad members standing around gossiping, right into the double doors leading into the house that Duke built.

"Okay, ladies, listen up," Coach Maddie called out to the room of chattering dance squad members. "Before we go out for our first practice of the New Year, we have some unfinished business to attend to."

Almost instantaneously, the entire room fell silent. Lauren, who'd taken a seat a few rows behind Lexi and Meghan and their crew, watched as Meghan tossed a knowing nod at her friends, like she just knew not only what the coach was going to talk about, but also that said subject would be all about her. Lauren gave a little eye-roll but, beyond that, tried her best to hide her emotions. Duke family motto: Never let them see you sweat. Lauren Duke motto: Forget them broads — Lauren Duke runs this. *Feel the ambience, heifas*, she smirked to herself. Lauren squared her shoulders, crossed her legs, and looked straight ahead.

"Let's start with the Candy Crave," Coach Maddie said. "A few moments ago, Lauren gave me the official report of the fund-raising efforts, and great news: Under Lauren Duke's leadership, and with the help of the squad, we managed to raise just over seven hundred dollars — a generous addition to our fund-raising account if I do say so myself. Great job, Lauren!" Coach Maddie added, kicking off the applause. When the hooting and hollering simmered down, Coach Maddie poured on a little bit more: "And Kayo, repeating a request from Ms. Duke, had a fantastic idea for how we should use the money. Kayo, do you want to tell the squad what you and Lauren had in mind?"

"Sure thing," Kayo said, standing up and facing the rest

of the team. "Well, as you know, our fund-raising efforts over the past few years under the leadership of Lauren Duke have far outpaced our goals, and while we enjoyed using the Candy Crave to satisfy Brookhaven's sweet tooth, we realized pretty early on that doing another fund-raiser really wasn't necessary. So Lauren suggested that we take a portion of the proceeds and donate them to charity."

"Humph, maybe she wants to give it to her father's legal fund," Caroline stage-whispered, eliciting a round of nervous laughter.

Lauren didn't hear her exact words, but she was pretty sure whatever they were giggling about over in Caroline's amen corner, it was at her expense. She tried to ignore it; Kayo and Coach Maddie were just getting to the good part.

"Anyway," said Kayo, pushing through the pettiness, "Lauren thought it would be a good idea to establish a scholarship for kids who attend a basketball academy at the West End Community Center."

Lexi sucked her teeth; Caroline and Meghan giggled and whispered and shook their heads and spread around their "I told you so's" good and thick.

"Fantastic idea," Coach Maddie said. "As a few of you know, I live in the West End, and while the community is on the verge, there's still a serious need for a youth outreach, and this is a fantastic start from the students of

Brookhaven, particularly since one of our core missions is to use our power and influence to give others a hand up. Way to go, Lauren!"

Lauren waved and smiled as her fans applauded; she made a mental note to thank Sydney for the idea. Pure genius.

"And that brings me to the other big matter at hand — the election of team captain," added Coach Piper, who walked into the room as the applause died down. "I didn't realize that the vote would be so contentious — in the past we've identified the person with the best abilities and the team has generally co-signed the choice, but this year, a few of you expressed interest in the position, so this season, we took a ballot vote."

Caroline, Lexi, and Meghan stopped giggling and sat at attention. The three of them seemed to lean in a little, as if stretching their ridiculous necks would somehow turn the tide in Caroline's favor.

"I'm happy to report that by near unanimous decision," Coach Piper said, pausing long enough to make everyone collectively hold their breath, "Lauren Duke will again lead the squad this season. Congratulations, Ms. Duke. Obviously, your reputation as a fearless, dedicated leader and dancer precedes you," she continued, barely heard over the applause, whistles, hoots, and hollers from the squad. After what seemed like an eternity, Coach Piper implored the girls to settle down. "Okay, Lauren, would you like to have a word with your squad?" she asked when it finally got quiet.

Lauren stood, but really, she hadn't thought she'd be asked to speak. She hadn't prepared. Saving grace: She'd just had her eyebrows waxed and Jamila had laid down her edges something fierce just last night, so she was looking fly. And that was all any girl needed. "Thanks, Coach," Lauren said, clasping her hands in front of her and smiling. "I just look forward to another fantastic year. And let me kick it off by inviting Kayo to be my co-captain; she's brilliant and has some hot moves I'd like to steal — er, um, I'd like her to teach us in some of our new routines. We're going to be smokin', y'all!"

The room burst into applause again.

Lauren continued to stand, doing her best Miss America wave to her fans. She gave a little giggle when her eyes locked with Caroline's; clearly, the tragic loser could barely keep her Tater Tots down.

So sick.

Lauren practically drooled thinking about all the different ways she would make the three of them pay.

It would not be pretty.

Lauren was practically bouncing out of the heavy glass door, almost all of the laughing, energetic dance squad in tow, when she looked up and saw him, sitting on the bumper of his car, Jay-Z pumping from his speakers and rattling the windows. He looked lovely and fresh, his white tee gleaming beneath his North Face down, his new Jordans peeking from beneath an oversized pair of Red Monkey jeans. His arms were folded, but he was smiling, his brown eyes practically sparkling when they finally found their mark: Lauren.

Her heart was racing. Here she was, standing in the parking lot in front of the building erected by her stepfather especially for her, in front of every girl who had just voted her conscience and made her the leader of Brookhaven's dance squad, in front of the tastemakers of her school, who, with the click of a SEND button to YRT, could blow up her spot to everyone who mattered in Buckhead; and there was the boy from the West End, in all his hood glory, standing there, waiting. For her.

Lauren looked to her left and then to her right; every last one of the girls following her like stray puppy dogs — even the trio of haters and their silly, useless, powerless, minions — were looking at Jermaine like he was a piece of red meat. "Damn!" she heard a few of them say. "Who's *that*?"

Lauren giggled and cleared her throat. "Um, everybody?" she said loudly. "You might want to get your camera phones ready — I know some of you will want to get the

YRT exclusive on this one. But do me a favor: Make sure you spell my man's name right," Lauren said, walking up to Jermaine and taking his hands in hers. "His name is spelled j-e-r-m-a-i-n-e. Get it right, hear?"

"You're officially certified," Kayo said, laughing and shaking her head. She walked up to Jermaine and extended her hand. "Hey, Kayo," she said, introducing herself. "Nice to meet you."

A few of the other girls sidled up to the couple, too, some introducing themselves, others staring and wondering in a not-so-discreet voice if he had any relatives as cute as him.

Jermaine, a lot embarrassed by the attention, wanted out. But who, he figured, was he to step in Lauren's spotlight?

"I trust you're here to take me out," she said.

"But it's my birthday," he laughed. "Shouldn't you be taking me out?"

"Not if you're driving," she said, eyeing his beat-up car. "Plus, a gentleman always plans."

"Well, I *am* a gentleman," he said.

"This much," Lauren said, "I know is true."

As she waved good-bye to her friends and her haters, she saw out of the corner of her eye a silver Saab pull into the space next to Jermaine. It was Sydney, bumping Jill Scott's "Golden" from her speakers like she was deliberately trying to blow out the custom-made woofers. "Hey!" Sydney said enthusiastically as she jumped out of her car, her radio still blasting.

"Uh, hey," Lauren said, peeking over her sister's shoulder to peer at her car, and then back at her twin. "What's up with you?"

"Oh, nothing's up with me. The question is, what's up with you, superstar dance squad captain? I just saw the news on YRT. Go, Lauren!" she said, giving a mock hoorah fist in the air.

Lauren cracked up at the sight of her twin, the unusually stiff and nonexcitable one — giggling and laughing and trying to do a fake cheer. "Why, thank you, sis," she said. "But, um, you should leave the cheering to me."

"Oh, you don't have to worry about that — that's all you, baby sis," she said as she surveyed the parking lot and took notice of how everyone was focusing on them. "Um, in case you all didn't know? My sister is the fire."

Lauren giggled. She didn't know what had gotten into Sydney, but she wasn't mad at it, either. "Hey," she said, "say hi to Jermaine."

Sydney twirled around and focused on Jermaine — the first time she'd set eyes on him since Rodney's funeral. A wry smile crossed her face as she switched her focus between Jermaine and Lauren and then to Jermaine again. "Well, I see somebody's trying her best to be the official

YRT cover girl of the year," Sydney laughed. "But I'm not mad at you. What's up, Jermaine? Good to see you again. Good to see you *here*," she added.

Jermaine smiled and nodded.

"It's Jermaine's birthday, and we were just about to go and celebrate. Wanna come with?" Lauren asked.

Sydney looked at her watch and considered all the things she had lined up for the evening — she had to study for an Econ quiz, start researching her Western Lit paper, start planning the spring calendar for Jack and Jill — the list went on and on. "I don't know," she said. "I have a ton of work to do . . ."

"Come on, " Jermaine pleaded. "It's my birthday. One cupcake."

Sydney hesitated and giggled a little. "If you get Lauren to spring for two cupcakes, I'll go," she laughed.

"That's a bet," Jermaine said. "I'm driving."

As Sydney collected her purse and locked her car doors, Lauren waved good-bye again to her friends and her haters and to the remaining gawkers, then walked to the passenger side and waited for Jermaine to open her door. It creaked open; Jermaine reached in and swiped at the seat.

"All set," he said. "Climb on in."

Then he rushed to the other side of his car and lifted the lever on the front seat so that Sydney could climb into the backseat.

"Turn that up a little," Sydney said as Jay-Z's "Dirt Off Your Shoulder" pumped through the speakers. "That's my song," she said as she settled into the hard leather seat.

Jermaine obliged, then put the car in drive, pulling out of the parking space as his charges, Sydney and Lauren, shouted the words to the rap and bounced in their seats. Jermaine laughed as he watched the twins flick invisible dirt off their shoulders — their bouncing and yelling rattled as loud as his speakers.

In Jermaine's rearview mirror, Sydney could see the girls of Brookhaven Prep standing there, mouths agape, wishing, no doubt, that they could be riding shotgun, too. Lauren was thinking the same thing as she caught sight of the girls in the side-view. Above their heads, in the distance, ever imposing, gleaming against the rich, blue sky, the squad building struck an impressive pose — THE DUKE HOUSE letters making it clear that this was still, and always would be, Lauren and Sydney's world.

Acknowledgments

DENENE

For God, who keeps opening windows for me when it seems all doors are closed — without His grace, I am surely nothing.

For my husband and darling daughters, Mari and Lila, and my son, Mazi: Thank you for encouraging my writing, even on the hard days when we'd all rather hit the park or watch ANTM than watch me bury myself in my MacBook again. You guys and the very furry, very sweet, extremely cute Teddy help me keep my eyes on the prize. For my Daddy, James Millner; my brother, Troy Millner; and my Mom, Bettye Millner: Thank you for loving me like no other. And for Angelou, James, Miles, Cole, and my in-laws, Migozo and Chikuyu: Thank you for your friendship, your laughter, your intelligence, and for providing us with the family structure we crave and love.

For Victoria Sanders, my agent extraordinaire: Thank you for using your beautiful mind to keep me working and constantly challenged.

For our editor, Aimee: Thank you for the encouragement. And for Andrea Davis Pinkney: Thank you for creating opportunities for me to keep writing; you are an extraordinary author, editor, and mentor, and I'm so happy to have worked with you.

And for Mitzi, my partner-in-crime: We wrote a helluva series, didn't we? We grew those girls up, didn't we? We're going to work together again, aren't we? We better. Because you rock.

And finally, thank you to Lauren and Sydney, for creating two years' worth of good times. I'll miss you.

MITZI

Every step forward begins with faith; so I thank God, Yemaya, Chango, and all the orisha and guides that remain by my side at all times.

Mommie, the phrase "thank you" isn't nearly enough for all that you have so selflessly given to me over the years. I am so blessed to be your daughter.

Daddy, even when I know that you don't have the slightest clue where I am or what I'm doing, I do know you love me. I'm a lucky girl.

Melissa, in choosing your own path, you constantly provide me with a true example of courageousness. Thank you.

To all my family and relatives who continue to support

and encourage me to pursue all of my wildest dreams — especially Tia Puchi and Mommy Sally — X's and O's.

To my beautiful godchildren — JJ and Sydney — you inspire me to create material that will be worth talking about when you become old enough to understand.

To my mentors — Dr. Ivy Mitchell and Joyce E. Davis — thank you for guiding me to the career of my dreams.

To my amazing and incomparable friends, every single one of you provides me with inspiration to create better stories and, more important, be a better Mitzi. Thank you for your patience, compassion, and encouragement.

To my dizz-ope writing partner, Denene, thank you for helping me create a phenomenal teen series. It is always a pleasure, my dear!

To Victoria and the diligent Scholastic team, thank you for seeing this series through all the way to the end. It's been a memorable ride!

And, of course, Drama. Through thick, thin, dark parks, and even stinky doggie farts, not a day goes by that I am not grateful for your companionship.

Last but not least, the success of the HOTLANTA series would not be possible without the support of countless unknown readers over the years. I am so appreciative of all those who have followed my byline from *Honey* Magazine to *The ABW Guide to Life* and forward. Thank you, thank you, thank you.

Outside the sky is weirdly dark and the air thick and humid, the way it gets before a storm. Sean leads me over to a navy blue Volvo. "Ta-da!" he says. The paint is scratched and the back bumper is covered in the remnants of bumper stickers that someone tried to tear off, but eventually gave up on — a piece of light blue with a lacy-looking white shape in the corner, a dark green sticker with everything torn off except for a white *UR*. Sean unlocks the passenger side and opens the door, then walks around to the driver's side and gets in. I get in, too.

There are four different plastic cups in the cupholder, and cups scattered all over the floor. On the backseat there's a black leather messenger bag closed with a shiny brass lock. The car smells like pine trees.

"Sorry about all the cups, you can just kick them out of the way," Sean says. "Iced coffee is my crack."

"What a coincidence," I say. "Crack is my iced coffee."

Sean laughs. "I knew there was a reason I liked you," he says. He shakes his head a little bit. He starts his car. "So where am I taking you?"

"I'm in the Sunrise Village condo complex," I say, "behind the A&P on Grays Avenue."

Sean starts his car, starts driving, neither of us says anything for a while. I watch his hands as he turns the steering wheel. I cannot recall ever having any sort of opinion about a guy's hands before, but his are beautiful.

"So . . . I have to confess something." Sean reaches up with one of his beautiful hands and pushes his hair out of his face. "I didn't really come here to tell you the rules of hide-and-seek." He pauses. "The truth is, Ellie, it's really not that hard of a game. And besides, you could just look it up online."

"The Internet is good like that," I say. My heart is starting to race. "Then why are you here?"

"The truth? I looked for you after the party and when I didn't see you I got worried. I thought maybe the fire ate you up. The fire department said everyone got out okay, but you just never know, I guess." He glances at me and then looks back at the road. "I remembered you said you worked at the coffee place, so I figured I'd just come by and make sure you were alright. I hope that doesn't seem stalkery or weird seeing as we only talked for like thirty seconds . . ."

"No, it's nice of you," I say. "I'm okay, thanks for checking."

"You don't look that okay actually . . . When I came in to Mon Coeur, you looked really sad. And at the party, too." Sean pauses. I don't say anything. "So did you ever find him?"

"Who?" I feel myself blushing.

"Whoever you were looking for at the party. Was it that guy with the bad tattoos?"

"Oh," I say. "Yeah. Sort of. I mean I thought so, only it turned out no."

"He isn't like your boyfriend or something, is he?"

"Ha!" I say. "Definitely not."

"Okay, good. I didn't think so. I mean, he didn't look like the kind of dude I'd imagine you usually date. He looked kind of like a loser."

And I'm oddly flattered by this comment, as it implies that I have actually ever dated anyone before. Which, of course, I haven't.

"So, tattoo dude didn't deliver?"

"He delivered his hand to my ass," I say. "So I delivered my knee to his balls. And that was it."

"Good for you," Sean says. "But why were you looking for him?"

I take a deep breath. And as I breathe in, I realize something, that I'm going to have to tell him the truth. It's not that I've somehow decided this is a good idea or anything, it's just what I'm going to do.

"I was looking for my sister," I say. "I haven't seen her in over two years." There's no going back now. We're stopped at a stoplight. I glance at Sean again. He turns toward me, nodding ever so slightly. I hope telling him isn't a mistake. "I didn't think *she'd* be there at the party exactly, I just thought . . ." I get the story over with as quickly as I can, just spit it out so it's out and I don't have to have the words in my mouth anymore. "So I showed her picture to tons of people but no one knew her but I thought if I found the guy who brought in the box, he might know something about where she was, or that someone at the party might." I look over at Sean but he's watching the road again. "But I was wrong." I feel my eyes filling with tears, but I blink them back. "So I guess that's why I looked sad."

"That's a pretty understandable reason," he says.

"My best friend Amanda thinks I need to get on with my life now. Stop focusing on my sister so much and just act, I don't know, like she never existed or something. It's been two years since she disappeared and nothing has changed." I inhale and exhale slowly. "I don't know, Amanda might be right, it *might* be time to give up now." I look down at my hands. "But I just don't know how to."

Sean is silent. And we both stare straight ahead at the rain pounding down.

"I think I know why I met you now," Sean says finally. And then I feel Sean place his hand gently over mine on the seat between us. "There are some things a person just never gets over, that the phrase 'get over' doesn't really apply to," he says. "And when one of those things happens in your life, it doesn't matter how much time has passed, or if you're sitting alone in your room or at a party surrounded by a hundred people, and it doesn't even matter if you're actually thinking about it or not because no matter where you are or what you're doing, it's still there. It's not just something that happened. It's become a part of you."

And then he shuts his mouth and keeps driving. This is it so exactly. And no one else I've ever talked to has ever really gotten it before.

He turns toward me, our eyes meet, and I'm just sitting there blinking. He grins, shrugs his shoulders, and tips his head to the side, all casual now. "Or, y'know, whatever." And I burst out laughing and it's a real hiccuping, doubled-over laugh, the kind of laugh I haven't had in a long time. And he laughs with me. Things are the funniest when they are a mix of sad and absurd and true.

"So you know what I'm talking about, then," I say.

"Something like that," Sean says.

"How do you know all of that?" I ask. "I mean, what happened to you?"

But as soon as the words are out, I wish I could take them back. The last thing I want him to think is that I'm mining him for his tragedies, the way I've felt so many others do to me. "Sorry," I say. "You don't need to answer that."

We are pulling into the apartment complex where I live now, the streetlights lighting up the inside of the car. Lighting up Sean's face.

"Seventeen-ten," I say. "Up there on the right." And Sean pulls up in the empty parking spot in front of my front door.

"Well," I say. "Thanks for the ride." I look out the window, there's so much rain pounding down it's like the whole world is underwater. It's like here, in this car with Sean, is the only safe place left on earth.

"No problem," he says.

I reach down and unfasten my seat belt. "So . . . um." I know I'm supposed to get out now, but I am struck with the sudden intensity of *how much I do not want to.* "Well . . . thanks again." I cringe, hearing myself. This is ridiculous. I have to go.

I start to reach for the door handle and glance over at him one last time. Our eyes meet and there's that flash again.

Sean takes a deep breath.

"I had a brother once," he says. His hair flops over one eye and he pushes it away. "But he died."

My breath catches in my throat. The rain starts pounding harder now, and there is thunder in the distance.

"What?" I blink.

I watch his mouth.

"My brother died," he says again. "So that's how I know about that stuff I said."

I raise my hand up to my mouth. "Oh God."

He smiles this sad half smile. "It was a long time ago." He looks down, looks back up, his face is flushed. "If there was even the slightest chance that I could see him again, that there was something I could do to make that possible, I would never stop trying. Ever. This is fate, Ellie, me meeting you, I think. Because I don't have a chance to get my brother back. Nothing I do can change the fact that he's gone. But maybe what I'm supposed to do now is help you." Sean pauses. "Do you think that sounds crazy?"

I shake my head. I feel something inside me warming up.

"So should I come in, then?" he says. "Maybe see the drawing?"

I hesitate for only the tiniest shred of a second, enough time for me to look through all that rain at the front windows of our building and remember that my mother is working the night shift tonight, which means she is gone now and won't be home until early in the morning.

"Yeah," I say quietly. "That would be great."

*   *   *

I realize, as we walk into my room, that this is the first time a guy has ever been up here.

I try and imagine how it must look to Sean, messy unmade bed, a dresser, a nightstand, a desk, a few items of clothing tossed around on the floor. It probably looks like no one spends much time in here, which is true since I'm almost always at Amanda's.

I sit on my bed and Sean sits in my desk chair and I continue explaining Nina's drawing. "So then I called the number on there but the guy didn't know anything, didn't even remember her. And the guy at the Mothership says he just found the book in the basement and it was practically empty when I was down there, and even if there were any more clues there, they're all burned up now."

Sean reaches out his hand and I give him the drawing. My fingertips brush against his, just for a moment. I am very aware of it. Sean holds the drawing close to his face and stares. He doesn't move, he doesn't blink, it doesn't even look like he's breathing. And I'm wondering if he's beginning to regret offering to help me since he is probably quickly realizing how futile this is.

"No pressure," I say. "I mean, or . . ." And then I stop because Sean's mouth has just dropped open, and then this huge grin spreads over his face. "Ellie," he says slowly. His eyes are shining. "Did you notice *this*?" He jumps off the chair and lands next to me on the bed. He flips the drawing over so I can see the fake credit card printed on the back.

"What about it?" My heart is pounding.

"This is a cardboard credit card." He taps it with his finger.

I nod, blinking. "Right."

"And do you know where people get these? With credit card offers in the mail . . ." Sean is nodding at me, trying to lead me to his conclusion. "So . . ."

I shake my head slowly. "So . . ."

"So, your sister turned eighteen only a couple months before she left, right? Credit card companies have this list, of all the people in America who are about to turn eighteen. So they can start sending them credit card offers right around their birthday and sucker them in."

"I'm not sure what you're saying."

"Chances are your sister got a ton of credit card offers in the mail before she disappeared, right? So what if she actually applied for one?" He turns the card over and points to the bank's name on the back. "Say from Bank of the USA? I bet we could sign into her account no problem since you're her sister. All we'd need is her Social Security number, and then we'd probably just have to answer a bunch of random security questions and the answers would be things like your mom's maiden name and other stuff you'd already know."

"Oh," I say. I try and force a smile.

"What's wrong?"

"It's a nice idea! And thanks for thinking of it!" I frown.

"You're frowning," he says.

"I just don't think it'll work."

"Why not?"

"It's too easy."

"But that," Sean looks me straight in the eye, his mouth curled into a mischievous little smile, "is exactly why it's going to."

To Do List:
Read all the Point books!

♡ 📖 ♡

Airhead
By **Meg Cabot**

Suite Scarlett
By **Maureen Johnson**

The Year My Sister Got Lucky
South Beach
French Kiss
Hollywood Hills
By **Aimee Friedman**

The Heartbreakers
The Crushes
By **Pamela Wells**

This Book Isn't Fat,
It's Fabulous
By **Nina Beck**

Wherever Nina Lies
By **Lynn Weingarten**

Summer Boys
By Hailey Abbott
Summer Boys
Next Summer
After Summer
Last Summer

In or Out
By Claudia Gabel
In or Out
Loves Me, Loves Me Not
Sweet and Vicious
Friends Close,
Enemies Closer

Hotlanta
By Denene Millner
and Mitzi Miller
Hotlanta
If Only You Knew
What Goes Around